Tempered Dreams

Pamela S. Thibodeaux

"For God does speak, perhaps once, or even twice, though one perceive it not. In a dream, in a vision of the night (when deep sleep falls upon men) as they slumber in their beds." Job 33:14-15

TEMPERED DREAMS
Book Two of the Tempered Series
By: Pamela S. Thibodeaux
Copyright © 2001

Publisher/Distributor:
Temperance Publishing, an imprint of
Pamela S Thibodeaux Enterprises, LLC
PO Box 324
Iowa, LA 70647

ISBN#: 978-0-9896728-3-2

Cover Design: Delia Latham (Delia's Designs)

Previous Publications:
Sept. 2005; ComStar Media, LLC.
Salem, Oregon, U.S.A.
ISBN: 1-933866-03-9

Dec. 2000; Writers Exchange E-Publishing Company
Atherton Qld 4883 Australia

All rights have reverted to Author

Note:
This is a work of fiction. Names, characters, places, and incidents either are the product of the author's imaginations or are used fictitiously, and any resemblance to actual persons, living or dead, businesses, establishments, events, or locales is entirely coincidental.

Praise for Pamela S. Thibodeaux

"Through Pamela's blessed ability to find God everywhere, even in secular song lyrics, she has written devotions guaranteed to touch the heart and remind the reader of our True Love, the Rose of Sharon." ~ Endorsement for **Love is a Rose** by Linda Yezak, Author, Editor Triple Edge Critique Service

*"**Lori's Redemption** is fast paced, lots of action, gripping storyline.... I loved it. It's gone straight back into my TBR pile."* ~ Clare Revell, author of "Monday's Child" series

"Thibodeaux leads the reader through from the first page to the last without once relinquishing control. She hooks them, holds them, and keeps them enthralled until the last line." ~ Review of **The Visionary** by Delia Latham, author of "Solomon's Gate" series

*"**In His Sight** caught my attention from the beginning and it made me wonder if I had given all to God as he gave all to me. Thank you, Pamela for a story that I would readily recommend to anyone who needs that extra encouragement!"* ~ Reviewed by Wendy for Happily Ever After Reviews

*"**Winter Madness** is a wonderful romance and an excellent example of Spiritual growth."* ~ Reviewed by Dee Daily for The Romance Studio

*"**A Hero for Jessica** is a good, sweet read charged with attraction but an emphasis on true love. I recommend it to women of all ages."* ~ Reviewed by Violet for LASR

*"**Cathy's Angel** is a short tale that is entertaining as well as inspiring. Well done!"* ~ Reviewed by Marlene for Fallen Angel Reviews

"Pamela S. Thibodeaux's motto is "Inspirational with an Edge!" Her short story **Choices** *lives up to those words and is well worth reading."* ~ Reviewed by Gail for Night Owl Romance

*"***The Inheritance*** was my first Thibodeaux work; however, it will not be my last! Her approach to writing about everyday life, while struggling to maintain strict Christian standards and values, is a glimpse into reality which we all must face from time to time."* ~ Reviewed by Brenda Talley for The Romance Studio

"If you have ever considered Christian fiction bland, then check out the **Tempered Series**. *It will be well worth your time."* ~ Amanda Killgore for Huntress Reviews

Dedication and Acknowledgements

All honor and glory belong to God for His wisdom, direction and strength to get through such a painful-yet-beautiful story.

This is dedicated to battered women everywhere; may you find the peace and joy offered through salvation, forgiveness, and the healing power of God's grace and mercy. To the people who counsel them and to the doctors who treat them, may God bless you in your endeavors. To the perpetrators of domestic violence and the children who are also their victims, may God reach your hearts and change your lives.

For James, in the spirit of forgiveness. Though painful, what we experienced was nowhere near this horrific or dramatic; for that I am eternally grateful.

And last but definitely not least, for my husband, Terry. Your love and support have paved the way for my dreams to come true. Thank you. I love you!

A special note of appreciation to Sandy Cummins, CEO of Writer's Exchange E-Publishing Co. for catching the vision and releasing *Tempered Hearts* as an e-book in Dec. 2000. Thank you, Sandy! May God continually bless you in all that you do.

And a very special **"Thank You"** goes to Lauron Sonnier (McCulloch) Stewart, President of Sonnier Marketing for the original artwork for *Tempered Hearts* and *Tempered Dreams*. You helped make my vision a reality...for this I'll forever be grateful. God bless you, Lauron!

Chapter One

Katrina Simmons awoke with a jolt when the car she rode in slammed into the bridge, spun twice and came to a sliding halt against the concrete wall. She sat a moment, stunned, her heart banging against her ribs, her breath escaping in ragged pants. Thank God there was no one around. Reaching over, she shook her husband. "Jack?"

He mumbled, eyes rolling languidly, and passed out.

Rage unlike anything she'd ever known roared through her. Fumbling with the door handle, she managed to get it open and climbed shakily out of the vehicle. A groan, more anguish than pain, escaped her clenched teeth as she considered the damage to her car.

"Great, Jack! Just great," she raged at her husband, who reclined in a drunken stupor. "You've finally done it! You've ruined my car!" she accused, kicking the door.

* * * * *

Dr. Scott Hensley settled in for the drive to New Orleans. It wasn't a long drive from Lafayette, but a trip he wasn't looking forward to. Mardi Gras in New Orleans was not the place to be. Putting the top down on his car, he reveled in the brisk evening air. A nearly full moon gleamed its glory against a backdrop of black velvet in the star-studded sky. A cacophony of night birds and insects sang in harmony, rivaling the sound of tires slapping on pavement. Much to his surprise, Interstate traffic was light. At the sight of an automobile accident, he slowed his vehicle and pulled over. Using his mobile phone, he called the police and climbed out of his car to check on the victims.

"Are you all right?" he asked, hurrying toward the young woman pacing alongside the car.

She whirled around with a screech, lunged through the window, and shook the driver.

"You drunken idiot!" she raged, punching him soundly on the jaw. She shook him again, winced, and shoved away to continue her tirade.

Being a wise man, Scott stepped back from the raging female as the sound of sirens pierced the air. Showing his Identification, he talked with one of the police officers arriving on the scene while the other officer spoke with the young woman.

"Did you see what happened?"

Scott shook his head. "No, I pulled up afterward. Looks like they hit the wall." He glanced toward the stretch of concrete median dividing one of the longest bridges in Louisiana and the United States. Most of its four lanes divided by water, the stretch of highway passed over the Atchafalaya Basin between Lafayette and Baton Rouge, making it a tedious section to travel with few exits. Endless swamps and cypress trees were the only scenery. They watched the young woman pace, answering in monosyllables. She turned in an angry whirl, gestured wildly, and then cradled her arm against her.

"She seems to be favoring her wrist," the officer observed.

Scott chuckled. "I'm sure it needs tending. She hit him."

The cop's eyes widened. "What? Who?"

Scott laughed softly and shook his head. "Her husband or boyfriend, whoever is driving. When I arrived, she was ranting and raving about him ruining her car. She lunged through the window, and punched him. I haven't had a chance to check on him. I doubt he's injured too badly. From what I can gather he's probably drunk."

"What did he do?"

Again Scott chuckled, feeling a tug in the region of his heart. The fiery little lady reminded him of someone he knew. Two people actually, someone he loved and someone he'd lost. "He just groaned and passed out," Scott answered, walking toward them. He presented his I. D. to the other officer, requesting permission to check her wrist.

Katrina balked at the offer. "I'm fine," she hissed, not caring about her wrist. All she wanted was for someone to drag her husband out of the car and let her loose on him!

Scott reached for her, turning her to face him. "Easy, Sweetheart," he said, his voice a soft drawl. "I won't hurt you."

She looked up at him, her eyes wide and angry; her cheeks flushed, and fainted. Scott caught her as she slumped in his arms. Picking up her small frame, he held her as the summoned ambulance arrived with sirens blaring. Carrying her to it, he waited as the EMT's opened the back and retrieved a stretcher before gently laying her there to examine her. Her wrist, swollen and purple, showed signs of a break. The golden band on her ring finger implied the driver was her husband. Other than restless stirrings, she seemed fine.

Covering her with a blanket from the ambulance, Scott watched the officers pull the driver out of the car. Gut-wrenching fury clawed through him when they hauled the huge bulk of a man from behind the wheel. A tad over his own six-foot height, the man was a giant compared to his tiny wife.

Where Scott's broad shoulders tapered down and narrowed to a slim waist and long, muscular legs, this guy was rock-hard. His chest was easily as broad and thick as his shoulders. He had a solid middle and bulky, muscular legs and hips, the build of a football player, wrestler or body builder. From his belligerent attitude, he obviously took advantage of it.

"You leave me in jail, and you'll pay for it, Katrina," he hissed, slurring the words, obviously unconcerned his wife lay passed out on a stretcher. When the young woman began to moan and writhe, Scott turned toward her.

"My baby," she whimpered. Clutching her stomach, she curled into a tiny ball and wept.

Scott noticed a widening stain of blood on her jeans as it seeped from her body. Pulling her against his chest, he did his best to soothe the trembling female in his arms. In all of his years as a physician, nothing prepared him for the array of emotions slashing through him. After she had quieted, never fully conscious, he lay her back down.

Walking over to the police car, he hailed the officer. "Add murder to his charges. She just miscarried," he growled, glaring at the man in cuffs.

It took a moment for the words to register on Jack Simmons's booze fuddled brain. He grunted. "Don't need no brats anyway," he slurred. His head rolled languidly, and he slipped into a drunken stupor once more.

Scott's hands clenched into fists and for one fleeting moment, he thanked God he'd taken an oath to preserve life. He could easily kill the man, so obviously unconcerned with his wife and unborn child that he'd driven, drunk, with her in the car. Domestic violence and child abuse were the two most hated diagnoses in the Physicians Desk Reference and he'd seen enough to leave no doubt in his mind that she had little, if any, say about the situation she was in.

The police drove off with the husband cuffed securely into the back seat, and the ambulance took her away. He watched their departure and then decided to follow the ambulance to see how she was. Turning on his c. b. radio, he communicated with the drivers and found out what emergency room they were taking her to.

"Well, she's from Lafayette, but we're closer to Baton Rouge, so we're taking her there," the paramedic replied.

Using his mobile phone, Scott put in a call to the hospital he was traveling to and bought some time. Instead of the seven in the morning to seven in the evening shift he'd originally been scheduled, Scott had it switched to the opposite. He pulled in behind the ambulance and talked with the doctors and nurses on staff in the emergency room at Baton Rouge General. Then he waited.

* * * * *

Katrina swam up from the pain-induced fog to awareness. Tossing in discomfort, she opened her eyes. Surprise and shock widened them as she gazed into the soft brown eyes of a stranger.

Scott moved closer when she stirred. He'd been watching her for hours. The sunlight streaming in the room bounced off the red highlights in her thick, golden hair, turning it into a fiery mass. Her skin, silky smooth and the color of a sun-ripened peach, made him wonder about the color of her eyes. Probably the blue or green that usually accompanied her coloring, he thought. Hazel perhaps.

Wrong.

They were brown; deep, dark brown, like two huge chocolate drops in a bowl of peaches and cream. He smiled tenderly and she glanced away with a blush.

"Do I know you?" she queried in a timid voice.

"I'm Dr. Scott Hensley. I was at the accident last night. I thought you might appreciate seeing a familiar face when you woke up. Can I get you anything or call someone for you?"

Her lip trembled as she shook her head. "My husband?"

Biting back a growl, he softened his reply. "In jail, Sweetheart. That's all I know."

"Good," she muttered, blushing at the relief she felt but still trembling with the fear. Jack always threatened to hurt her if she ever had him put in jail or left him if he landed there on his own. This morning she didn't care. He'd caused her pain for the last time and cost her the one thing she wanted most in life—her baby. The minute she returned home, she planned to call a lawyer.

Scott watched the emotions cross her lovely, fragile features and fought back the urge to take her in his arms. Professional ethics insisted he remain objective, but it was difficult to adhere to ethics when a lone tear escaped from one of her tightly closed eyes to leave a trail down her silky cheek. He waited and watched, his heart cringing, as she fought valiantly against the tears, and lost. Her breath started to hitch and she succumbed to the sobs wracking her small frame.

Forget ethics.

Sitting on the bed, Scott pulled her into his arms and held her against his chest. The icy reserve he'd built around his heart over the last several years began to melt under the onslaught of her tears. His fingers sank into the luxurious softness of her hair while the other hand caressed her back in a soothing manner. Her sobs subsided into soft, hiccupping sounds; silence ensued.

Katrina stiffened fearfully when she realized the strength in the arms of the man holding her, arms of a stranger, of a man other than her husband. Grinding her teeth in mortification, she pushed herself away, a hot blush warming her cheeks. "I'm sorry," she mumbled, not daring to look him in the eye.

"It's okay, Sweetheart. I'm a doctor. I won't hurt you. Are you sure there's no one I can call for you? Your mother or some other family member?"

She shook her head. "No. No one," she admitted, knowing her mother wouldn't be able to come even if she wanted to. Her stepfather would see to that. Coming from a long line of abused women, Katrina was determined to break the pattern. Never again would a man take advantage of her.

Scott's voice broke into her thoughts. "Is there anything I can do?"

"Leave me alone." She turned away knowing her words were rude and not at all grateful for the comfort he so easily and gallantly offered.

Totally unprepared for that answer, Scott frowned. He'd dealt enough with grief and pain to know when a patient was talking out of emotion, lashing out. He respected that. But coming from someone so tiny, so fragile, so vulnerable, it seemed out of place. He remembered her fury the night before and bit back a grin. Maybe not.

"Okay," he said, brushing the thick mane of red-gold hair off her face then stood. "I need to be going, anyway." Still, he hesitated. Something about her pulled at him. Maybe her fragile beauty or the subtle waves of fear. Perhaps the gentle elegance of her fine, porcelain-like features giving the impression of a china doll, or the fiery passion he had witnessed last night.

He shook himself mentally, maybe he was just tired.

With a slight shrug he walked around the bed and toward the door. Turning, he got a glimpse of the tremble that shook her slender frame. He walked back to the bed, reaching for his wallet and pulled out a business card.

"Look, here's my card. If there's anything, anything at all I can do for you, please don't hesitate to call." He wrote the phone number to the hospital in New Orleans where he would be for the next couple of weeks. She remained silent as he set the card on the bedside table.

With another subtle caress, he brushed the hair off her cheek and felt her stiffen. Of their own accord, his knuckles swept gently across her cheek again, soothing. He bit back words of comfort. It was evident though needed she didn't want them. Turning quietly, he left.

Trina's fingers trembled when she reached for the card and noticed he resided in the same town as she. Questions rolled around in her head and all she could do was speculate about the answers. Dr. Scott Hensley. Who was he? What did he want? Was he like this with all of his patients or just the helpless females?

* * * * *

The two-hour drive to New Orleans passed without further incident; giving Scott plenty of time to think about the woman he left behind. Something about her stirred memories long since buried, some better off forgotten. Unable to resist, he picked up the phone and dialed the hospital. Requesting her room, he waited for her to answer.

"Hello?"

"Mrs. Simmons..." he hesitated. What was he supposed to say? He didn't even know why he called! Clearing his throat, he tried again.

"Katrina, I'm serious about what I said. If there's anything you need, please feel free to contact me."

"Dr. Hensley," she huffed out a sigh. "I know you're aware that I'm a married woman. I don't know what you want from me, but you won't get it. I'd appreciate it if you just leave me alone," she insisted, slamming the receiver into its cradle. Men! Her mind screamed, drowning out the voice in her heart chiding her for the unfairness of her attitude.

Put ever so completely in his place, Scott hung up. A smile crossed his face as he thought about the defiant tone that belied the soft, sensual voice. Maybe it was time for a challenge in his life. He sighed, wished once again he was going anywhere but New Orleans, and slipped a cassette in the deck. Soft, soothing Jazz notes oozed out of the speakers as his mind roamed lazily along the path of his career.

In all of his years as a physician, his one desire—the desire to help those in need—was finally being fulfilled in this job. He was one of the leading physicians for the Louisiana Charity Health Care System, a system which served the needy. One of the joys of being on contract with the State was traveling to different facilities and working with various people. One of the disadvantages was not being able to refuse. But at least he no longer had to journey with missionaries to do the good he so desperately wanted to do. He'd given up on that after the death of his wife and parents.

Leaving his home in Texas more than six years ago hadn't been an easy decision, but a necessary one. Necessary for his sanity. Home was too full of memories. Memories he hadn't dragged out in a long time. Memories which surfaced now. His jaw hardened and fists clenched in automatic defense against the swift tug of anger followed by sorrow and grief that always accompanied the recollections of his wife and parents, and how they died.

He'd been on a three-month mission in South America. His family had flown down to visit him his second month there, his mother and father always so proud, and Melissa, his wife. He'd been swept away by her passion, not seeing until it was too late there was very little substance beneath. Though not a happy marriage from the beginning Scott did his best to adhere to his vows. Still, he was on the verge of divorce when he received the offer to travel with the missionary. He'd known then, even as he knew now, the trip had only been an escape hatch and that when he returned home he'd have to make some serious decisions about his marriage.

As fate would have it, he went home sooner than expected when the plane they occupied was blown out of the air by terrorists. To date, their deaths were recorded as a senseless, unsolved tragedy.

He'd returned to Bandera, Texas to bury his family. Unable to deal with the grief, the heartache and the guilt, he sold the ranch to his friend Craig Harris, who then turned most of it into an arena and campground. The house was turned into a Bed & Breakfast, and the charity rodeo the Rockin' H had hosted for over thirty years was now held there. The rest of the year, it was merely an extension of the Rockin' H. Guests came and went at the B & B, giving a substantial monthly income, which, at Craig's insistence, Scott retained. That decision made, Scott had moved on. Craig and his family still remained his closest friends. Now, when he returned to Bandera for a visit, it was with joy, joy tempered by memories and heartache.

His mobile phone rang once, jerking Scott out of his revere, which was a good thing since he nearly missed his exit. When it didn't ring a second time, he shrugged it off, knowing if it were important, whoever it was would call back. Arriving in New Orleans, he ordered flowers to be sent to Mrs. Katrina Simmons then took a much needed nap.

The next ten days flew by with little time to dwell on the fiery little lady in Baton Rouge General, but she was always in the back of his mind, making him smile.

From the weekend before to the weekend following Fat Tuesday, New Orleans ran wild, parties ending in fights,

fights ending in brawls, brawls ending in injury or death. It was rough to say the least. New Orleans was notorious for its parties and passions.

Beautiful and old, the city graced the banks of the Mississippi river, as it had for more than a hundred years. In the old days, the French filled this port city with style and elegance. To date, it still held all the magic and beauty, with its river walk, shops and boutiques, French Market and, of course, the notorious Bourbon Street. Restaurants offered the best of French Cuisine and nightclubs offered the best in Jazz music. New Orleans was a beautiful place to visit, but Scott wouldn't want to live there, especially during Mardi Gras.

Scott knew the city and its people would settle down after Fat Tuesday. Rich in tradition, they would shelter in for the Lenten season, repenting of their wicked ways and drawing closer to God. This spiritual side increased the charm of New Orleans. Full of life, the people exuded laughter, love and faith, but like all of God's children, they had their rebellion and tantrums. During Mardi Gras, these aspects came out in the worst ways.

* * * * *

Katrina stared at the single, rebellious rose still alive amongst the bouquet of dead flowers. The arrangement had graced her kitchen table for almost a week now. A smile curved her lip. That one rose reminded her of him, the strange doctor with his tall good looks and Texas drawl. Stubborn too, she thought, but a gentle stubbornness. Trina knew she'd never met a man like him before.

Taking the flower from the center of the bouquet, she placed it in a slender vase. Burying her nose in its soft fragrance, she inhaled deeply, then exhaled on a sigh. This one rose spoke so boldly of life, life and hope, especially considering the rest had long since been dead.

A tear rolled down her cheek and emotions swarmed through her as she faced the sad facts. No life existed in her marriage, and no hope. Nothing left to cling to after nearly ten years of abuse. There was only now, her life and her future, if she wanted one, if she wanted to live long enough to have one.

Trina knew the facts, the statistics. Most battered women lived frightened, lonely lives, if they lived at all.

For some unknown reason, she had survived through the years of abuse, first as a child then as a wife. Trina found it hard to believe it was God who looked after her, not after all she'd been through and tolerated in the name of love.

Despite everything, she still believed in the sanctity of marriage. But she could no longer consider her's a true marriage. Until suffering the loss of her child, she'd never faced the fact that what she lived in for the past nine and a half years was not a marriage. Not in the real sense of the word. In truth, it didn't even come close. Trina knew what she had to do. Picking up the phone she called Legal Aide.

Chapter Two

Katrina locked the door behind her and sighed. In the four days since she had called Legal Aide, she'd been busy. At the advice of her attorney, Sam Ortego, she took half of the money out of the checking and savings accounts and removed her name from both. She'd packed up all of Jack's things, dividing the household items as fairly as possible after showing a list to Sam, and stored them in the shed in the yard. She'd had the locks changed on the doors of the tiny house they rented and contacted the landlord to tell him of the situation. He, in turn, made sure all of the windows had screens on them and that they were nailed shut. Jack would literally have to break in to get to her.

Walking into the kitchen, she tossed her mail onto the counter and put the kettle on to boil for a cup of tea. Turning toward the table, she caught sight of the single rose which, against all odds, continued to thrive in its vase. Taking it out of the window, she carried it to the table and set it down. Tenderly fingering a silky petal, she smiled.

"I don't know if you're a special breed of flower or just a stubborn one, or if you're a symbol of grace, beauty, and hope from God, but you sure are beautiful," she spoke softly, feeling a little foolish talking to a yellow rose.

Yellow rose of Texas.

The thought made her think of the strangely tender doctor she'd met that night. Shaking off the foolishness of her ponderings, she buried her nose in the soft petals, inhaling deeply its sweet scent. "I think it's the latter," she whispered.

In the ten days following her return home after the accident, Trina had done a lot of soul searching, and more praying than she'd done in years. Scriptures from the Bible that had been stowed away most of the years of her life, and throughout the years of her marriage, assured her of what she had known in her heart for a long time. Hers was not, and never had been, a true marriage.

Though he'd spouted the words 'wives be submissive to your husband' at her longer than she cared to admit, Jack had never upheld his part in the scripture: To love your wife as Christ loves the church. According to the Bible, he represented everything opposite of love, and she felt sure she was doing the only thing left to do—get on with her life, and, though she hadn't set foot in a church for years, she also wanted to renew her faith.

Finally free at thirty, she had so many options open to her. Work, school, a future. What little money she had wouldn't last forever, but she was free!

And alone for the first time in her life.

To add to her worries, her mother had called, concerned that by getting a divorce, Trina went against the church's teachings.

"I was never married in the church, Mom. In their eyes I've never really been married at all. Not that I agree with that completely, but it leaves me options in the future.

Besides," she admitted softly, "I'm not worried about the church right now. At this moment, all I'm worried about is living to be thirty-one. I'm sure, if all the facts were known, the church, any church, wouldn't condemn me to life in eternal hell when I've been living in hell on earth. If it does, then I don't need a church. What I need is God. And that's not what God wants for us, Mom."

Trina hesitated, hoping against hope the words wouldn't go unacknowledged then continued.

"God knows I've tried, Mom. I've given the best ten years of my life to this fiasco called a marriage and all I've gotten out of it was bruises and broken bones. I've paid with my self-esteem and self-respect, and at the expense of my baby. I can't give anymore."

Her stepfather condemned her for not sticking it out. But what could she expect from two people who'd lived in a living hell for their entire adult life and were too reluctant, too scared or too proud to change?

The prospects for her future were so different and so exiting, they scared the living daylights out of her. A sob caught in her throat as guilt rose to choke her. "Oh, God," she whispered. "I'm so unworthy. I'm so afraid. And I...," she hesitated. What was she? Unsure? Afraid she was making a mistake? Afraid God wanted her to stay in the situation? She shook her head. He couldn't! Could He?

Resting her head on her arms, Trina let the tears come. Cleansing. Renewing. Refreshing. Like fresh drops of rain renewed the flowers of the field. Then she heard it, the gentle, reassuring voice of the Lord: All have fallen short of the Glory of God.

Oddly, instead of more guilt, those words filled her with hope. It sprang to life, a tiny flame flickering in her heart; hope and healing, which could only be found in God's forgiveness.

If only she could convince her mind it was real.

The whistle from the steaming kettle drew her attention. Welcoming the diversion, she rose to pour water over the bag of herbal tea, inhaling deeply as it seeped its soothing flavor into the cup. Sorting through her mail, she was surprised to find a letter from Jack. The words it contained didn't surprise her one bit. Reading the threat, all too real, all too frightening, she called Sam and read it to him.

"Don't worry, Honey," Sam Ortego soothed, seething inwardly. "I'll take care of it."

The very next morning, he had a restraining order placed against Jack. A few phone calls uncovered the fact that Jack's sentence for DWI was three thousand dollars and thirty days. Since it wasn't his first offense, the judge had denied bail and had him detained in the East Baton Rouge Parish jail where he still had twenty days to serve. After that, all hell would break loose. Acting on a very real sense of urgency, Sam had Trina's divorce papers drawn up, filed, and served to Jack there.

A week later the second letter from Jack threatened even more. Katrina didn't respond, but brought it to Sam. For now she was safe. As long as Jack remained behind bars, he was no real threat to her. The bulk of her worries revolved around what would happen once he was released. Until that day, she would continue to look for a job and pray, finding her strength and courage in God.

* * * * *

Katrina smiled with relief and anticipation. She had a job! Working as a waitress in a nightclub wasn't exactly the kind of job she'd hoped for, but it enabled her to have her days free for school. In the three-and-a-half weeks since the accident, she'd done a lot of research and decided on the course of her future.

Financial aide and help from other sources enabled her to go to school. She enrolled at Acadiana Technical College for an Associate Degree course in Accounting with the option of going for a full degree afterward. Though the financial aide would enable her to go to school virtually debt free, it would not be enough to totally support her along the way. She still had to pay rent and utilities. Being single, she didn't qualify for any other type of assistance from the Government, and she didn't want a dime from Jack. All she wanted from him was her freedom.

Undaunted, she'd searched for a job that would keep her days free and pay enough to help with her expenses. She'd had several offers, but when she explained her circumstances, hoping to get assistance from her employer in upholding the restraining order against Jack, she'd always been turned away; that is, until she walked into The Cowboy Club.

* * * * *

Jodi Bourgeois, manager of The Cowboy Club, took to her immediately and assured her she had all the qualities of a perfect waitress; she was petite, pretty and friendly. He approved her application, gave her a uniform which consisted of black shorts, white blouse, a gold sash and garter, and advised her to keep her wedding ring on. She was less likely to have any trouble if she wore it. However, if that proved to be wrong, all she had to do was locate a security officer.

Well known for its peaceful good times, the club was protected and its reputation upheld by weapon-carrying security guards. Its clientele consisted mostly of the upper echelon of Lafayette's society. The people who went there did so to have a few drinks and to listen to the best variety of music around. No drunkenness or disorderly conduct was allowed, and highly trained waitresses and bartenders monitored the patrons' alcohol intake.

When Trina showed Jodi her restraining order against Jack and explained her situation, he had shown her a sign placed strategically throughout the place: We reserve the right to refuse entrance and/or service to anyone.

Jodi requested a picture of Jack and promised he'd give it to all of the guards so that Jack wasn't even mistakenly allowed on the premises. Since the guards always escorted the waitresses to their car, she wouldn't have to worry about being attacked in the parking lot either.

Working Tuesday through Saturday evenings gave her thirty-four hours a week. She would make minimum wage plus tips, which she'd been told ranged anywhere from fifty to one-hundred-and-fifty a night. She would start training tomorrow evening.

After two weeks of working she was deemed a natural. She loved it! She loved the atmosphere; the smell of cologne mixed with cigars all enshrouded in a thin veil of soft lights and smoke; the music—a mixture of soft rock, pop and country, both new music and old classics. The people, young and old, were all friendly, all professional. Doctors, Lawyers, and Indian Chiefs. Trina had laughed at that until she found out the man who made the claim actually was a descendant in a long line of chiefs from one Louisiana's native tribes.

She'd only had a couple of encounters from regular customers who, she'd been warned, always flirted with the new girls. One of them sidled up to her with the old familiar line, "Hey, beautiful, where've you been all my life?"

Trina gave him her sweetest, most innocent smile, raised her left hand and replied, "Married." To which he fell all over himself apologizing. No one had bothered her since. She was there to work. Period. They respected that.

She made good money too, which was nice. In just over two weeks she earned enough in tips to pay her rent for the month with a little left over, which she deposited into savings for future use. School was a bit of a challenge but actually fun. So far the hours she worked hadn't interfered with her classes or study time. All in all, she was pleased and excited about her future. She figured Jack was probably out of jail by now, but, so far, he hadn't contacted her.

Hurrying toward table eight in her section, Trina prepared to take the customers order.

"Hi!" She smiled brightly, lighting the candle on the table, which seemed to defy her intentions. Rolling her eyes, she replaced it with one from the next table and tried again.

"I'm Katrina. I'll be your..." her voice trailed off as she gazed into the sparkling eyes of Dr. Scott Hensley.

Scott grinned, surprised and pleased to have finally run into her. He'd often wondered and prayed he would. "You'll be my what?"

His eyes shone with mischief, his voice lowered to a husky tone. Trina flushed. Everything about his presence made her nerves hum. "Waitress," she managed on a suddenly dry throat.

"How've you been?"

She smiled. "Okay, busy. May I get you something?"

"Bourbon and water. Alternate that with a coke. Oh, in case I forget," he stopped her hasty retreat with a wink. "Two's my limit." Katrina laughed. The silky, tinkling sound made Scott think of wind chimes.

"You don't seem like the type to forget anything," she remarked.

Know it, Sweetheart, he thought as she walked away, the subtle sway of hips crowding his mind.

She returned shortly with his drink. "Here you go. I'll be checking on you, but if you need anything don't hesitate to flag me down. We usually get busy around ten so I might be a little slow in getting back to you after.”

“Katrina?”

She stopped her nervous chatter, and eyed him; her eyebrow arched, waiting for him to continue.

“You still have my card?” She nodded, a flush rushing to her cheeks.

“You haven’t used it.”

“I haven’t needed anything.”

Her smile was sweet, shy and caused hope to well up inside him despite the fact that a gold band still encircled her ring finger. “Well, we’ll just have to see about changing that,” he teased.

His grin coaxed a bigger smile out of her. “Thank you for the flowers, by the way. You know, one rose lived about two weeks longer than the rest. It died just the other day.” She didn’t dare tell him she’d pressed it into her Bible with his business card, unable to forget his face, or voice, or the depth of kindness and gentleness he’d shown her.

“What kind of rose?” Scott asked, knowing he’d ordered roses of every color.

“A yellow one.”

His grin was smug. “Made from good stock, those yellow Texas roses.” Trina laughed.

“Right,” she remarked and made her escape.

Though she waited on him faithfully, she didn’t have much time to chat. The next evening when she arrived at work a dozen yellow roses awaited her. The card simply said: Think of me. It wasn’t signed. It didn’t have to be.

He didn’t show up that evening, or for the next two. Come the weekend, Trina didn’t have time to wonder what Scott was up to or if he would show up, but he remained in the back of her mind, making her smile.

Work, not lack of desire kept Scott away. He began his month long shift of evenings the weekend following his encounter with her. He often wondered how she had received the roses, and if she liked them. Did she think about him every time she looked at them, or as often as he thought about her? Everything about her intrigued him, and he could hardly wait to see her again. He cursed himself for not asking if she was still married as the ring on her finger indicated.

For someone who believed in the solemnity of marriage, he sure hoped not.

* * * * *

Katrina reached for the phone, its shrill ring startling her out of a deep sleep. Glancing at the clock, she groaned. She'd intended to study longer but had fallen asleep with her head resting on her arms and her book beside her.

"Hello?"

The voice brought her instantly awake.

"Katrina, I want to talk to you."

"Talk, Jack. But you'd better make it short and sweet. I don't have the time or the energy to fight with you." Oh, how she hoped she sounded tough, convincing.

"I don't know what you think you're going to pull, but it won't work. I'm fighting the divorce all the way."

She shrugged wearily. "Whatever, Jack. Is that all you wanted?"

"I want my stuff."

"It's in the shed. You have a key on your key ring. Call before you come to get it, and make sure you have a police escort." Rubbing her tired eyes, she fought back tears and the wave of fear.

"You're not allowed on this property alone. It's in the restraining order. All of your things are well packed. Very neatly, I might add. I gave you the television; I hate it anyway, and split all the dishes between us. You can have our bedroom suit. It wasn't much of a marriage bed anyway. I kept the one from the spare room. All of your gifts from the past ten years as well as your sports equipment are in there. If you have any problems, contact my attorney."

He snorted. "I'll contact you anytime I please. And I'll come by whenever and however I want you bi...."

Trina sighed and hung up the phone, effectively cutting off that overused word. She wasn't the bitch, never had been regardless of how much Jack wanted to believe and tried to make her believe otherwise. The phone rang again. She answered, and hung up immediately when he began to curse and yell into it, then took the receiver off the hook.

Trina didn't sleep that night, nor for the next two. Jack passed by every hour or so, blowing his horn. She called the police but was told they couldn't do anything unless others complained about him disturbing the peace. They could give him a warning but that was all. As long as he didn't enter onto the property, he wasn't violating the restraining order

She prepared for work Tuesday evening with a heavy heart and tired mind. The battle had begun. Experience taught her it would be a long, rough one, and that it would probably get real nasty before it was all over.

Only God knew how right she was.

Chapter Three

Scott brushed the thick, black waves off his forehead and put on his hat. It had been a long time since he'd dressed in jeans, boots and a hat, but funny, it didn't feel strange at all. Tucking his shirttail a little more snugly into the waist of his jeans, he eyed his reflection, pleased with what he saw.

Though forty-six, he still had the physique of a twenty year old. His shoulders were as broad, waist as narrow, hips as slender, legs as toned and muscular. His hair, except for a few silver streaks at the temples, was just as it had been twenty years ago. His moustache, full and well trimmed, graced the curve of his upper lip. The word sensuous came to mind and he grinned, remembering the many occasions he'd been told not to ever shave it off because it was so sexy.

Whistling, he picked up his keys and wallet and headed out the door. Excitement curled in his gut, as he thought about the evening ahead, hoping to see Katrina again. It had been a long time since he'd felt the pull and tug of desire at the mere thought of a woman, a long time since he'd felt anything at all in the deep, private regions of his heart. Perhaps too long.

Stopping by the florist, he picked up a single yellow rose. Arriving at The Cowboy Club, he took the rose from its wrapping and carried it with him. Requesting a seat in her section, he waited for Katrina to appear. A frown crossed his face when another girl approached him.

"Katrina's not here. I'm filling in for her."

"Where is she?"

"She called in sick."

He frowned again. "Oh. Well, can you tell me how to reach her?"

She smiled. "No, I'm afraid we can't give out that information."

Scott pulled a twenty-dollar bill out of his wallet. "Really?" he queried, tossing it on her tray and giving her his most charming smile. Her eyes lit with mirth.

She nodded. "Really." She hesitated. "I know her phone number is now unlisted but I believe her address hasn't changed." She eyed him meaningfully giving just enough information to find out what he wanted to know and not get herself in trouble.

He grinned. "Why didn't I think of that? Thanks, Sweetheart. Keep the twenty."

She eyed the rose and waited, her eyebrow arched in hopeful expectation.

"Sorry, the rose goes with me," he teased, chuckling at her disappointed frown.

"Figures," Ramona muttered, watching him walk away. The man didn't walk, she noted, he strolled. His whole being oozed sensuality. Mona knew she'd never seen a better-looking specimen of the male species and felt a tug of envy toward Katrina.

Stopping at the first convenient store he came to, Scott borrowed the phone book and looked for Katrina's listing. Without hesitation, he drove to the address listed by J. Simmons, and knocked on the door.

"Who is it?"

Her beautiful voice was weak, leery.

"It's Scott. Scott Hensley." His eyes narrowed in concern when she opened the door and glanced around before turning wide, wary eyes to him. Like bruises on her creamy skin, dark circles beneath them enhanced the paleness of her complexion.

"What do you want?" Katrina asked.

"What's wrong?" he countered.

She shook her head. "I haven't been sleeping well."

"Is there anything I can do?"

Trina shook her head. "No. I'm sorry you made the trip all the way over here."

"Katrina, wait." He stopped her from closing the door, held out the rose, and watched as tears filled her eyes.

"For me?"

His smile was tender. "You see any other gorgeous red-head around here?"

She shook her head; positive he wasn't talking about her. "I'm sorry. I can't keep accepting these from you. I..." her voice broke as she struggled with the emotions which threatened to overwhelm her.

She hadn't slept in days. Jack constantly called or drove by. She saw him standing or parked across the street, watching her house. Watching her. She had called the police several times only to be told there was nothing they could do unless he threatened her in some way. Didn't they understand his simply being there threatened her? Physically. Mentally. Emotionally.

Scott pushed his way in the slightly ajar door. "Talk to me, Katrina," he urged. "Maybe I can help."

She shook her head. "It's my ex-husband. He's been bothering me, but not enough to worry the police. He's probably watching right now. You can't come in here," she protested, when he stepped inside her living room.

Scott shrugged. "Bull. Let him watch. We'll leave the door open and sit in full view. He doesn't intimidate me."

"But he does intimidate me," she hissed, panic bubbling up to choke her. "I have final exams tomorrow, and if I don't get some rest and study, I'll never pass."

"So study. Or rest. I'll stay here and keep you company. I won't bother you."

Despite herself she was impressed with, and afraid of, his insistence. Insistent, arrogant men had been her undoing. Trina had no desire to get involved with another one.

She snorted. "You've been bothering me since the day we met," she snarled, quailing inwardly at the thought of his reaction. Her opinion had always been met with anger. Or sarcasm.

Scott grinned. "Really?"

Her eyes widened in surprise at the teasing light in his.

Scott chuckled. "That makes us even then, 'cause you sure have been bothering me."

He watched as she paced, glancing over her shoulder in a nervous gesture, opening blinds and curtains, turning on lights as she went. When she walked back to him, he reached for her, surprised and concerned when she recoiled from his touch. "I won't hurt you, Katrina."

The promise rang clear and true in his soft voice. Much to her dismay, tears filled Katrina's eyes and rolled slowly down her cheeks. Her breath began to hitch as she lost the few remaining shreds of control to his tenderness. With a sob, she let him pull her in his arms.

"Oh, please," he groaned. "Don't cry, little one. I can't bear it when you cry," he soothed.

Which only made her cry harder. "I don't know why you're being so nice to me," she wailed. "We don't even know each other. You don't know me. You don't know anything about me or what I've done or what I've been through. If you knew, you surely wouldn't be here."

"I don't care what you've done or what you think you've done that's so bad. I don't know why, either, but I do care about you. I'd like to get to know you. Besides, I'm nice to everyone. I'm a doctor." He tried to tease but it didn't work.

"I don't need a doctor," she sobbed. "I need a bodyguard."

"Well," he smoothed the hair off her flushed face. "I can be that, too."

Trina looked up into the serious eyes of the man holding her so gently. "You don't know what you're getting yourself into by hanging around here," she whispered in a quiet, frightened voice.

"Jack always swore if he couldn't have me, no one else would either. I wouldn't put anything past him." Scott smiled; a soft, dangerous smile which accentuated the angry glint in his eyes.

"Jack doesn't scare me. From what I've seen, his type are usually more bark than bite when it comes to dealing with someone their own size." He frowned, remembering several cases to the contrary. "Most of the time anyway."

Stepping out of his arms, Trina eyed him thoughtfully. "Yeah, you probably could hold your own against him."

He chuckled. "Know it, Sweetheart," he assured, pulling her against his chest once more and holding her until he felt her relax.

She pushed herself out of his arms. "So, what do I have to do to get you to leave so I can study?"

He shrugged, unable to hide his disappointment. "Ask."

Trina blushed, unable to bring herself to say the words in light of all he'd offered. "How about a glass of tea?"

Picking the rose up from where he'd dropped it, Scott offered it to her again. "I like that idea much better than leaving."

Taking the rose she did what any woman would do and buried her nose in the soft petals. Turning, she led him into the kitchen, filled a vase with water for the rose and prepared them something to drink.

They talked for hours. Although she didn't share her darkest secrets with him, she did tell him some things about her childhood and marriage. He, in turn, told her about his childhood. Though he didn't go into detail either, he talked about his marriage and the death of his parents and wife. He even helped her study. Close to midnight, he decided he'd better leave. Standing in the doorway, he waited while she went throughout the house closing drapes and blinds and making sure everything was locked. She returned to his side much more relaxed than she'd been when he arrived.

He smiled down at her. "All locked up tight?"

She nodded.

Cupping her face in his hands, Scott wrestled with temptation. It had been a lovely evening and he didn't want to rush her or scare her off.

"I want to kiss you," he whispered, unable to keep the huskiness out of his voice. He felt her blush, watched as the color rushed to her cheeks, saw the pulse throbbing in her throat, and fought the urge again. Her eyes were wary, confused, and afraid.

His smile was tender, as was the light in his eyes.

"But, I don't think you're ready for that yet," he admitted with a heavy sigh, then grinned. "So, I'll let you off the hook tonight. Almost," he amended with a chuckle, pressing his lips to her cheek. "Sleep tight, little one. I'll see you soon. Good luck on your exams tomorrow."

With that he left, waiting until she closed and locked the door behind him before walking to his car. That girl had been through hell and back in thirty short years. Scott had a feeling her life story contained a whole lot more than what she revealed. His eyes scanned the area, taking in the silence. Though there was no sign of Jack, he couldn't shake the feeling that something just wasn't right. He drove home with a heavy but hopeful heart and a nagging sense of worry.

It was a while before Katrina went to sleep but she welcomed the silence and the tender sense of joy and hope which filled it. For the first time in her life, she felt wanted, pretty, special, and, for the first time in a long time, she felt hopeful that she could have a normal relationship with a man sometime in the future. Even if Scott Hensley wasn't that man, she knew she had found a friend, a true friend. She fell asleep with a smile on her face and slept soundly for the first time in days.

The next afternoon when she arrived home a dozen yellow roses arranged in a beautiful vase were awaiting her. With a gasp of delight she bent down and stroked a silky petal before picking them up. Fumbling in her purse, she searched for her keys, overwhelmed with joy. Her pleasure was short-lived however, when Jack jumped up on the porch. Temporarily paralyzed by fear, she jammed the key in the lock on a surge of adrenaline. But she wasn't quick enough. Jack grabbed her by the hair and pushed her into the house just as the door opened.

"I see you've been entertaining already. Damn bed ain't even cold. What's the matter couldn't wait until the divorce was final before letting someone else take my place? Quite the bitch, aren't you? Or did he pay you? What? Money? Roses?"

Trina put down the flowers with a trembling hand and turned to face him, hoping to diffuse his anger. His face was twisted with rage, his whole being reeked of alcohol. Still she tried. "No. Jack, it wasn't like that. We're just friends...." her voice trailed off at his snort of disbelief.

"Don't you dare lie to me," he snarled, grabbing her by the shoulders and giving her a rough shake. "I told you Katrina, if I can't have you, no one will. By the time I get through with you, lover boy won't want you either."

The back of his hand cut off her protest. Holding her by the arm he hit her again and again, beating her worse than he ever had before, abusing her verbally and physically. Tossing her on the floor he followed her down, punishing her with his fists until she struggled no more. Once he had her in a state of total submission, he abused her as he often had during the years of their marriage, forcing himself on her battered and bruised body until all she could do was lie still and pray it was over soon and that he didn't kill her or her chance of having children. Finishing, he tossed her aside with a grunt.

Towering above her he snickered, a brutal sneer on his face.

"Think lover boy will want you now?" he taunted. "Wonder what your lawyer will say once he finds out we've been together. You know the divorce proceedings have to start all over if you and your ex make love."

With a sadistic little laugh and a crude comment, he knocked the flowers over, shattering glass and water, then left.

Katrina drug herself to the door, locking it, and heard his cruel banter. Sinking to the floor, she covered her ears in an effort to drown out the hated voice. She didn't move or relax until she heard his truck engine roar to life and drive off. Then and only then did she succumb to the tears she'd held at bay. It always excited Jack more when she cried and begged him to stop hurting her.

Oblivious to the glass cutting her knees she began picking up the roses one at a time, clutching them to her breast as sobs tore from her in painful torrents. Pulling herself to her feet, she squinted through rapidly swelling eyelids to dial 911. Sheer luck, or the grace of God, kept her awake and lucid long enough to ask for help and give her address. Swallowing convulsively, she attempted to dislodge the thick lump of bile clogging her airways as nausea overwhelmed, followed by complete darkness.

Trina came to in an emergency room, conversation between the nurses trickling through the fog of pain. She felt the tug and heard the ripping as they cut her clothing to examine her further. Wincing when a blood pressure cuff was strapped on her arm, she opened her eyes, locking gazes with the nurse taking her vital signs.

The nurse smiled, a tiny, tight, movement of her mouth. "Can you tell me your name?" she asked, her voice soft but professional.

Katrina nodded, speaking through swollen, cracked lips. The nurse continued asking her questions: How old are you? Can you tell me what happened? On and on, she questioned until she got the answers she needed. Patting her gently on the hand, she spoke softly. "Dr. Hensley will be here shortly."

Katrina groaned in horror. "Oh, please. Is there another doctor? A woman maybe?"

The nurse eyed her with suspicion but shook her head. "Don't worry, Honey, Dr. Hensley is the best around. He's very gentle, very thorough, very professional." Leaving the room, she hailed Scott who was returning from making rounds.

"What do we have?" Scott queried, seeing the pain and fury in his favorite nurse's eyes.

"Domestic abuse. And rape."

Scott's gut churned with suspicion and fear, and a gnawing sense of knowing. "Who? Where?" He reached for the chart. No! Oh, God, no, he pleaded silently. Shoving the chart at the nurse he strode to the trauma room where one lousy look confirmed his worst fears.

"Oh, God," he whispered. Jerking the door open, he walked in. Gently cupping her face in his hand he asked, "Did he do this to you?" Trina nodded, tears streaming down her cheeks. "Call the police," Scott ordered.

"No!" Katrina wailed.

Her eyes widened with fright despite the swelling.

"Please, just call my lawyer and my job. He'll take care of the rest." Scott nodded.

"Do it," he demanded of the nursing assistant. "I'll be back," he promised, his voice soft and broken.

Hot on his heels when he stormed out of the emergency room, Barbara Johnson, head nurse, watched in complete, stunned disbelief as the unflappable Dr. Hensley came completely unraveled. He leaned against the wall and banged his fist on it, wishing to God it were the face of one Jack Simmons. Curses, muttered with violent ferocity, flowed from a mouth which always had a smile and a friendly comment. Tension—dark, dangerous, and animalistic, oozed from him until, spent, he sank against the wall, his fists skinned and bloody.

"Oh, Barbara," he moaned, his voice harsh, eyes fierce. "Look at my hands. How am I supposed to take care of her now?"

Not exactly sure what to say, Barbara led him into the doctor's lounge. She bathed his hands with a damp cloth, doctored them up, and bandaged them. "You want me to call someone to come in? Dr. Guidry, maybe?"

He and Mike Guidry had hit it off well from the beginning, often trading shifts or filling in for each other. Scott shook his head. "No. I'll take care of her. I'll call him later, and see if he'll fill in for me the next few days."

"Okay. Ready?" Barbara asked. He gazed at her with a blank, haunted look in his eyes and shrugged.

"Ready as I'll ever be. God, give me strength and tenderness," he pleaded, in a soft under breath.

Barbara smiled. Scott wasn't known as the divine physician simply for his looks. His spirituality put him in a league of his own. Lending silent support, she helped put Katrina at ease while Scott proceeded with his examination.

Tears of shame and humiliation streamed down Katrina's cheeks as she choked back sobs.

Scott's hands, though white-knuckled with strain were gentle. His voice, tight and low, was tender as he explained each step of the examination. His eyes, dark and dangerous, were filled with compassion and pain. He winced when she cried out, apologizing for her discomfort and embarrassment.

Finishing the examination, Scott covered Katrina as shivers of aftershock began to shake her slender frame. "Get her a room. I want her admitted for observation. I also want x-rays and cat scans to check for internal injuries. I don't think there are any, but we need to be sure."

Barbara left immediately to do his bidding.

Sitting beside her on the bed, he waited, brushing the hair off her face and talking soothingly until her lawyer arrived. He left them alone for a few minutes and called Mike Guidry.

Sam Ortego called the police. They took statements from him, Katrina, Scott and the paramedics who brought her in then set out in search of Jack prepared to arrest him on a whole slew of charges including violation of a restraining order, domestic violence, assault, battery, and rape.

Chapter Four

Katrina opened her eyes slowly and looked around the room. The door and furniture wavered, black spots danced in her vision, blurriness made her stomach reel. Swallowing hard, she forced down the wave of nausea. Her pain, which had been dulled by sedation, came back in full force. The moan she tried to suppress escaped in a whimper. Scott appeared at her side immediately.

"Hey, little one, can I get you anything?"

She shook her head. "I hurt." His eyes darkened.

"I know, Sweetheart. Hang on, I'll get you something." He'd been by her side since they moved her to a room last evening. Ringing for a nurse, he ordered a pain shot, hoping to make her a little more comfortable.

A wary silence filled the room while they waited. Once the shot was administered, Katrina smiled slightly over at him. "Why are you still here?" she queried in a soft, timid voice.

"Where else would I be?" Scott asked.

She tried to shrug, winced instead. "Working. Or home."

"I wouldn't dare leave you alone right now."

"Why?"

"Because, that's what friends are for," he answered, a gentle rebuke in his tone.

A tear slipped down her cheek. "He ruined my flowers," she whispered, sadness clouding her voice. "He said you wouldn't want me any more. I tried to tell him we're just friends but he didn't believe me. I tried to stop him."

"He's wrong," Scott bit out through clenched teeth. Sitting beside her, he gathered her against his chest, rocking her tenderly, until the torrent ended in soft sobs. Needing to get out and get control of his raging anger, he forced a smile.

"If you're okay for a while, I think I will go home and at least shower and change."

Trina nodded, her eyelids drooping as the medication he'd ordered took effect.

Knowing she would sleep for a while, Scott left. He decided to contact Sam Ortego. He and Katrina's lawyer had talked for quite sometime the night before. Today, he wanted to know what had happened when the police arrested Jack.

Sam bit back his own rage when Scott Hensley called. "He's out."

"What?"

"Said it wasn't him. No proof, no witnesses. He had an alibi."

"No proof? He left his handprints all over her!" Scott raged.

Sam sighed. "I know. But there's not much we can do right now. It's her word against his, and he's saying he didn't do it, and them being legally married, well, it's a tough call. On top of all that, there's no prior record of abuse. Other than DWI, he's squeaky clean. Slippery bastard," he muttered then continued.

"The assault and battery may stick; we'll have to wait and see. He has one of the slimiest lawyers in town representing him. He'll find a way to get Jack out of it. Jilted husband, temporary loss of control, jealousy, pain, anguish - I'm sure he'll have a briefcase full of excuses for Jack's actions. However, the judge did reiterate the restraining order. Jack's not to go within a one mile radius of where she lives or works."

Scott snorted. "He broke it once, he'll break it again."

"Probably so. We'll just have to see what we can do to protect her." Sam had some ideas, but, not really knowing where Scott fit into Katrina's life, he kept them to himself.

Scott had other plans. Working the day shift would enable him to check on her quite often, which he did. He stayed as late as he could during the evening, using the excuse of visiting hours to leave. No one would enforce visiting hours on him, but it was a good excuse. Then he parked by her house, watching and waiting for some sign of Jack. He didn't wait long. Three nights after the attack, Jack showed up, snooping around her house and banging on the door. Holding onto his temper, Scott watched and waited until Jack left, then followed him home.

As a doctor, he abhorred violence. As a man, he felt supreme, primitive satisfaction at the surprised look on Jack Simmons's face when he opened his door to be greeted by a hard right and an equally hard left. Unprepared, the punches left Jack sprawled out on the floor. "Come on, big boy," Scott urged, his voice deceptively soft. "Beat me up."

"I don't even know you," he whined.

"That's right. You don't. But know this, the next time you're feeling manly, beat up on someone your own size." A surprised look crossed Jack's face and he struggled to his feet.

"You must be the fella hitting on my wife."

"Ex-wife," Scott corrected. "And a real man never hits on a woman."

"Aw, man, she's just a whore..." A backhanded fist which had him spitting blood cut off the rest of his words.

Jack slammed against the wall with a thud, proving the old adage that the bigger they are, the harder they fall. Eyes, black as midnight and just as dangerous as that bewitching hour, dared him to move.

Scott's fists clenched and unclenched as he struggled to control the fury raging through his system. "If you ever go near her again, I'll kill you. Do you understand?" he queried in a soft, deadly voice. Scott had pegged him correctly when he said Jack was probably more bark than bite when matched up against someone his own size. Wiping his mouth with the back of his hand, Jack nodded and whimpered, too cowed to move, much less stand up.

Instinct told Scott Jack was not above attacking from behind, so he backed out of the house until he reached his car.

Jack never moved, but his eyes watched each step the man took. It was quite a revelation for him to realize he would not be quite as free to bother Katrina. She had a hero on her side—a tall, dark, dangerous hero. A chill raced down his spine.

When Scott arrived at the hospital the next morning, Trina was gone. She'd left AMA: Against Medical Advice.

Calling Mike to fill in for him again, Scott went to her house, then her job. No one he spoke with knew where she was or had heard from her. No one. Going back to the hospital, he paced the doctors' lounge. Worry and fear warred in his soul until he was frantic.

"Someone has to know where she is," he muttered to Mike. "Did she leave alone?"

"No. A cab picked her up."

"When?" Scott demanded, raking his hand through his hair in an agitated gesture.

"Five-thirty," Mike answered.

"Why? Where would she go at five-thirty in the morning, Mike? Do you have any ideas?"

Mike shook his head, eying Scott with wary confusion. He'd never seen Scott so tied up over a patient. After what Barbara had told him about Scott's reaction when Katrina had been brought in, Mike worried about his friend.

"I'll tear this town apart until I find her and when I get my hands on the idiot responsible for her leaving, I'm going to hurt him!"

"Scott, calm down!" Mike insisted. "Listen to yourself, man. Who is this girl? What is she to you?"

"She's...we're...I..." *Love her.*

Scott slumped down into a chair. In that instant, his mind admitted what his heart had known all along. He loved her. More than that, he was in love with her. From the moment he'd set eyes on her, he had known they were destined. Being a wise man, he kept the knowledge close to his heart, knowing if he blurted it out, Mike would surely think he was one card shy of a full deck. Burying his face in his hands, he regained control of his raging emotions.

"We met not too long ago," he admitted with a sigh. "She's come to mean a great deal to me in a very short time. I'm just worried."

Mike grinned. "Well, doctor, sounds like love to me," he taunted. "About time, too."

Scott grunted but refrained from comment. Once his heart and mind calmed and were in total agreement with each other, he was able to think a bit more clearly. If anyone knew Trina's whereabouts, Sam Ortego did. Calling him, Scott ran into another brick wall. If Sam knew, he wasn't telling.

After two weeks of days filled with worry and sleepless nights, of watching her house and place of employment and staking out the school campus, it all came to an end. He arrived at work for his evening shift and on the counter, a single rose rested in a glass vase. The card simply read, *Thank you.*

He walked around, questioning everyone. All they knew was it had come for him earlier that day. A smile tugged at the corner of his mouth, excitement filled his soul. She was okay, and she hadn't forgotten him.

One week later another rose appeared with the message, *Thinking of you.*

"Okay, Katrina," he whispered. "We'll play it your way. As long as I know you haven't written me out of your life, I'll wait." Though it drove him crazy, he did just that, wondering when and where it would all end. Or begin again. One week after the last rose appeared, he received a call.

"Dr. Hensley?" At his assurance, the caller continued. "This is Sam Ortego..."

"Where's Katrina? What's wrong?"

Sam rubbed his eyes with a tired sigh. "I can't tell you that."

"Then we have nothing to discuss," Scott insisted.

"Wait! Dr. Hensley, please, just hear me out." Sure that Scott hadn't hung up, he continued. "I will tell you she's somewhere safe. The reason I called is to ask a favor of you. Would you come to court tomorrow morning? Nine o'clock."

"What's going on?"

"I'm having nothing but trouble from Jack Simmons. He's balking, refusing to sign the papers, insisting that he see

Katrina for himself. So far I've been able to convince the judge she is safer staying away, but the judge is getting tired of Jack and his attorney's antics. I'm bringing up the attack again, hoping to convince him to grant the divorce with or without Jack's signature. I was hoping you could show up to be a witness and back me up."

Scott's jaw clenched as he thought about paying Jack Simmons another visit. But he couldn't. He'd felt justified before, but now he wanted more than justification. He wanted vengeance. He wanted Katrina free of Jack, and he wanted Jack out of her life for good.

"Vengeance is mine says the Lord," a Voice reminded him.

"I'll be there," Scott assured Sam.

As fate would have it, he arrived late. He walked into the courtroom to hear Sam plead with the judge to revoke his decision that Katrina must appear before him that afternoon. His entrance garnered the judge's attention.

"May I help you?"

All eyes turned toward them as Sam walked up to Scott and shook his hand. Sam turned back to the judge.

"Your Honor, this is Dr. Scott Hensley. He was the attending physician the night Mrs. Simmons was rushed to the hospital after her estranged husband paid her a visit. It is my request, on behalf of my client, that Dr. Hensley is allowed to comment on Mrs. Simmons condition that night."

"I have the reports, Mr. Ortego," Judge Elkins shook his head with a sigh. "There are no doubts as to the condition of your client that night. What this court is concerned with is her condition now, and whether or not this marriage is salvageable."

"Your Honor, I can assure you there is no hope for this marriage. And I can further assure you Mrs. Simmons has no intentions of reconciliation or even contact with Mr. Simmons. Once again, Your Honor, I beg of this court to grant her the divorce with a permanent restraining order against her husband."

"Your Honor?" Jack's attorney raised his hand in an attempt to get the judge's attention.

Scott turned toward them. There was no mistaking the message in the dark eyes, the set jaw, the clenched fists. Jack heard it loud and clear. He grabbed his attorney's arm, whispering in his ear.

Stomach churning with the bile of defeat, the attorney addressed the court again. "Your Honor, my client has decided to sign the papers without further contest."

"Finally," the judge muttered. "Petition for divorce is granted as well as the restraining order. This court is dismissed."

* * * * *

Katrina held Scott's business card to her heart for the millionth time in nearly two months and for the millionth time she wondered how he was, where he was, what he was doing and if he was thinking of her. A tiny smile tugged at her lips as she thanked God again for life and for freedom.

Her nightmare had ended. Sam had pushed and prodded, cajoled and coerced, coming just short of bribery to get her divorce finalized, and to get a permanent restraining order against Jack. No one knew why but, oddly, after weeks of fighting it, Jack had agreed to the divorce and the restraining order. She still couldn't believe it was true. She'd received her papers an hour ago and now her newfound freedom beckoned her home.

In the time that she stayed in hiding, Trina had found a new job which she worked incognito. Just yesterday she'd rented a new apartment. Her stuff had been moved quietly last night. She had kept up with school by special arrangement, doing most of her work from the women's shelter where she'd been hiding since she left the hospital. Now she could get on with her life. Now she could relax and heal, both mentally and emotionally.

With the war over and her life just beginning, she wondered what the future held in store.

* * * * *

The first thing Scott noticed when he strode into the doctor's lounge was the yellow rose. It had been three weeks since the last one, and two weeks since he'd appeared in court at the plea of Katrina's attorney. His heart thudded thickly in his chest when he reached a trembling hand toward the card. Laughing softly, he chided himself for acting like a teenager. Picking up the card he read, then re-read.

308 W. Jefferson Apt. C.

Glancing at his watch, he swore softly. He still had three hours to go before his shift was up. Calling the florist, he had eleven roses delivered to the address on the card. The twelfth, he'd deliver in person.

* * * * *

Katrina wiped her hands on her jeans before reaching for the doorknob. She wasn't prepared for the sudden case of nerves at the thought of having Scott over for dinner. Nor did she expect the quick jolt of pleasure at the sight of him standing at her door and holding one rose. And absolutely nothing had prepared her for the surge of joy when she opened the door and he swung her up in his arms twirling her around until, breathless and laughing, she insisted he stop and put her down.

He complied, keeping one hand on her waist and holding the rose with the other.

"Where have you been? I was worried out of my mind! I've missed you! I can't ever remember missing someone so much!"

Taking a deep, trembling breath, Trina stepped out of his embrace. "C'est tout," she said.

Scott frowned. "What?"

She grinned. "How long have you lived in Louisiana?"

"Six years."

"And you don't know what C'est tout means?" she teased.

He chuckled shaking his head. "I can talk a mean streak of Spanish, but French has always eluded me. I could never get my tongue just right," he joked, tucking his tongue in his cheek and trying to talk around it. He grinned at her giggle.

"Have a hard time talking in English sometimes, too," he added in that same voice thrilled to hear her laughter.

Trina shook her head, pushing her hair back from her face. "I've finally figured it out. You're crazy."

He smiled, stepping closer to her. "If I am, sweetheart, it's all your fault."

She rolled her eyes, shook her head, and laughed. "I always get the blame."

He grinned. "So what exactly were you trying to tell me that I'm too linguistically impaired to understand?"

"C'est tout. It's over. Finished."

Scott's eyes narrowed with a frown. "But we've only just begun, sweetheart." He knew what she meant, but wanted to hear the words straight from her sweet, little mouth.

"I'm talking about my fiasco of a marriage," Trina admitted, her eyes fluttering demurely, a flush warming her cheeks.

Lifting her chin, he waited until she raised wide, wary eyes to his. "Are you okay with that? Really?" he asked.

Tears rushed to her eyes. Trina blinked them back, not wanting him to get the wrong impression. Taking a deep breath, she tried to explain.

"Yes and no. I mean... all I've ever wanted was to be married and have a family. Part of me mourns the loss. But a bigger part, the part that wants to live to a ripe old age, rejoices. It's long since been over, almost from the beginning. It just took a long time for me to give up the dream."

"Don't give it up, little one. Never give up your dreams. Sometimes you just have to wait for God's timing before certain dreams come true."

"Is that the voice of wisdom or age talking?" she teased.

Scott chuckled, brushing a thumb across her lips. "Probably a bit of both," he admitted, fighting the urge to kiss her.

As though reading his thoughts, Trina took a step back. The fear returned, gnawing at her, making her feel inadequate, unworthy. "How about some dinner?" she offered, a shy flush covering her cheeks.

"Sounds nice," Scott agreed, smothering a groan of frustration. Take it slow, he warned himself, real slow.

Over dinner, she told him where she'd been and what had happened since he'd seen her last.

Scott frowned when she told him about the women's shelter. "I wish you'd have let me know."

"I thought about it, wanted to, had to fight not to call you and at least let you know I was all right. That's when I had the idea to send the rose. It was simple and couldn't be traced back to me. Sam said the less people who knew where I was, the safer I would be."

"I wouldn't have even contacted you, if that was necessary for your safety."

"I know, but he is my lawyer. He's been working overtime to get this mess cleared up. I owed him that much, at least, for all he's done."

She continued her story, telling him of Jack's actions. "Can you imagine? After all the fighting, he just all of a sudden," she snapped her fingers for emphasis, "agrees to leave me alone. For real." Scott's eyes sparkled with mischief.

"You don't say?" he queried, his expression carefully polite, his tone laced with innocent sarcasm.

Katrina heard it and peered at him through narrow, suspicious eyes.

"You wouldn't have any idea as to what made up his mind would you?"

A triumphant smile tugged at his lips. "Not me," he denied. The grin gave him away.

"You didn't?" She gasped. "No, don't tell me. I don't want to know," she added, holding up her hand. But she knew. It made perfect sense now. Jack had been urged, convinced, coerced into leaving her alone. *Thank God.*

They talked for hours, late into the evening. Close to midnight, Scott reluctantly decided it was time to leave. Adamant, he waited until she'd checked to make sure everything was locked.

"But no one knows where I live. My address and phone number are unlisted," she protested.

"So? Check anyway," he demanded.

Rolling her eyes, she made a show of checking all the locks, calling out one room and window at a time, until she stood before him again.

He grinned.

She smiled.

Cupping her face in his hands, Scott once again wrestled with temptation. "Trina," he breathed, urging her closer to his body. "One kiss," he pleaded, his lips covering hers in a soft, tender caress. Utilizing the strength of a saint, he kept it light, choking back a groan.

Katrina trembled. The gentleness of his hands and the tenderness of his lips were at odds with the tension in his body. Where she welcomed one, she feared the other.

"'Night, little one," he whispered, biting back the words: *I love you.* Talk about scaring her off. She would certainly high tail it and run if he let that slip so soon.

Katrina stood mesmerized by the dark eyes. She'd never been treated with such kindness or so much tenderness. It was wonderful! It was scary. She didn't deserve such sweetness. A flush of embarrassment rushed to her cheeks.

"Good night," she whispered, stepping out of his reach.

"Hey." He stood firm, keeping a light hold on her arm. "What's this?" he queried, brushing his knuckles across her cheek.

She shrugged her cheeks bright red, fear back in her eyes.

Scott fought not to grind his teeth in frustration. Kissing her on the forehead, he retreated a step. "I'll call you," he assured her. "Soon," he promised, relieved at her shy smile. Reining himself in, he took another step back. "I'll wait right here until I hear the dead bolt click into place."

Reluctant, yet relieved, Katrina closed and locked the door, remaining there until she heard his car back out of the drive.

Unable to get her reactions to him out of his mind, Scott called the minute he arrived home. "Is everything okay, Sweetheart?" he queried, smiling at her soft reply. "Okay. Sleep tight. Sweet dreams."

"You, too," Trina murmured. Tucking the phone against her heart, she hugged it to her, unaware he still held it to his ear.

Scott heard the erratic beating of her heart. Clutching the phone he fought back a groan and listened without saying a word until the dial tone rang clear and loud. The echo of her heartbeat reverberated through his dreams.

Chapter Five

"How are you doing, Sweetheart?" Scott asked, hoping to see her tonight. All week he'd looked forward to the weekend. He hadn't dropped by Katrina's house or even seen her since the Saturday before. Not wanting to push, he'd talked to her only a couple of times. Tonight, though, he wanted to see her and to hold her.

Katrina shrugged slightly to herself. "Okay."

Scott could feel her tension over the line and frowned. "Feel like having company tonight?"

"If you want to."

Something was wrong. He could sense it, hear it in her voice. "What's the matter, Trina?"

Again she shrugged not willing, not able, to put her feelings into words. Depressed, alone, she feared she would end up an old maid without any children, afraid she'd be alone the rest of her life. "Nothing."

"So," he began, his voice soft and hesitant, "do you mind if I come over?"

"It doesn't matter."

Scott ground his teeth. He could understand her reluctance to say what she really felt for fear of starting an argument, but she needed to get past that, and learn to trust him.

"It does matter, Katrina," he chided in a gentle tone. "It does matter. It's a simple question. A simple yes or no will suffice."

"Okay, then," she huffed. "No. I don't feel like having company." A tense silence flowed across the lines.

"Okay. Well, I guess I'll talk to you later, then."

"Now you're angry," she accused. Men! They were all alike. As long as they got their way everything was fine, but stand up for yourself a little bit, and they puffed up like a child. Or went crazy on you. Her eyes widened when she heard his soft chuckle.

"No, Sweetheart, not angry. A bit disappointed maybe, but not angry. You never have to worry about me getting angry for you speaking your true feelings. Call me later if you feel more like talking. Okay?"

She agreed, her voice soft, hesitant.

Scott hung up the phone and growled to himself. It would be a long night! After a restless hour of flipping through the channels on television, his phone rang. Craig sounded horrible when Scott answered. His daughter, Amber was refusing to sleep after a childhood nightmare had returned the night before. He listened with sympathy and concern while his friend explained what was going on. They talked for a few minutes before hanging up. A wave of homesickness assailed Scott when he placed the receiver in its cradle. Within minutes, the phone rang again.

"Hello?"

Hearing Trina on the other end sent a thrill coursing in him. "Is the offer for company still open?" she asked.

Scott grinned. "Sure is, little one." His voice softened. "You want to tell me what's bothering you?"

Trina shrugged not knowing how to express her feelings. "I don't know. I'm just a little depressed I guess."

"Know what you need?"

"What?"

"Dinner and a movie, dancing 'til dawn, then breakfast, after which, you can sleep the day away."

"Really?"

"Doctor's orders."

She emitted a tiny laugh. "Well, Doctor, should I go alone or have an escort?"

"A beautiful lady never goes alone," he chided.

She snorted. "Well, I should have no problems then."

Scott frowned at her tone of voice. "What do you mean by that?"

Her laugh was harsh. "Oh, please. We both know I'm not so beautiful that I'd have to worry."

"I think you are," he assured her. "And I've seen some beautiful women in my time."

Katrina flushed at his intimate tone, felt oddly chastised. "Well, Doctor, do you have any idea where I might find an escort for this evening?"

"Are you asking me for a date?"

"Of course not," she tried her best to sound offended. The giggle gave her away.

Scott chuckled. "I'll be there in half an hour."

When he arrived she was still undecided as to what to wear, and near tears.

"Hey, hey," he soothed. "What's the deal? Jeans and a blouse are fine. Or a dress." He shrugged. "Cut-offs and sneakers suit me. We don't have to make a big deal out of it."

Trina blinked back the tears. "I really don't feel like going out."

Scott reached for her. "Talk to me, Katrina," he urged. "Tell me what's wrong."

Raking her fingers through her hair, she glared at him. "I miss him."

"What?"

"I miss Jack. I mean, I've never been alone. I left home when I married him. I'm no good at being alone. I..." her voice trailed off, she struggled with tears.

"Katrina, you're not thinking of going back?" he asked, unable to hide the concern in his voice.

"Now, that would be stupid, wouldn't it?"

"It wouldn't be the wisest decision in the world," Scott agreed. *Not to mention it would break my heart.*

Trina rolled her eyes. "Boy, that's an understatement," she muttered. 'I don't know what I'm going to do," she insisted, throwing up her hands in exasperation. Her eyes narrowed when he swung her up in his arms and carried her into the living room.

"What do you think you're doing?"

"I'm going to sit right here," he plopped down on the couch, "and hold you while you cry." Her eyes darkened as tears rushed to fill them.

She tried to blink them back, to fight them. She lost. With a soft moan, she succumbed to the deluge which had threatened all day. Sinking her face in his shoulder, she soaked his shirt with tears.

Clueless on how to comfort her, Scott held her while she emptied her heart. His hands ran over her back in a soothing caress, but he didn't dare shush her. When the sobs subsided into soft, hiccupping sounds he kissed the top of her silky head. "Feel better now?"

"No."

He grinned at her defiant tone. "Cry some more, then."

"I thought you couldn't stand it when I cry," she wailed, a torrent of fresh sobs escaping.

"I can't," he whispered, his voice husky and tender, wishing he could take away the pain and confusion she felt. "It's tearing me apart," he assured her.

His sweet words only made her cry harder. "I'm sorry," she sobbed. "I don't know what it is. I mean, I thought, I hoped I was pregnant. I want a baby so bad and..." she trailed off, embarrassed at her revelation. "I mean, I know it wouldn't be easy or smart to be tied to him the rest of my life through a child, but I've always wanted a baby."

"I understand, Sweetheart," he soothed. His heart clenched at her pain. His body tightened with need at her sitting so vulnerable on his lap. "You're still young. You'll have your baby. I promise."

His voice was husky, thick. Trina heard it and felt the response of his body. She shuddered with fear, struggling slightly to pull herself together and get up.

Scott tightened his hold on her. "Oh, no, you don't," he argued. "You're not running away. I will not force you into anything you don't want. I would never hurt you like that, but I'm not letting you up until you relax. Just trust me a little bit."

"I do trust you," she insisted, but remained stiff, tense and rigid in his embrace.

"Trina, Love" he soothed, brushing the hair off her flushed face. "Please don't be afraid of me," he pleaded, his lips caressing her face with feathery kisses.

The endearment was her undoing. No one had ever treated her with such tenderness.

Scott felt her relax. Her soft moan of surrender reacted on him quicker than the strongest aphrodisiac. He groaned, pulling her more firmly against him. One hand sank into the thick, luxurious softness of her silky hair while the other held her against his body. His mouth covered hers in a hungry kiss, drinking deeply, greedily, of her sweetness. His lips clung to hers; molding and shaping them to his until each ragged, painful breath he took robbed her of her own.

He heard her whimper as fear once again deprived him of her full surrender. He loosened his hold by degrees, lessening the pressure of his lips until she lay passive in his arms.

When Trina came to her senses she lay limp in his arms, devoid of even the slightest hint of sanity. Her fingers were curled in the thick, black hair showing through the open collar of his shirt. She could hear his harsh, uneven breathing; feel the thudding of his heart, keeping rhythm with her own. A flush of embarrassment covered her cheeks as she eyed him through lowered lashes. His head was thrown back, his face taut, eyes closed. A tiny smile crossed his lips as he tugged her hand free from its grip, urging it toward his mouth. She heard his low, triumphant chuckle when he brushed his moustache over her knuckles then uncurled her fingers to bury his lips into her palm. Her body responded with an answering shiver. Awed, and a little afraid of her reaction to him, she tugged gently at the hair above his upper lip.

"Ouch," he whispered. "Witch."

When he opened his eyes, they sparkled with mirth and desire.

"So beautiful," he whispered, kissing her fingertips, his eyes capturing hers in a heated embrace. "So sweet. So full of passion."

So innocent, he thought, when another blush covered her cheeks. She didn't have to explain that, although she'd been married for nearly ten years, she wasn't very experienced in the way of men. He could sense it. Her only experience had been that of fear and violence. Though she aroused a violent lust within him, Scott determined to be gentle with her, and patient. He figured he would be certifiably insane long before he made her his own.

His arms tightened around her for a brief hug before he uncurled his long frame off the couch. Setting her gently on her feet, he let her slide along his body, watching the display of emotions on her face and in her eyes. His smile was tender as he caressed her lips with his own once more. "What do you say we pick up a pizza or Chinese, and take a drive? I know a lovely little spot where we could picnic."

"Now?"

"Yeah, now; a moonlight stroll along the bayou and a picnic under the stars. Sound good?"

"Sounds dangerous. And romantic," she parried.

A teasing light sparkled in her dark eyes. He grinned, not missing the hidden meaning in her words. "No more dangerous than staying here, alone, where there's a soft, warm bed," he argued, cupping her tiny waist in his hands and pulling her closer to his body. "And I'm a sucker for romance."

"Okay. Okay," she agreed stepping out of his embrace. "I'll go wash my face and brush my hair; then we can leave."

"Don't be long," he ordered, aware of the husky note in his voice. "I can't bear to have you out of my sight for more than five minutes."

"Right," Trina muttered, rolling her eyes for emphasis. "Know what I'm really hungry for?" she queried once they were on their way.

"What?" Scott wanted to know.

"A great big hamburger, a huge order of fries and a chocolate shake."

"Hamburger? Those things are bad for you. They're loaded with sodium and contain all sorts of fillers."

"And pizza's good for you?" she queried.

Scott grinned at the sarcasm in her voice. "Pizza is a full course meal," he argued, ticking the ingredients off with his fingers. "Bread, meat, cheese and vegetables."

Trina grunted. "And enough salt and fat to last you a week."

He laughed. "Right. We'll have it your way. Hamburgers it is."

"And fries and a shake," she reminded.

"I'd like to know where you're going to put it all, little one."

"Just watch. Jack used to say he would rather buy my clothes than feed me. That was when he was nice to me, before we were married and things went to hell," she added, swallowing hard the lump of tears clogging her throat.

Scott reached over and caressed her cheek. "It's all over now, Sweetheart. It can only get better."

"Promises, promises, promises," she remarked, smiling at his gentle laugh. Stretching, she raised her arms heavenward, breathing in the fragrant night air when he put the top down on the car. With a laugh, she shook her hair free from its ponytail and let the wind transform it from sleek silk into a tangled mass.

Scott grinned as she transformed from a scared, confused woman into a laughing, free-spirited, little girl. A silent vow echoed through his mind, settled in his heart: Her life would be heaven on earth from this point on. After that kiss, he'd destroy anything or anyone that tried to come between them.

Arriving at his destination, he led her over to a tiny gazebo way out in back of a large plantation house. Lighting an old-fashioned coal-oil lamp, he unloaded their food until it lay before them like a feast. "We'll eat before it gets cold, and then take a walk."

Katrina looked around wide-eyed. "Where are we? Does anyone live over there?" She nodded toward the house.

"We won't get into trouble, will we?"

Scott grinned, his eyes sparkling. "Nah, I can come here anytime I want."

Crossing her arms over her chest and tapping her foot expectantly, she waited for him to explain.

"Eat," he ordered with a laugh, a subtle, husky chuckle which assured her he was teasing.

Trina shook her head and frowned. "Not until you tell me where we are. I know that look, Doctor, you're hiding something from me. If you don't tell me, I'm going to start walking," she threatened. "I think I can find the general direction of town."

"You are so pretty when you're in a huff." He chortled. "Reminds me of an angry kitten. All you need is a little cuddling and you'll start purring."

"I scratch and bite, too," she warned with a cat-like hiss.

"Oh, I'm scared now."

"Scott, I'm serious. You'd better tell me where we are and who you know that lives in such a big, beautiful house, otherwise I'll get really angry." She tried to sound tough and threatening. She really did.

Scott tossed his head with a shout of laughter. "Oh, please, you're scaring me to death."

"Jerk," she huffed.

"Eat your supper, little one, before it gets cold. Then I'll give you the grand tour."

"The grand tour?" Her eyes widened in surprise. "You live here?"

"Guilty," he confessed. "Welcome to *The Palace*. When Amber and Ace were younger, they came to visit. One look and Amber dubbed it the palace." He chortled at the memory.

"Who's Amber and Ace?"

Over dinner and the next two hours he told her about his best friend Craig, and Craig's family. They took a walk along the bayou and, as promised, he gave her a tour of his home and grounds.

"You'll have to come and spend the day sometime soon. The house is full of mystery and beauty. The place takes on a whole new identity in the daytime."

"I'll bet," she said, awe and wonder reflected in her soft voice. "Why did you bring me here?"

"Can you think of a lovelier spot to have a picnic?" he asked.

Trina shook her head.

"It's special to me, and I wanted to share it with you. I knew you didn't feel like being part of a crowd, and, to be honest, I didn't either. I just wanted to be with you." Raising her hand to his lips, he kissed it. "Only you."

Alone, even with darkness all around, she could see the glow in his eyes. It terrified and thrilled her at the same time.

Scott pulled her gently in his arms, breathed her name, and covered her lips with his in a tender caress. Keeping a tight rein on his emotions, he kept the kiss light, teasing, tempting, a promise of more to come.

Chapter Six

"Have any plans for tomorrow?" Scott asked. For two weeks he'd spent every spare moment with Katrina. Though wary of rushing her or scaring her off, he stayed in touch by phoning and dropping by. More often than not, he ended up staying longer than he'd planned, but he found it difficult to leave once he was with her. She didn't seem to mind the company, assuring him it didn't bother her when he dropped by unannounced.

Katrina fingered the silky petals of one of his most recent gifts of yellow roses. Her apartment never lacked of fragrance. The huge, beautiful, yellow flowers graced nearly every room. She smiled.

"I'm thinking of going to church," she admitted.

Scott smiled to himself. As their relationship developed into a more trusting one, she talked of her desire to return to the church of her childhood. She told him of the things she loved the most, the things she disagreed with and the things she didn't understand. He had encouraged her to attend, but to his knowledge, she hadn't as of yet.

"That's great, Sweetheart. What time?"

She shrugged, frowning into the phone. "I'm not sure, probably early. Before I chicken out."

"Trina, there's no harm in going back," he chided. "You may not feel comfortable right away, but it's always a good way to start. From what you've told me, you're feeling closer to God every day. If you feel the desire to go back to church, I'm sure He won't mind. Besides, no one will know anything about you that you don't share with them. There's no law saying you have to confess everything all at once, or anything right away, or anything at all, for that matter, no Biblical law I know of. That's between you and God, and He already knows what's happened and why. God doesn't judge us, Trina; He merely offers love, mercy and forgiveness. You know that. You've already experienced it to some degree. Maybe going to church is His next step for you."

"I know," she admitted. "But, I'm just not sure yet."

He waited while she hesitated, praying silently for words of wisdom and guidance for her.

"I'm just so afraid of making a mistake. The church is big on Reconciliation and the Sacrament is based on Scripture, though I don't know exactly where. I wish I understood more. Maybe then I'd know what God wants me to do."

A thought occurred to him. "What are you afraid of, the judgment of God or the judgment of men?"

She stammered. "Both, I guess."

"Then it's not time. Maybe all you need to concern yourself with at this point is getting comfortable with going back to church and getting comfortable with God. You have to trust in the forgiveness of God before you can trust in the forgiveness of man."

"But isn't that what confession is all about? Receiving, through the Sacrament of Reconciliation and penance, the forgiveness of God?"

"I don't know, Trina. I know very little about your religion. Only the things you've told me," he admitted. "But I think it's a wonderful idea."

"You really think so?"

"Yeah. I really think so. How about lunch afterwards?"

"Would you like to go with me?"

Scott hesitated, wanting to, but unsure if he should be intimately involved in this part of her life just yet. "I guess...I mean.... Sure, I'd love to."

"You don't have to. Maybe it's something I need to do for myself."

He chuckled. "Are you taking back the invitation?"

"No. You just seemed kind of hesitant. I don't want you to feel obligated."

"Obligated? Honey, I'll grab any excuse to be with you," he teased, imagining her blush.

His imagination wasn't mistaken.

Trina felt her cheeks grow hot. "Okay. Ten o'clock?"

"There's not an earlier service?"

"Eight-thirty."

"Perfect. Then we can have breakfast and lunch."

"Are you trying to fatten me up?" she asked.

Scott laughed, a hearty, husky sound which had her smiling in return.

"I doubt that's possible, Kitten. I've seen the way you eat, and you haven't gained an ounce."

* * * * *

The next morning he picked her up bright and early. They shared a quick, light breakfast before church.

Though he'd never set foot in a Catholic church, Scott hesitated in the doorway, awed by the quiet beauty of the little country place. Sunlight streamed through the stained glass windows and reflected off the well-worn pews. He gazed in amazement at the statues of the patron Saint, the Holy Mother and the infant Jesus, having no doubt that love and talent went into the making of them. A work of art in itself, the Crucifix hung on the wall behind the altar. The suffering and love captured so marvelously on the face of Jesus sent an ache, like a shaft of hot iron, straight through him.

Following the Mass as closely as possible, he watched Trina out of the corner of his eye, saw tears fill her eyes, and wondered if they were of sadness or joy. He squeezed her hand in a gesture of support. When the time came to share the Peace of Christ, he lifted her hand to his mouth in a brief but tender kiss, before turning to greet his neighbors.

He sensed her tension and desire when the time came to receive Communion, and left with an admiration for the simple beauty of the service. Though some might consider it ritualistic, the heart of the prayers and the reverence with which they were recited touched his heart and warmed a place deep in his spirit.

Raised in the Baptist faith, Scott found more gratification in a one-on-one relationship with God rather than the structure of formal religion. However, he could see why many would find comfort knowing that, no matter where they were in life, the Mass would always be there, unchanging, solid, and strong. Like God.

Over lunch, he listened with interest as Katrina explained everything she could remember about the religion she'd been raised with, and how she'd strayed during her teen years and during her marriage. It angered him to think a man would force his wife to abstain from the religion of her youth just because he didn't understand or appreciate its uniqueness. But then, no one had ever accused Jack Simmons of being much of a man.

Intrigued, Scott vowed to learn more about her religion and hoped to be a source of knowledge, and possibly comfort, for her during her journey back to the Lord. He encouraged her to continue to seek the Lord on her own and to return to church as often as she felt led to do so. It certainly couldn't hurt; and it just might prove to be the greatest source of comfort and healing for her after all she'd been through.

They spent the whole day together. Not wanting it to end, Scott coaxed her into seeing a movie, after which he planned on taking her to dinner. "Want something?" he queried.

Trina grinned. "Popcorn."

Scott smiled. "Make it a large," he told the attendant. "We'll share."

Katrina smiled sweetly. "And add a peanut butter cup."

Scott looked down at her, an eyebrow arched in teasing. "You just polished off half a cow, where do you plan on putting all this?"

She giggled. "Can't have popcorn without chocolate."

Scott shook his head winking at the young man behind the counter. "Don't you just love women with healthy appetites?"

Neither he nor Trina missed the innuendo. He grinned, nodding in agreement as her cheeks grew pink. "Yes sir. Especially one as pretty as she is," he added.

Scott slipped his arm around her waist. About as subtle as a Pit Bull and just as possessive. "That she is," he admitted, eying the young man with a pointed look.

Katrina rolled her eyes and winked at the young man who was grinning from ear to ear. "Thank you," she said, smiled pleasantly and reached for the popcorn and candy while Scott grabbed their drinks. Once seated, they chatted while waiting for the previews.

Scott watched as she munched on popcorn along with eating a peanut butter cup. He frowned. "That's disgusting."

She frowned back. "No more disgusting than peanut butter and banana sandwiches." One of his favorite snacks.

"That's healthy," he countered, with a guilty grin.

Trina smiled. "Fact, doctor? Or simply professional opinion?" she teased. "Have you ever tried popcorn and chocolate?"

"Don't think I want to."

She grinned. "Close your eyes."

"Why?"

"Just do it." He did. "Okay, now open your mouth," she instructed.

He shook his head. "I'm afraid of what you're going to feed me," he teased.

"Use your imagination. No, don't," she ordered as though reading his thoughts when he grinned that arrogant, roguish grin. "Just taste it Scott. It's wonderful. First you take a bite of the chocolate, then, while you can still taste it, the popcorn. You like a Snickers candy bar, don't you?"

He nodded.

"Well, it's the same principle. Salty and sweet. You know, peanuts and chocolate. Try it," she urged.

"Okay." Closing his eyes he took a bite of the candy. Careful to be gentle, he grabbed her finger with his teeth and licked the chocolate off.

Trina gasped. "Stop it, before I spill this on you," she warned, then regretted the words the minute they were out of her mouth. Especially when she heard his throaty chuckle.

"That could be interesting," he teased.

She snorted. "You're a jerk."

He chortled. "You're adorable."

Trina had the grace to smile. "I guess I asked for that," she admitted with a blush. He agreed that she did.

The movie, a wonderfully funny romantic comedy, made them laugh and tease each other until tears of hilarity streamed down their cheeks and their sides hurt.

After the show and too full from lunch and movie snacks, they opted for Scott's special garden salad, which he whipped up at her house after picking up the ingredients at an all-night market. Not wanting the evening to end, Scott reluctantly checked with his answering service to find out if there were any urgent calls. He grinned when the operator told him the only urgent call was from someone named Craig.

"He wouldn't leave his last name; said you'd know who he was," she explained.

"No problem," he assured with a laugh before hanging up to dial Craig's number.

"Where've you been?" his friend demanded upon answering the phone. "I've been trying to reach you all day. All I ever heard was 'he's out. I'll give him the message you called' from some snippy little answering service."

Scott laughed. "I'm entitled to a day off, aren't I?"

Craig chuckled. "Not unless you check in with me first." Then he told Scott of their vacation plans.

Scott hung up the phone with a whoop. "Alright!" He swung Trina around by the waist. "Next week! They're coming next week. I can't wait for you to meet them!"

"Who?"

"Craig, Tamera, and the kids. I'm going to put in for a few days off. Think I'll take them down to White Castle and New Orleans. Want to come?" She frowned, looked hesitant.

"I don't know."

"You're still out of school aren't you?"

She nodded. "Yes, but what about my job?"

He shrugged. "Take off."

"And who's going to pay my bills?"

"I will."

She shook her head. "I don't think so," she countered.

"Aw, c'mon Trina. If you need help, I'll help. I'd really like for you to meet them."

"What if they don't want to meet me? Or don't like me when they do?"

Scott felt an immediate surge of irritation. "Why do you do that? Why do you think no one will like you? They'll love you, not only for who you are, but because I love you."

She stared at him wide-eyed. "What?"

He groaned. He hadn't wanted it to come out that way! No choice but to play it out, he nodded. "Yes, Trina. I love you," he assured, his voice quiet, sincere. "I didn't want to say anything just yet. Didn't want to rush you or scare you off. But, these things have a way of coming out when you least expect them to. The truth usually does."

Katrina's cheeks grew warm at his admonishment and admission. "I..."

Cupping her face in gentle hands, Scott cut off her reply with a tender kiss. "You don't have to say anything, Sweetheart. I know it's kind of sudden. And soon. I'd rather you say nothing than something you're not quite sure of yet. Or don't mean at all."

"I don't know what to say," she admitted, awe and wonder reflected in her soft voice.

He grinned. "Just say you'll come with us."

"But," she hesitated again.

Scott swore under his breath at the fear and anxiety in her eyes. "Trina, don't be afraid of me, or my friends. No one will hurt you."

Shame darkened her eyes, tears trailed down her cheeks. "I know. It's just that I'm afraid you're wrong, and they won't like me after they find out about my past."

He ground his teeth in agitation. "You don't know them. I do. They would never be so shallow as to judge you for something you had very little, if any, control over. What makes you think I'll go into detail about your past anyway?

Do you think my love is so superficial that I'd do anything to embarrass or humiliate you?"

"I guess not," she admitted avoiding his gaze, ashamed that she was afraid he'd do just that. "I'll go if you want me to."

Scott hesitated this time. He wanted her with them, but not because she felt pressured or obligated to go and certainly not if she was afraid of causing a strain between them if she didn't. "Look, if you don't want to go just say so. You don't have to do what I want, whenever I want. You're feelings count here too. Don't give in just to avoid a discussion."

"It's not discussions I want to avoid. It's a fight."

Raking his fingers through his hair, Scott suppressed a growl. "A difference of opinion doesn't always end up in a fight, Katrina." His voice was soft even though he was unable to disguise the agitation he felt.

"Then why are you getting angry?" she countered, stepping away from him.

It was the ultimate show of fear. Scott closed his eyes and prayed for guidance and tolerance. What would it take for her to get over her fear and to trust him?

"Trina," he sighed, clenching his fists to keep from reaching for her. "I love you, Trina. I swear I will never put a hand on you in anger." He held one out to her beseechingly.

"I'm not saying we'll never disagree or argue, but I promise, on everything I hold sacred, I will never hit you."

She eyed him but a moment before placing her trembling hand in his. Moving forward, she put her arms around his waist and took the next step in relinquishing the fear.

He hadn't noticed he held his breath until it rushed out in a sigh of relief. Wrapping his arms around her, Scott hauled her firmly against his chest. Lowering his lips, he captured hers in a tender embrace.

Her head tilted, lips parted, body swayed in unconscious surrender. His reaction resembled that of a starving man offered a feast. Pulling her more firmly against him, Scott devoured her sweetness. His mouth clung to hers in deep, hot, relentless pursuit until he was sure she trembled from desire and only desire.

"Trina," he breathed. "Sweet. Beautiful. Love," he moaned, pulling her up in his arms, his lips moving to caress the tender skin showing through the open collar of her shirt.

"I want you," he admitted, tugging gently at the buttons. "I want you so much." He felt her stiffen as she realized how close he was to losing control.

"No!" she pushed away, struggled out of his grasp. "Please," she pleaded. "I'm not ready."

Scott forcefully reined himself in and got a hold on his emotions. "Okay," he whispered, his voice thick. "Okay. Just let me hold you," he pleaded, pulling her in his arms once more.

Picking her up, he carried her to the couch, settling her on his lap. Sinking his fingers in the thick mass of red-gold hair, he buried her face in his shoulder as she trembled in his arms.

"I'm sorry," he whispered. "You're just so beautiful I get carried away."

"Blame it on me," she teased, in an effort to calm her raging senses.

He grinned. "I'm not blaming you. Yeah," he contradicted. "I guess I am. It's not my fault you're so beautiful you take my breath away."

"Right," she snorted. "I'm so beautiful. My legs are too short, my breasts are too small, and my hips are too big. And you think I'm beautiful. You, doctor, need your head examined. Or your eyes."

Scott glared at her, irritated beyond belief at what he was hearing. "That low-life son-of-a-bitch really did a number on you, didn't he?"

Trina gasped, surprised and shocked at his anger. "I was just joking."

"Well, it's not funny. You're constantly putting yourself down, and I'm sick of it!" Lunging from the couch, he carried her into the bedroom and stood her in front of the full-length mirror.

"Look at yourself," he insisted, urging her chin up with his hand, determined she see herself as he saw her.

"Your skin is like silk, all peachy and soft." He brushed his knuckles down her cheek. "Your hair is like satin, thick and shiny, makes me think of..." he hesitated. How could he describe the rich gold shot with equal proportions of red? he wondered, running his fingers through it, pulling her head back against his chest and placing a kiss on it.

"Makes me think of a fiery sunset. And those eyes," he groaned, forcing himself not to turn her around to face him. "Big and luminous and incredibly rich. Like two huge chocolate drops in a bowl of fresh peaches and cream. Those lips," he traced them with his thumb, "soft and full, beg to be kissed."

His fingers trailed down her throat and over her shoulders until he cupped her breasts in his hands. "Feel perfect to me," he breathed, giving them an intimate squeeze. Releasing the tempting flesh, he continued, running his hands over her torso to cup her waist. "Beautiful," he assured her, his voice thick and husky. "So tiny. I can almost clasp my hands together, you're so tiny."

His hands continued their torturous journey, cupping her hips. With a gentle tug, he pulled her firmly against his body. "Flared just right," he hummed. "Baby-making hips. Watching you walk, with that subtle sway of yours, drives me crazy," he confessed.

"And those legs," he rolled his eyes with a satisfied grunt. Turning her around, he picked her up, and wrapped them around his waist.

"Not long, true. But incredibly slender and well toned. The sexiest pair of legs I've seen in a long time. And I see plenty of them in my profession," he admitted, stroking her thigh.

"You have an abundance of energy, and depths of untapped passion which shows in the way you carry yourself, the glow you radiate, and the way you laugh and cry, with all of your emotions. That in itself is a turn on. Knowing when you love, you'll love with all of your being, that you'll hold nothing back, and you'll give yourself freely and completely. I know you haven't been loved like that before, and it's hard for you to trust you ever will, or can. But I love you, Katrina. I love you like that," he whispered.

With a soft moan, he kissed the tear which slipped from her eye. "I love you, Kitten. I think you're beautiful and it hurts me when you brush off a compliment or put yourself down."

"I'm sorry," she whispered, and hung her head, feeling confused, hopeful and ashamed all at once.

"Don't apologize," Scott insisted, lifting her chin with a gentle finger.

"Just quit. Okay?"

Her smile, albeit a wobbly one, was brilliant as his tender words sank deep into her heart and mind. "Yes sir, Doctor Hensley," she complied as meekly as possible.

He chuckled. "This is the only time I'll allow you to call me sir."

"Thank you," she whispered, brushing a lock of hair off his forehead. "You make me feel beautiful."

"I hope you never get tired of hearing it. Or of hearing how much I love you. Now that it's out, I doubt I'll be able to keep from saying it."

Katrina bit back her response. She loved him too, but was so afraid; afraid of not being worthy, of it being too good to be true, and of herself, that somehow, she would mess it up; that she wasn't as passionate as he imagined. Jack never seemed satisfied unless he hurt her.

It never dawned on her the lack was in Jack, not herself and that Jack had made sure she never entertained the thought. So, she reveled in the pleasure of Scott's words, basked in the warmth of his touch and kept her feelings and fears to herself.

Scott saw the play of emotions on her face and in those beautiful eyes. Recognizing what he saw, he felt a tug of pain and anger. Determined to be patient, he allowed her the privilege of privacy and respected her silence. *For now.* The day would come, he vowed, when she would open up and let him show her the love she deserved and he so desperately felt.

Chapter Seven

Scott buried his face in his hands with a weary sigh. This had been one of the worst days of his career, and it was barely noon. One emergency after another kept everyone in the hospital on their toes. Then to top it all off, one of the regular patients, a child whom they'd pulled through one crisis after another, died after a week in the Critical Care unit.

Mike had lost it while administering CPR. Sobbing, he begged and pleaded, alternately praying and cursing until he couldn't work anymore. Scott had to practically drag him away from the little boy's side so he could take over in the attempt to revive the child. But it wasn't meant to be. Then came the horrid task of telling the parents. A perfect ending to a perfectly wretched morning.

Raking his fingers through his hair, he choked back a sob. I'm getting too old for this, he thought. If this morning wasn't bad enough, he hadn't heard from Katrina since he left her apartment two nights ago.

The memory of that evening played back with vivid clarity in his mind, and he wondered if he'd overstepped his boundaries and scared her off. Had she thought his declaration of love was false? Too soon? Frightening? Had he been too rough in his attempt to help build her self-esteem? Had he succeeded or failed? Helped or hurt?

The man in him insisted he'd been right while the doctor in him examined his methods. Pushing his lunch tray aside, he swallowed the hard lump of nausea lodged in his throat. Though he couldn't choke down a bite if he wanted to, hospital food still left a lot to be desired.

"Come in," he grumbled, not turning to greet whomever had the indecency to interrupt the first few precious moments of quiet he'd had in hours. He didn't move until he felt the hands gently massaging the tension out of his shoulders.

Katrina smiled to herself as he rolled his shoulders with a lusty sigh and relaxed under her tender administrations.

"Just what I needed, Barb," he remarked. "Knew there was a reason you're my favorite nurse."

"Who's Barb?"

Scott opened his eyes, swung around at the voice, and pulled her in his arms. "Trina! Where on earth have you been? I haven't heard from you in days."

"Who's Barb?" she asked again.

He grinned. "My favorite nurse. We've worked together for years."

She arched an eyebrow at him. "Oh, really?"

"You don't think I'd let just anyone rub my shoulders do you?" he queried, laughing when she struggled in his grasp.

"Don't," he insisted, resting his forehead against hers. "Hold me, Trina," he pleaded, his tone soft. "It's been one hellacious day."

Concerned at the weariness in his voice, Trina relented. Pulling his head against her breast, she ran her fingers through his hair. Her arms tightened around him automatically and her hands ran over his back and shoulders in a soothing caress as he filled her in on his morning. Words didn't come easily to her, so Trina said nothing, offering her support in silence; doubting anything she'd say could ease the pain and grief evident in his voice.

Scott tightened his arms around her. Here, in her embrace, he'd found the peace he'd sought since escaping into the doctors' lounge twenty minutes ago. A smile tugged at his lips as they traveled up the smooth, silky flesh of her throat to nibble at her chin.

"Barbara," he began and felt her stiffen. "Is a very competent, very happily married nurse whom I've worked with for the past five years." He gazed tenderly into her dark eyes. "Efficient as she is, she does not have your magic touch, Kitten," he assured, his voice husky, his lips covering hers in a tender caress.

She smiled, regarding him with laughing brown eyes. "I knew that," she lied glibly, giggling at his throaty chuckle.

"Yeah, right," He agreed, his smile all-knowing. "So, are you gonna tell me what you've been up to the past couple of days?"

"Working. Marcy's been sick, and Sarah had to stay home because her little boy has chicken pox. I pulled a double Monday and yesterday, and I have to be in at three this afternoon. But," she smiled warmly. "Since I'm such a valuable employee, willing to help out in a pinch, Mac gave me Tuesday off along with my scheduled days of Wednesday and Thursday and I don't have to be in until three on Friday."

Scott laughed. "So that means you can go with us?"

She nodded.

"Tell Mac I love him. I'm going to be pretty tied up this weekend too. And Monday. But I'm off Tuesday through Sunday. Guess that means we won't see much of each other until next week," he remarked, frowning at the realization.

"Guess not," she agreed.

Shifting in his chair, Scott pulled her across his lap, cuddling her against his chest. "Well, in that case..." he muttered, burying his hands in her hair and his lips on hers in a hungry gesture.

"Scott," she mumbled, struggling slightly. "Suppose someone sees us?" Without effort he rose with her in his arms, walked to the door and shoved the lock firmly in place. Not breaking stride, he turned and laid her gently on the cot, pinning her down with his long frame.

"What are you doing?" Trina hissed, shocked and touched, and, despite herself, aroused at the intimate contact.

"Gotta get in a week's worth of hugs and kisses," he muttered, stopping her struggles with a gentle caress and her protests with his mouth. "Do you know how long I've wanted to hold you like this?" he whispered, feeling her tremble beneath him.

She shook her head.

Her cheeks were flushed, her lips slightly parted. A shiver of need coursed through him. Scott groaned, brushing his lips across her forehead.

"Too long," he assured, pulling her soft form firmly against his long frame. "Actually I'd like to more than simply hold you like this. Much more."

Fear slipped in, lurking in the dark depths of her eyes and cut him like a knife. His smile was tender, as was his touch.

"But not here, not like this. You're much too precious for that. I understand you need time to trust me, and yourself. I love you, Katrina," he whispered, and he wanted to show her. Desperately.

A knock on the door stopped him from seducing her where they lay, from showing her that what he felt for her was beautiful and so right. Strong, yet tender. Fierce, yet gentle. There would be no shame, only joy. No pain, only pleasure.

"What?" he barked.

"We have an ambulance on the way," a hesitant voice answered.

Swearing softly, he assured whomever it was he would be right out. Pulling Trina up, he smoothed the rumpled mass of red-gold hair off her face. Cupping her cheeks in his hands, he kissed her with all the tenderness he possessed. "Promise you'll call. No matter what the time," he mumbled against her lips.

She nodded, smiled shyly, and promised.

Scott walked her to her car, for the first time in his life hating his profession, despising the demands on his time that separated him from the woman he loved.

* * * * *

Scott hurried home. The Harrises would be in shortly if they hadn't already beaten him there. Joy swept through him at the sight of the dark blue Suburban parked in the drive. Carrying a sandwich tray, he opened the door just in time to see a small boy, shrieking with laughter, race down the stairs. His sister followed on his heels. Balancing the tray, he shoved it at the girl and swooped the boy up in his arms.

"Hello, beautiful," he greeted the lovely dark haired, seventeen-year-old with a kiss on the cheek. "What's going on?" he asked the grinning boy in his arms, whose gray eyes shone with laughter and mischief.

"I took Sissy's phone card."

"Brat," Amber Harris muttered, well versed in the antics of her eight- year-old brother Ace, who, even when not cooped up in a vehicle all day, was wired hotter than an electrical fence.

"This it?" Scott asked, taking the card from the boy and slipping it in his pocket. He turned to Amber.

"Since when do you need a phone card to make a call from here?"

"I wanted to call a friend back home. I got my own phone and phone line for my birthday. I was going to charge the call, so I wouldn't have to worry about time limits."

"And since when do you have to worry about time limits over here?" he asked, his dark brow lifting in an irritated gesture.

"She's going to call Stanley," her brother interrupted before Amber could answer. In a singsong voice, he continued: "Sissy and Stanley sittin' in a tree, k-i-s-s-i-n-g. First comes love, then comes marriage, then comes Sissy with a baby carriage."

"That's right," Amber assured him, her eyes narrowed into shimmering slits of sapphire. With a poke in the ribs, she tickled her brother, grinning at his delighted shriek.

"And if the baby's a boy, I'm going to drown it so he doesn't grow up to be a brat like his uncle. Or grandfather," she muttered under her breath.

Scott chuckled. So that's how the wind blew. A boy, he thought, wondering how her father was handling the situation. By her remark, he would guess not too well. "We'll discuss phone arrangements later. Where are your parents?"

"In the kitchen."

The sudden, enticing, aroma of coffee confirmed her statement. With a nod, he headed in that direction, still holding the boy protectively in his arms. Amber followed with the sandwiches.

"Anybody home?" Scott called out.

Craig Harris turned to greet his friend who walked into the kitchen carrying his son. "Sandwiches?" he asked with a frown. "All day on the road, and we get sandwiches?"

Scott chuckled. "Well, when I told the maid you were coming to visit, she quit. Said she wasn't putting up with the two of us," he teased, welcoming the hearty hug from the other man. "Hey, gorgeous," he greeted Craig's wife, Tamera, with a wink.

Tamera smiled, shook her head, and lifted her cheek for his kiss. After all these years, it still surprised her that the two men looked so much alike. Tall and hard framed, they stood an identical six feet. Broad shoulders, narrow waist, long, muscular legs, dark hair; they looked enough alike to pass for twins. Raised on neighboring ranches, they'd survived the gossip and rumors surrounding their parentage, and came through as the best of friends. Theirs was a friendship which had survived and strengthened over the past forty years. Taking the sandwiches from her daughter, she placed them on the table and ordered everyone to wash up before dinner.

A lull in the conversation around the dinner table allowed Scott the opportunity to address his friends with the question burning in his heart. His gaze rested on each a full minute before locking with Craig's. "I hope you all don't mind that I've invited a friend to tag along with us tomorrow?"

He turned to Amber. Slipping her hand in his, he raised it to his lips. "You won't mind sharing your room, will you, Beautiful?" Before she could answer, he turned to the little boy. "And, you won't mind sharing a room with me, will you, Ace?"

Everyone gazed at him in surprised pleasure, except Ace whose gaze was alive with curiosity. "Is it a boy?"

Scott grinned. "No. It's not a boy. It's a lady. A very special lady."

Ace frowned. "Well, does she have a son?"

Again, Scott grinned. "No. Not yet."

Craig chuckled. "Well, that answers that. Of course we don't mind."

"And you should know better than to ask," Tamera scolded, chiding him with a firm look.

Amber leaned over and kissed him on the cheek. "Yeah," she agreed. "And if it is she who has put that sparkle in your eyes, I can't wait to meet her."

"The sparkle's only for you, Sweetheart," he assured as he had since the day she was born, laughing at the warm color that rushed to her cheeks.

After supper, the men slipped out on the patio for a chat. Amber went upstairs to use the phone, while Tamera settled Ace down for the night.

"So," Craig began, "tell me about this 'friend' of yours. What's her name?"

Scott's eyes danced. "Katrina, and she's beautiful; petite but tough. She's young and sweet and vulnerable and, despite all she's been through, incredibly naive. There's a natural strength in her she's coming to recognize and use. She's been going through some rough times, and a real nasty divorce, but she's holding up. She's got the most beautiful laugh. And her hair..."

He shook his head at a loss as how to describe it. "It's thick and silky, and the most unusual color. Not red, not gold, but an intriguing combination of the two—like a fiery sunset. And she has the most beautiful brown eyes," again he hesitated.

"Big and soulful and incredibly, rich, brown. Like dark, liquid chocolate."

Craig chuckled. "Liquid chocolate? I've never heard of anyone having eyes like liquid chocolate," he teased. "Looks like you've got it bad." His eyes narrowed. "What do you mean, a real nasty divorce?"

Scott knew Craig well enough to know he asked out of concern. He nodded in answer to the unspoken question in his friend's eyes. "Let's just say I know exactly how you felt about Tamera twenty years ago." His voice lowered a notch, fists clenched in automatic fury at the thought.

"It's a good thing I took an oath to preserve life, cause I could kill the bastard. Had to stop myself from doing so," he admitted.

"Good for you," Craig muttered. Knowing him so well, he too nodded to the unspoken question in Scott's eyes. "Goes without saying, Buddy," he assured him. "Not a word."

"Not even to Tamera?"

Craig frowned. "I don't usually keep things from her."

"I know, Craig. And I understand and appreciate your feelings on the matter. It's just that she's so afraid you all won't like her, and I promised I wouldn't say much about her past," he shrugged, sighed.

"I've already said more than I should. I know I can trust you. And Tamera. Use your best judgment. Man, I've missed y'all," he admitted.

Craig grinned. "We've missed you too. We'll just play it by ear," he promised, as his daughter joined them.

When Scott took Amber for a stroll along the bayou, Craig went upstairs to join his wife and say good night to his son. As comfortable here as at home, he answered the telephone when it rang. "Hello?"

"Hey, everyone get in all right?"

Craig smiled, winking at his wife. "Sure did, Sweetheart."

"Good. Guess I'll see you in the morning," Trina remarked.

Craig chuckled. "Can't wait to meet you."

Trina gasped. "You must be Mr. Harris. I'm sorry, I thought you were Scott."

"It's Craig, Darlin'. Scott's out walking with my daughter. Shall I tell him you called?"

"Please."

"You got it. I'm sure he knows how to reach you?"

"Yes, I can't wait to meet you and your family. Scott has talked so much about you."

"Warned you, did he?" Craig asked with a chuckle.

"Not at all." She smiled to herself. But I've got a feeling he should have, she thought as she hung up the phone.

* * * * *

Ace had two speeds: stop and wide open. He raced into the kitchen at his usual pace. "She's here! I saw her drive up."

Scott stood up from the table. "I'll bring her in here to meet you all." He grinned at Craig's soft chuckle. "Haven't seen her in a week," he admitted with wink, leaving them laughing behind him.

Opening the door before she could knock, Scott took Trina's suitcase from her, put it down, and pulled her in his arms. "Man, I've missed you like crazy this week."

Trina flushed sweetly. "I've missed you, too," she admitted, rising up on her toes, her arms sliding around his neck, her lips reaching up to receive his kiss.

"C'mon in, everyone's dying to meet you."

She took a deep breath, ran a hand over her hair, and walked with him into the kitchen. Her eyes widened, as a man who could pass for Scott's twin rose from his seat. She turned to Scott, the question hovering on her lips.

He laughed. "No, we're not brothers. But we are best friends. Sweetheart, I'd like you to meet Craig Harris."

In a gallant gesture, Craig took her hand and raised it to his lips. "Your description didn't even do her justice," he chided Scott. "She's far prettier than you said."

Trina's cheeks grew hot. "Nice to meet you, too, Mr. Harris."

"Craig," he insisted.

Her eyes lowered demurely and she nodded.

Craig, in turn, introduced her to his family. "This is my wife Tamera, Amber, my daughter and my son, Ace."

Katrina smiled shyly and nodded 'hello' at each woman. "Nice to meet y'all," she remarked then turned to the little boy. "You too, Ace."

Ace's eyes widened when she smiled down at him and offered her hand. In a gesture emulating his father, he raised it to his lips. "Wow," he whispered, awed. "Is that your real hair?"

"Ace! Where are your manners, young man?" his father asked, unable to suppress the amusement in his voice. His rebuke won him a glare from his young son.

"Well," Ace insisted, his voice mutinous. "It's pretty."

Trina smiled. "It's okay, really," she assured Craig, then turned back to Ace.

"Yes, it's really mine. Want to tug on it?"

He shook his head. "No, I mean the color. Is it real or did it come out of a bottle?"

Katrina laughed, and squatted eye level with the little boy. "Yes, it's real. Feel."

He reached a tentative hand, stroked a silky handful. "Wow! What color is it?"

She shrugged, her eyes dancing merrily into his inquisitive gray gaze. "Don't know really. Some people call it blonde, some red, and some strawberry. Can you imagine having strawberry hair?" she queried, wrinkling her nose in disgust.

Ace grinned and shook his head. "I like it," he admitted.

Scott laughed. "Hey, boy, you flirting with my girl?" he teased, watching color warm both Ace and Trina's cheeks.

"I think she's pretty," Ace admitted, chin high, eyes daring Scott to argue.

Craig chuckled and shook his head with a sigh. "Oh please, Ace, one child at a time fancying himself in love is enough for me." His daughter's eyes narrowed into shimmering slits of sapphire but Amber bit back her retort at the warning look he gave her.

In a lightning swift change usual of him, Ace transformed from awed to insistent. "Can we go now?"

Scott looked at his watch. "Time for one more cup of coffee."

Amber nudged her brother before he could protest. "C'mon, Brat, we'll load Miss Katrina's suitcase in the truck and make a quick pit stop before we get on the road."

"Thanks, Sweetheart," Scott said, kissing Amber on the cheek.

"One cup," he promised Ace, pouring one for Katrina and refreshing everyone else's.

Chapter Eight

The drive started out peacefully enough. Katrina found herself sandwiched between Tamera and Amber, while Scott sat up front with Craig. Ace was delegated into the back seat with some of the luggage.

"Remember this spot, Katrina?" Scott asked, when they passed the area on the Atchafalaya Basin Bridge where the accident which led to their meeting had occurred.

"It's a bridge," Amber remarked.

"It's where we met," Scott informed her.

"How?" she asked, intrigued. "I know. There was an automobile accident. You rescued her out of the tangled mass of a burning car, and you've been inseparable ever since."

Scott laughed. "Not quite that romantic, but close. Huh, Kitten?" He grinned, addressing Trina before she could answer.

"Amber writes romance stories. One day we'll see her name on the New York Times Best Seller List."

Amber laughed. "Yeah, but it might not be Amber Harris."

"No, it'll be Morrison," Ace piped up from the back where he was playing computer games on Amber's lap top.

Amber caught her father's glare in the rear-view mirror and gritted her teeth against the instant retort. "I was referring to a pseudonym. Little boys should be seen and not heard," she insisted, reaching over the seat to jab a finger in Ace's ribs. "Got it, Brat? Be careful with that."

She turned back to Scott. "So tell me. What really happened the night you met Katrina?"

He grinned, enjoying the teasing. "What, and spoil the romantic version you've invented?"

Katrina swallowed hard the lump of emotion suddenly clogging her throat. "I wouldn't say it was romantic at all, considering what I lost in that accident."

Scott turned and Trina saw the apology in his gaze even as it hovered on his lips. "I'm sorry."

She shook her head. "It's okay. Some days are harder than others."

An uncomfortable silence hung heavily in the truck. One look at the devastated expression in her eyes and Tamera knew Trina had lost a child in the accident. She reached over and hugged her. "You don't have to explain, Katrina, or apologize. We've been there. Craig and I lost three babies before the Lord blessed us with Ace."

Trina clung to the warmth and understanding Tamera offered. "Oh God, three? I don't know if I could live through it again." She trembled, sniffing back the tears.

"You could if you had to. Just trust in God, Trina, and He will give you the desires of your heart."

"I'm finding that out," she admitted.

Scott apologized again then turned to Craig with a sigh. "Guess we've become insensitive clods in our old age."

Feeling a need to recapture the gaiety of earlier, Amber unfastened her seatbelt and slipped her arms around her father's neck. "Oh," she began, in a voice laced with sugary sarcasm. "I wouldn't go so far as to call you insensitive," she assured him, then spoiled the relief by adding: "But, I'll be happy to let you know when that changes."

Craig couldn't help but chuckle. "I'm sure you will," he remarked, reaching back to caress his daughter's face when she leaned forward and kissed his cheek.

Katrina saw the pleading look in Scott's eyes and quickly unfastened her seatbelt and slid forward to hug him.

"There's an old saying," Amber continued, settling back and buckling her seat belt. "Count your blessings in the midst of trouble." She turned to Trina as she sat back and buckled up.

"Knowing what Mama went through, I can imagine you find that difficult to do. But, I'm sure you have much to be grateful for."

Scott winked at Katrina with a grin. "Yeah. You have me," he reminded.

Grateful for their efforts, Katrina smiled at Amber then Tamera. "That's supposed to make me feel much better I'm sure. I'll have you know this is the most hard-headed, insistent, arrogant man I have ever laid eyes on."

Tamera laughed. "Just wait," she warned. "You haven't seen anything yet. Now that those two are together, we will have our hands full."

"Darling men, aren't they?" Amber joined in the teasing. "It's okay, Mama, I'm here to help you out. We'll cure them of their antiquated, chauvinistic attitudes."

Tamera smiled at her daughter. "I have a feeling your young Mr. Morrison has the same tendency toward chauvinism Amber, so be careful what you say."

Amber shook her head. "Don't worry, Mama, I can handle Stanley."

At the heated look from her husband, Tamera dropped the subject.

"Three against two," Craig remarked, fighting the irrational surge of irritation at the mention of the new man in his daughter's life. "That's not very fair."

Scott chuckled. "We've got Ace on our side."

Amber giggled. "Ace knows where his bread's buttered," she countered, turning to Ace. "Don't you, Brat?"

"I'm not a brat," he challenged, engaging in the familiar banter with his sister.

"Yes, you are," she insisted. "You've been a brat since the day you were born."

"But you love me, anyway," he argued, regarding her with laughing gray eyes.

"Yeah," she agreed, unable to dispute his point. "But you're still a brat."

Katrina listened to the teasing between Amber and Ace. She had never heard the word brat used as a term of endearment. But it was evident by the tender expression on Amber's face and the glow in her brilliant sapphire eyes, she meant it in exactly that way.

The first stop on their trip to New Orleans was to visit Nottoway Plantation in a community called White Castle, Louisiana. The beautiful old plantation stood on the banks of the Mississippi river. They listened with interest as the tour guide told the legend of how the plantation got its name, and how, during the Civil War, Union soldiers confiscated the home.

Fascinated, Amber listened avidly to the story about the original owner's daughters who were married in the house, how the home was used for a model in the famed Gone With the Wind movie, and how it was restored to its original grandeur after years of misuse and neglect. She asked endless questions and turned wide, pleading eyes to her father when she found out the servant's quarters were now rented out like hotel rooms. "Can we stay a night?"

Craig shook his head. "Not this time, Amber. We've already got reservations in New Orleans."

Unable to hide her disappointment, Amber bit back her arguments and took advantage of the many pamphlets and brochures offered by the tour guide. She selected a tiny replica of the house as a souvenir from the gift shop and eagerly accepted her father's offer that they eat lunch in the lavish dining room.

Creative juices primed and running wide open, she worked steadily on her lap top computer the rest of the way to New Orleans.

They timed their arrival to coincide with Ace reaching the end of his ability to sit still. After unloading the truck and checking into their rooms, they opted for a nice, long swim to help him work off some of his energy, and then planned their activities for the following day.

"I thought we would go out and eat tonight, maybe hit a few night clubs and listen to some jazz music," Scott offered. "That is, if you don't mind leaving the kids, and Amber doesn't mind baby sitting."

"Hey, it's my vacation too." Amber protested, though not too fiercely. "Do we get to eat too?"

Scott grinned down into her teasing sapphire gaze. "How about pizza? We can have it delivered. There are movies on pay per view, and the pool is open until ten. And, there's a phone in your room," he added, laughing at her father's narrowed, steely glare.

Craig fought back his fatherly instincts while Tamera fought down her protective ones. "Do you think it's safe?" she asked Scott.

He nodded. "This is one of the finest hotels, and they have plenty of security."

Though she hadn't hit the water herself, Amber offered to stay out and let Ace swim while her parents, Scott, and Trina got ready for the evening. She settled into a lounge chair with her computer planted firmly on her lap. "No running," she warned Ace, lowering her sunglasses so he could see she was serious. "See that sign," she nodded toward the board boasting Pool Rules. "If I have to call you down one time, we're going to go in. Got it?"

He nodded, shot her a charming grin, dove in, and fought the urge to throw water at her. If she hadn't had that computer on her lap, he would douse her but good.

As if reading his thoughts, Amber lowered her glasses again. "Don't even think about it," she warned.

Scott led Katrina to the room she would share with Amber. Lifting her hand to his lips, he grinned down at her. "I sure like your swimsuit," he admitted, his eyes sweeping over her in an appreciative gesture.

Trina wrapped the beach towel more firmly around her, her cheeks flaming. "I bought a one-piece because I thought it would cover more." She winced, thinking about the French cut thighs and scrap of material which revealed almost as much as it covered.

"Too bad I couldn't return it after trying it on."

He chuckled. "Fits just right," he assured, enjoying the way her cheeks flamed and eyes flashed. Pulling the key out of the pocket of his swim trunks, he unlocked her door and held it just out of her reach when she stepped into the room. "It'll cost you to get it back," he teased.

"It usually does," she muttered. Holding the towel firmly in place, she stood on her toes and brushed her lips across his cheek.

"What do you call that?"

"I call it more than you deserve and all you're going to get if you don't stop acting like a male chauvinist pig and give me that key."

He chuckled, lifted her up and kissed her thoroughly. "Yes, Ma'am," he remarked, setting her back on her feet and handing her the key.

"Hey," he whispered, his fingers brushing over her cheeks in a tender caress. "I love you."

Though he didn't expect a reply, the curve of her lips and glow in her eyes were answer enough. For now. Moving two doors down, he entered the room he and Ace would share. Craig and Tamera's room was in-between, with doors that adjoined the three.

Dinner was a quiet, intimate affair in one of New Orleans's finest restaurants boasting of French cuisine and jazz music. Katrina joined in the laughter as Craig, Tamera, and Scott regaled her with tales from their past. She laughed with them as the two men reminisced about their childhood.

"Did you two ever fight?" she asked, when there was a lull in the conversation.

Craig grinned at Scott, the memory as fresh as though it were the day before. "Only once that I recall. Remember, Scott? The day you bloodied my nose for calling you Ritchie."

Scott chuckled. "We were waiting for the school bus. Craig and I had been bickering at each other," he shrugged, "over what I can't remember."

"Over Sally Smith," Craig reminded him.

Scott grinned. "Yeah, that's right."

"Wait a minute," Tamera interjected. "Who is Sally Smith and how come I've never heard of her?"

"It was, what, about second grade?" Craig asked.

Scott nodded, and picked up the story. "I think so. Anyway, I've always hated being called Ritchie. Craig knew it. Everyone knew it. Being the tough guy he was, he started taunting me with it, threatening to tell Sally my real name was Ritchie, not Scott. Didn't matter it's Richard Scott, not to mention I wasn't much for fighting. My father was a minister, and he always warned me I'd be in big trouble if I was ever caught fighting." He chuckled, recalling the memory.

"I warned Craig more than once to shut up. Finally, I belted him one. I think it was at that time we realized we were equally matched, and no one would ever really come out the winner in a confrontation. Once Sally found out we were fighting over her, she wouldn't have anything to do with either of us."

He laughed. "We decided then and there that nothing, not even a girl would come between us again. And it hasn't." He winked at Tamera.

"Well, it almost did. Once. Over you."

She arched an eyebrow. "Really?"

Craig chuckled. "No. Not really. Tell the truth now, Buddy, you weren't serious when you threatened me with having a bit of competition on my hands over her. Were you?"

Scott shrugged. A teasing grin tugged at the corners of his mouth. "I'll never tell," he taunted.

The teasing led into the story of how they met. Tamera had been hired as resident veterinarian for the summer by Craig's grandfather. It hadn't been love at first sight between her and Craig, seeing as they'd clashed from the onset. But, when she was hurt in a riding accident, Craig was forced to examine his heart and realized he'd lost it to her from the beginning.

Deeply touched by the love shared by the three, Katrina felt blessed to be welcomed so wholeheartedly into the relationship. Heart overflowing with emotion, she leaned toward Scott. "Well, Doctor, are you going to bloody my nose if I call you Ritchie?"

Scott's gaze rested a full minute on Trina's mouth before lifting to hers. "No," his husky voice lowered a notch.

"I have a more effective, and far more pleasant way of shutting that pretty mouth of yours."

Though her cheeks flamed red, Katrina had the grace to laugh. "I guess I left myself wide open for that one."

Tamera reached over and squeezed her hand. "Not really. Anything and everything you say will be turned against you with these two. I warned you earlier we'd have our hands full." She rose from the table.

"I think I'll go call and check on the kids before we take our stroll down Bourbon Street."

Katrina rose also. "I'll go with you."

Craig eyed Scott as Scott watched the women's departure, his eyes following Trina's every move. "She's lovely, Scott." Craig said, nodding in approval when his friend's gaze turned to meet his.

"Really sweet. I can see why you're head over heels. It's about time, too," he added, when Scott grinned.

Scott shrugged. "Can't hurry love. You, above all, should know that."

Craig laughed and reached for the check. "My treat, Buddy," he insisted when Scott protested.

"It's good to have y'all here, Craig."

Craig slapped him on the back. "Good to be here."

* * * * *

Piled up in the bed in her parent's room with Ace sleeping beside her, Amber talked on the phone with Stanley. The doors to both her and Ace's room were open so she could hear if the phone rang. When it did, she asked Stanley to hold on, then ran to answer it. It was her mother.

"Yes, Mama, everything's fine," she assured when her mother asked how they were. "I'm on the phone with Stanley in your room. Ace is sleeping. I'll move him to his bed in a while. Y'all have a good time, and don't worry," she urged.

Tamera laughed at her daughter's tone of voice. "It's a mother's prerogative to worry," she said.

"We probably won't call again, Honey, because it's getting late. Don't leave Ace alone, just stay with him there in our bed. And don't stay on the phone too long; you need to rest. We've got a busy day planned tomorrow. Give Stanley our love," she added, then chuckled at her daughter's remark.

"Yes, your father's, too. Though if you tell him I said so, I'll deny it."

Amber giggled. "Okay, Mama. He's on hold, so I'd better get back."

Katrina smiled when Tamera hung up the receiver. "Craig doesn't seem too happy Amber has a boyfriend."

Tamera laughed. "That's an understatement. He can't stand the thought of his little girl growing up."

"She's really blessed to have him love her so much," Trina remarked.

Tamera didn't miss the pain and longing in her new friend's eyes. She hugged Trina. "Tell her that, will you, Trina?"

Katrina accepted the embrace with a smile and a nod, promising to do so.

* * * * *

For the next couple of hours, the four of them strolled down the famed Bourbon Street, enjoying the smell of food and sound of music oozing out of every open door along the strip. They took a walk along the river before turning in for the night.

Arriving at the hotel, Craig carried his daughter into her room, while Scott carried Ace into theirs. Everyone settled in for the night, looking forward to the next day's adventures.

Chapter Nine

Wednesday morning dawned bright and clear. After breakfast of bengits and café-au-lait at the famed Café Du Monde, the sight seeing began. Excitement filled the air as they visited the Audubon Zoo, the Aquarium of the Americas and took a horse-drawn carriage ride through the city. A trolley car took them to a restaurant where they feasted on seafood po-boys and iced tea. After lunch, they headed out again for the afternoon.

Their afternoon consisted of a tour of Bourbon Street, so Amber and Ace could get a glimpse of its magic. The air was alive with sights, sounds, and smells of the French Market. Artists hawked their talent on street corners and along the river walk; break dancers and singing quartets performed for pocket change. Tourist shops offered momentary relief from the humidity. An occasional breeze off the Mississippi river cooled the sultry summer heat.

After a few moments of watching a clown twist balloons into exotic shapes, Amber urged her mother and Katrina into yet another souvenir shop. Craig and Scott opted to stay and let Ace continue watching while waiting for his balloon. With a promise to return in twenty minutes, the women headed off.

Stepping out of the shop five minutes later than promised, Katrina froze. Two doors down and heading in her direction was Jack. He noticed her before she had a chance to slip back through the doorway.

Breaking into a sprint, he caught up with Trina and grabbed her by the arm. "Well, well, look who I've found," he crooned to no one in particular, "my sweet, little wife."

"Ex wife," Katrina corrected, jerking her arm in an attempt to free herself from his grasp. "Let me go," she insisted when he tightened his grip.

"Restraining order isn't enforceable outside of Lafayette," he taunted, pulling her up short. "You're coming with me."

He was drunk, as usual, or hung over. His clothes were rumpled, hair disheveled, eyes bloodshot. On a surge of fury and fear, Trina jerked free of him. "Oh, no, I'm not."

"Katrina?" Tamera's voice was a welcome sound as she stepped up next to her.

Katrina looked at her new friend, her eyes begging Tamera for understanding, and help. "This is my ex husband. He was just leaving," she said, giving Jack a pointed look.

"Not going to introduce me to your friend?" he asked, eyeing Tamera lewdly.

Tamera felt the hair on her neck stand up and her skin crawl. "Let's go, Trina, the men are waiting." She took Katrina protectively by the arm and turned to put her other arm around her daughter.

Jack's wolf whistle and crude remark about a threesome, made them all stiffen. Before they could step away, he blocked their exit. "You're not going anywhere, Katrina."

Tamera spotted her husband and felt an overwhelming relief at the sight of his tall frame followed by a tiny tug of alarm at the fury in his gaze. Fury evident by the twitching muscle in his jaw.

As the men approached the scene from across the street, Craig put a warning hand on Scott and a protective one on Ace.

"Problem, ladies?" he queried, moments before Scott grabbed Jack by the arm, whirled him around, and shoved him away from the women and up against the wall.

"I told you I'd kill you if you ever went near her," Scott muttered through clenched teeth.

"Scott, no!" Katrina pleaded, apprehension evident in her soft voice. "Please, he's not worth it."

"Did he touch you? Any of you?" Scott asked Tamera, not loosening his hold.

Tamera glanced at Trina. There was no mistaking the panic in her eyes, or the pleading in them. She turned back to Scott and shook her head. "No."

"Scott." Craig's voice was soft, coaxing. "Let him go. I'm sure he'll think twice before approaching her again. Won't you, pal?"

Jack nodded, not daring to say a word.

Craig put a restraining hand on Scott's shoulder and said his name again.

Scott tightened his grip, ground his teeth and fought the urge to pummel Jack Simmons's face into a bloody mass against the wall. Tension surrounded them like a thick, dark cloud. With a snort of disgust, he flung Jack away.

"Consider yourself lucky, my man. This time. But be warned, I won't hesitate again. I'll beat you within an inch of your miserable life," he assured, giving Jack a hard shove.

"I'm sorry," Katrina raised tear-filled eyes to Craig, then Tamera. "I'm so sorry."

"Stop apologizing!" Scott turned on her in an angry whirl. "No one is blaming you."

The anger in his tone cut her like a knife. She stepped away, eyes flashing, chin lifted in subtle defiance.

"I'm apologizing because I'm sorry it happened in front of the children." Her breath hitched, but she clung to the few remaining shreds of her composure. "It shouldn't have happened in front of the children."

Turning on her heel, she headed in the direction of the hotel.

"Trina, wait." Scott stepped forward, reached for her.

She pulled away. "Don't touch me!" Fighting tears with every breath, she glared at him. "I'll not be man-handled again. By any man. Ever."

Scott raised his hands in defeat. "I'd never man-handle you, Katrina," he assured, his voice edged with anger despite his attempt at a softer tone.

She acknowledged the remark with a curt nod before her eyes sought Tamera's. "I'm going back to the room for a while. Please, continue your sight seeing. I'll be fine." Without waiting for a reply, she turned in the general direction of the hotel.

Amber felt Katrina's pain as if it were her own. "Trina, wait!" she called out. "You shouldn't go alone."

Trina turned and shook her head but continued to walk away. "Don't worry, he won't bother me again. He's too scared. Besides, he's probably half-way out of the city by now."

"How can you be sure he's not lurking in a doorway somewhere?" Amber asked. "Please, don't go."

Because he's a coward," Scott interjected before Trina could answer. "And a bastard in the first degree."

Swallowing the lump in her throat, Amber glared up at Scott. "I never thought you could be so insensitive!"

"Amber!"

She shook her head at her father, and held up a hand, cutting off the admonishment before he could utter it. "She shouldn't go alone, I'm going with her." Turning, she ran after Katrina.

"Great," Scott groaned raking his hands through his hair in an agitated gesture. "Really smart move," he muttered. "After months of being gentle and patient, I blew it in one lousy lapse of self-control."

Craig bit back his retort. It was evident by the self recrimination Scott didn't need to be told he'd been rough on Katrina. Instead, he put his hand on his friend's shoulder, motioned for Tamera and Ace to follow and led them into a nearby deli & pub. Making his way to a table, he went to get everyone something to drink.

"Who was that man?" Ace wanted to know.

"Someone Miss Trina knew before," his mother answered.

"I don't like him. You should have punched him," he told Scott.

"Out of the mouths of babes," Scott muttered.

"No you shouldn't have," Tamera insisted. "We are called to love, not violence," she reminded her son. "Fighting doesn't solve anything."

"But he was being mean to y'all." Her young son remained adamant.

She shook her head. "Doesn't matter. Jesus says to turn the other cheek. Scott was right not to hit him."

"Then why is Miss Trina mad?"

Scott chuckled in weary humor as Tamera tried to answer Ace's questions.

"Miss Trina isn't mad, she's just upset."

"No. He's right," Scott argued. "Mad as a hornet's nest. Has every right to be, too."

Tamera rolled her eyes and relented. It was obvious she wasn't going to get through to either of them in their present frame of mind. With an imploring look at her husband, she rushed Ace off to wash his hands.

Craig sat across from him and leaned forward, his eyes searching Scott's. "You were a bit rough, Buddy. Any fool can see she's in love with you. And scared to death."

"Well, that makes me a bigger fool than the rest, 'cause I sure can't see it."

Craig laughed. "Happens to the best of us, Buddy. When it comes to the women we love, sooner or later, we leave ourselves wide open for stupidity and put our foot all the way in it."

"How encouraging," Scott mumbled.

Craig's whole-hearted laughter made him smile. Pushing away from the table, he stood, glanced at his watch then down at his friend. "I'm going to talk to her, if she'll listen. See y'all later?"

Craig nodded. "We'll take Ace around a little longer, try and get his mind off this and onto something better, then head back to the hotel for the evening. Maybe we'll catch a riverboat tour tomorrow before heading home."

"Sounds like a plan."

On the way to the hotel, Scott wondered what he would say. What could he say when all he wanted to do was take her in his arms and hold her until she forgave him? Silently he prayed she would allow him the privilege.

* * * * *

In the hotel room, Amber sat, holding Trina while she wept; heart wrenching sobs which tore from her in painful torrents.

"You really love him, don't you?" she asked, when Katrina's sobs turned to soft, hiccupping sounds.

"Yes. And I'm so afraid."

"Your ex-husband was abusive to you?" Amber asked. Trina nodded.

"God. It must be horrible to live that way."

Katrina raised tear-drenched eyes to Amber's. "It is," she admitted, her tone weary and sad. "And the pain and fear don't go away easily, even after the papers are signed."

"Scott would never hurt you that way. You know that, don't you?" Amber insisted.

"Yes," Trina admitted.

"You know he loves you. It's written all over his face every time he looks at you."

"I know that, too. I'm just still afraid to make a commitment. Afraid I'll make a mistake. Again."

"Normally I'd argue with you on that," Amber said, her eyes narrowed into shimmering slits of sapphire. "But after today, I'm not so sure. I never thought Scott would be so irrational. Now, my Daddy is another story. He's overprotective and irrational, especially when it comes to me or Mama. I'm seventeen, and he still treats me like a baby. Scott's always been the more levelheaded of the two. But..." Puzzled, she shrugged and shook her head.

Katrina smiled, remembering her promise of the night before. "Your daddy loves you very much. You are so blessed to have a father who cares like that. So many girls' fathers don't care. I've never known a man who loves and respects his wife and daughter the way your father does."

Amber sighed heavily. "I know. And I'm trying to remember that." She broke off at the knock on the door.

"Bet that's Scott. Do you want to talk to him yet?"

Katrina nodded, slid off the bed and headed toward the bathroom to wash her face. "I'll be out in a moment."

Amber opened the door and looked up into the troubled brown gaze of the man she'd known and loved all of her life. He smiled down at her.

"I'm sorry, Amber. I was out of line," Scott said.

"I'm not the one you should apologize to."

He cupped her cheek with his hand. "Yes, you are. And I am. I'll apologize to Trina, too, if she'll listen."

Amber wrapped her arms around his waist. "I'm sure she will. Love's not always easy, is it, Scott?"

He hauled her against him, hugging her to his chest, stroking the dark hair streaming like liquid silk down her back. "No, it's not, Sweetheart. But when it's right, it's worth the fight, and every moment of pain. You may be too young to understand just yet."

"I understand more than people give me credit for," she interjected, pulling away to look up at him.

He nodded, kissed her head. "I'm sure you do, Sweetheart. You've grown up pretty fast. Too fast." He hugged her again.

"Be patient with the men you love, Amber. We're a bunch of hot heads when it comes to the women in our life," he added, as Katrina walked out of the bathroom.

Though he spoke to Amber, his eyes beseeched the woman he loved.

Katrina's heart melted when she heard the tender plea and saw the pain and the pleading in his dark eyes. She waited a moment while Amber disengaged herself from Scott's embrace then walked toward them. Without hesitation, she took his outstretched hand.

The breath he hadn't known he was holding escaped Scott in a relieved sigh. Pulling Trina firmly against his chest, his lips covered hers in a tender caress. "I'm sorry I lost it like that," he whispered against her mouth.

"I don't like it when you're angry."

Picking her up, he held her tightly against him. "I wasn't angry at you, just the situation."

"I know." She brushed the hair off his forehead. "But I still don't like it."

"I'll try to remember that," he promised, resting his forehead against hers. "I've got a surprise for you, if you'll come with me."

"What?"

He glanced at his watch. "We haven't got much time. Hurry and change into the dress you wore last night. I'll meet you back here in ten minutes."

"Where are we going?"

He hesitated a moment, reluctant to leave her even for the ten minutes. Pulling her in his arms again, he lowered his lips to hers for a long, luxurious, taste of her sweetness.

"How about," he whispered, brushing his knuckles across her cheek, "Mass at the St. Louis Cathedral?"

Her eyes widened, cheeks flushed with pleasure. "Really?"

"Oh, wow! I've heard it's a beautiful church." Amber said.

"It is," Scott agreed. "I toured it the last time I was here. But we've got to hurry if we want to make the evening Mass."

"Want to come along?" Trina offered.

Amber smiled. Yes, she did. But she shook her head, sensing Scott would prefer it if she didn't tag along. She knew him better, loved him longer, and, tiny though it was, saw the flicker of disappointment in his eyes when Trina issued the invitation.

"No, thanks. I'm sure Mama and Daddy will be back soon. But, maybe we can visit the Cathedral tomorrow?"

Though he'd rather cut off his arm than hurt her, Scott couldn't stop the flash of relief when Amber declined. "It's a promise, Sweetheart. Now hurry if you want to change," he told Trina. "I'll be back in five minutes."

One of the city's most notable landmarks, the St. Louis Cathedral faced Jackson Square in what is known as the heart of Old New Orleans. Katrina stood amazed at the gracious beauty of the church with its three steeples and roots dating back to the early 1700's.

The Mass was executed with such reverent beauty there was no doubt the presence of the Lord resided within the lovely building and in the hearts of its inhabitants. Filled with an incredible sense of peace, Katrina stayed in prayer long moments after the service ended.

Scott waited patiently by her side, prayerful, thankful. When she rose from the pew, he stood and took her hand. Slowly they walked through the church and out into the Square. She looked at him in surprise when he hailed a carriage.

"Where are we going?" Trina asked. "Don't you think we need to get back?"

Scott pulled her against his side, wrapped his arm around her and hushed her questions with his finger on her lips. "I want to be alone with you a little while. Do you mind?"

She shook her head and allowed him to help her climb into the carriage. Since they'd taken a tour of the city earlier, Scott paid the driver for his silence. They sat quietly for a moment then he lifted her chin with his finger. "I love you, Kitten," he whispered huskily, tracing her lips with his thumb.

Trina felt the warmth of his words, the heat of his touch, and shivered.

"Cold?" he queried, wrapping his arms more securely around her and hugging her against him.

She shook her head. "No. It's a beautiful night for this, full moon, billions of stars, warm, balmy evening."

He chuckled. "Kind of romantic, huh?"

She nodded.

They sat in companionable silence while the carriage made its way through the city and along the river walk. The gentle clip-clop of the horse's hooves lulled them into a quiet, peaceful state. Moonbeams danced off the Mississippi river only to reflect their brilliance in the twinkling stars. Scott reveled in the scent of her hair and the feel of her snuggled up against him. Caressing her face, he cupped her cheek in his hand and brushed his lips across her forehead.

"Trina, I'm really sorry about today."

"Shh," she admonished, placing her finger against his lips. "I guess I should be grateful you're so willing, so eager, to protect me."

"I'd move heaven and earth to protect you, Kitten. I love you," he whispered, his lips covering hers in a tender caress.

His tenderness was intoxicating, his warmth seductive. Sliding her arms around his neck, Trina melted into the kiss. Like a flower to sunlight, she opened to the feel of his body pressed intimately against hers and to the taste and feel of his mouth gently molding her lips to his.

Scott pulled her closer and closer, until she was trapped against his chest, both of his hands fisted in her hair, his mouth feasting greedily on hers.

As quickly as it disappeared, sanity returned. Scott held her tenderly against him, stroking the silky, red-gold mass streaming across her shoulders. "Trina," he breathed. "You are so beautiful."

She brushed her lips across his. "You are such a sweet, gentle man. I love you, Scott. Whether I'm ready for it or not, I can't deny the truth any longer. I love you, and it scares me to death. Please," she pleaded, "be patient with me. Give me time to know my own heart before asking me to give it fully to you."

"Take all the time you need, Sweetheart. But know this, when you do, I'll never give it up. And I'll never break it," he vowed.

"Thank you," she whispered.

"No, thank you. You've given me a beautiful gift tonight, Trina. You've given me your love and your forgiveness. I can't ask for more than that. I only hope you realize how precious you are, both in God's sight and in mine."

Her smile was tender, wistful. "I'm beginning to," she said.

The quiver of doubt in her voice pierced Scott's soul. God, he prayed silently, help me show her. Help her believe.

Forgive her doubt and her unbelief. Pulling her firmly against his chest once more, he kissed her.

"Say it again," he whispered. "I never thought I'd need to hear the words, but, Trina, tell me again that you love me."

Framing his face in her hands, she whispered the words again. They rang through his heart in a melody of hope and settled in his soul like a song of joy.

Chapter Ten

Craig awoke early the next morning. Sunlight streamed through the window. As usual, he was up with it. Sliding quietly from the bed, he opened the door to his son then daughter's room to check on them. Everyone was sleeping soundly. Tamera stirred behind him.

"Craig?"

Locking the doors, he returned to his wife's side. "Just checking on everyone," he murmured. "Go back to sleep."

Her smile was tender as she snuggled in his arms. "You too."

"You know me better than that. Once I'm up, I'm up."

"And you expect the whole world to be up, too," she admonished in a sleepy voice.

He chuckled, brushed his lips across hers. "Not the whole world. Just those in mine."

"I hope Scott and Trina got things straightened out last night."

Running his hand down her arm, he curled his fingers around hers. "I doubt he would be sleeping quite so peacefully if they hadn't."

"I'll bet he looks as sweet and boyish as you do when you're sleeping. All the worries of the world smoothed off your brow, a smug little smile on your face while you dream youthful dreams of happy-ever-after."

Lifting their entwined hands to his mouth, Craig kissed her palm. "I can assure you, my beautiful wife, there was nothing boyish or youthful about my dreams last night." His body hardened, remembering.

Tamera felt the familiar rush of pleasure at the feel of his hard body curled around hers. Turning, she caressed his cheek, brushed her fingers through his hair and covered his lips with hers. "Really?" she murmured against his mouth.

The press of her slender frame against his and the quiet invitation in her eyes was all the encouragement he needed. Pulling her firmly against him, he reveled in the sweet ecstasy which always awaited him in her arms. Sated and utterly content, he held her while she drifted off to dream once more.

Before long, he heard the sounds of people stirring in the adjoining rooms, muffled laughter from Ace's, the shower running in Amber's. He watched as the silhouette of Scott and Ace crossed in front of his window to the room on the other side. Careful to be quiet, he slid from the bed and took a shower. After slipping on a pair of jeans and a shirt, he ran a comb through his hair then opened the door and walked barefoot into his daughter's room.

Ace was curled up next to Trina, so was Scott. He held her against his chest while she nursed her first cup of coffee. Amber had just finished blow drying her hair.

"Where's Mama?" Ace wanted to know.

"Mama's still sleeping, so let's keep it down to a minimum roar," his father answered.

Amber winked at Trina. A gesture her father missed. "I'm seriously considering getting this mop cut up to six inches below my ears."

"No, you're not," her father retorted.

"It's my hair," she argued.

"I'm your father, and I say you're not cutting it."

"I'm seventeen. I think that's old enough to decide how to wear my hair. Don't you, Trina?" she asked in wide-eyed innocence, trying hard to suppress the smile tugging at the corners of her mouth.

Scott's chuckle cut off Trina' reply. "Don't answer that," he warned with a wink. "No matter what you say, you'll get in trouble."

Craig shook his head, eying his daughter with a pointed look. "As long as you live in my house, you'll not cut it."

She tossed the brush at him. "You take care of it, then."

Craig caught the brush with a smile. "My pleasure." He sat on the edge of her bed and waited while she curled up at his feet as she had when she was little, but hadn't in a long time. "Who's counting?"

Amber sighed, almost purring with pleasure at the long, soothing, strokes of brush against scalp. "Just brush. I'll let you know when to quit."

Craig laughed softly. "Yes, ma'am. What's on the agenda for today?" he asked Scott.

"Well, the riverboat tour we talked about," Scott began.

"And you promised we'd tour the St. Louis Cathedral," Amber reminded.

"Sure did," Scott agreed.

"That's where y'all went last night?" Craig asked.

"Oh, yes," Trina gasped, glowing. "And it was so beautiful! I can just imagine how lovely it is with sunlight streaming through all those stained-glass windows and I can hardly wait to go back today and visit the gift shop."

Craig nodded, grinning at her exuberant response. "Sounds good to me. I thought we'd order up breakfast so Tamera can sleep in for a change. It's not often she gets to sleep late."

"Not often she wants to sleep late," the woman in question answered from the doorway. Tying her robe snugly around her waist, she walked over and gave her husband a kiss. "Morning, everyone."

Ace scrambled from the bed to give his mother a hug. "When are we leaving?"

Craig laughed. "Give your mother a chance to wake up, Ace."

Tamera laughed and hugged her son. "Just like your father. Up with the sun and raring to go."

Scott kissed Katrina, got up, and stretched. "That makes three of us. How long will it take you ladies to get dressed?"

"Daddy's not through brushing my hair," Amber protested.

Tamera settled on the floor next to her daughter. "And I'm next."

"Me, after," Trina chimed in.

Scott arched an eyebrow at her and shook his head. "He's not brushing your hair."

Trina's heart thrilled at the possessive note in Scott's voice. "Why not?" she taunted, enjoying, perhaps for the first time in her life, the simple pleasure of teasing.

Scott knew she was teasing. Wonderful though it was to know she felt comfortable enough to do so, he couldn't stop the quick surge of jealousy at the thought of Craig brushing her hair. He shook his head again. "If any man gets his hands in that hair, it'll be me."

"I don't know, Buddy," Craig piped up. "I've got a lot more practice than you," he added, winking at his wife when Tamera nudged him with her elbow.

"As you can see, they fall at my feet to have these magic fingers in their hair."

Scott's eyes narrowed. "It'll be broken fingers if you lay one on her," he grunted.

"Oh, please," Ace broke in. "Don't argue about it. Scott, you brush her hair, and I'll brush Mama's so we can go."

Tamera laughed and scooped Ace up in her arms. "I don't think so, little man, you'll be brushing tangles in my hair instead of out," she teased, tickling him into squeals of laughter.

"That's right," Amber agreed, grabbing a handful of his silky, blond hair. "You can't even get the tangles out of your own hair, much less someone else's."

"Help me," he pleaded between fits of giggles.

Scott promptly rushed to his rescue. After breakfast, he carried Ace piggyback to their room so they could brush teeth and comb hair before heading out.

Like cotton candy floating on the breeze, huge, puffy, white clouds drifted in the heavens. Katrina couldn't remember a time when the sun was so bright, the sky so clear and blue, or the air so fresh as it was standing on the deck of the Delta Queen.

The women banded together like the three musketeers wielding truth against injustice in the form of male chauvinism as they toured New Orleans from aboard the riverboat. Although seeing the city from the Mississippi River was exciting, their visit to the St. Louis Cathedral was the climax of her morning.

Even the bright light of day couldn't dim the beauty of the church. Just as she'd imagined, sunbeams streamed through the stained-glass windows creating tiny rainbows which danced in the air and reflected off the well-worn pews. The peace of Christ was a tangible thing within its walls, His presence unmistakable. So much so, that when Trina looked at Scott there were tears in her eyes.

"He's here," she whispered.

Her words struck a chord. He looked around for signs of Jack.

As though reading his thoughts, she shook her head. "God is in this place. Don't you feel Him?"

Scott smiled tenderly, and nodded. He chose his words with care. "There's no doubt the Holy Spirit of God dwells in special places of worship. Some more than others. But Trina, His desire is to dwell in here." He touched her heart.

"Take what you feel in this place and carry it with you, knowing God is within. That's when you'll find your greatest peace, your greatest strength. The Bible says I will never leave you nor forsake you. Jesus said, 'The Kingdom of God is within you.' More than anything God wants to live in our hearts and minds. He wants us to know He's there, to trust in that and to believe in His presence from the deepest part of our hearts and souls. Then and only then will you experience the kingdom of God on earth."

Trina couldn't stop the tears which started with his words, tears of love and peace, of joy and gratitude. She let them flow freely. Reaching up, she cupped Scott's cheek in her hand.

"I love you," she whispered, feeling the truth of those words deep in her heart. She let them settle there and take root, like tiny seeds of hope and excitement for what the future might hold.

Scott pulled her against him, resisting the urge to crush her lips to his. "Thank you."

Though he didn't say it, she felt the depth of his love clear down to her soul, much like the love of God. In that moment, Trina knew she was well and truly blessed. Taking Scott's hand, she led him to a pew, knelt beside him, and thanked God for the blessing of his love.

Running his hand down her hair in a subtle caress, Scott whispered he would meet her in the gift shop.

"I won't be long," she promised.

"Take as much time as you want."

"I could stay here all day."

"Well," he countered, grinning, "Not that long." With a tender wink, he rose and made his way to the gift shop at the church's entrance.

Katrina stayed a few moments longer meditating on Scott's words, opening up to the presence of God, and inviting Him to fill her with His Holy Spirit. Rising, she stepped out of the pew, genuflected low before the altar, made the sign of the cross and walked quietly to join the others.

Browsing through the assortment of religious articles, she chose a few things and joined everyone else outside.

"What did you get?" Scott asked.

Trina withdrew the gifts from the bag and handed them out. "It's not much, I know, but I wanted to get everyone a little something. These are prayer cards, or novenas," she explained handing each person a card with a picture on it.

"What's a novena?" Amber asked.

"It's a special prayer said to a certain Saint. See, the prayer is on the back." She turned Amber's card over.

"Yours is to the patron Saint of writers and journalists. Tamera's is the patron Saint of mothers. Your father's is the patron Saint of fathers and Ace's is a special prayer to his guardian angel."

She turned to Scott. "Yours is the patron Saint of doctors."

"What's it for?" Amber asked, intrigued.

Trina shrugged, flushing with embarrassment at her lack of true knowledge. "Well," she began, hoping to explain to the best of her ability.

"I've never really participated in a novena, but I've heard of people who have. You pray the prayer asking the Saint to intercede for you for a certain petition. Some people swear they work. I don't know. But, I believe it's not any different than asking you or someone else to pray for me. A lot of people think it's worshiping the Saint, but I don't believe that. I mean, if we ask each other to pray for us, what's wrong with asking a Saint, who is already in the presence, of God to pray for us?"

Tamera reached over and hugged her. "It's a beautiful thought. I, for one, will cherish it."

"Me, too," Amber insisted as everyone agreed. "Wow, the patron Saint of writers, huh? I may have to do a little research on this."

Katrina flushed with pleasure at their whole-hearted acceptance of her beliefs and the graciousness with which they received the simple gifts. She turned to Scott.

"What did you get?"

He shrugged. "Nothing."

She saw the teasing light enter his dark eyes and knew he wouldn't tell, but her curiosity was aroused. "Then what's in the bag?"

He grinned. "What bag?"

"The one you're holding."

"This one?" He held it up.

She rolled her eyes. "Yes, that one."

He shrugged. "Not much."

Amber giggled, Craig laughed and Tamera chided Scott for teasing.

"Look what I bought for Stanley," Amber said, showing them a gold cross on a sturdy chain.

"It's beautiful," Trina breathed. "I hope he likes it."

"He's a fool if he doesn't," Scott remarked.

"So," Trina began. "I guess you're not going to share your purchases with us?"

He chuckled at her insistence and handed her the bag.

"For me?" she asked, pulling out a book which addressed many of the questions about Catholicism and one on the history of the St. Louis Cathedral.

He nodded. "There's one more for you," he insisted, reaching in his pocket.

He handed her a tiny box and Trina's heart jumped into her throat. Her hands shook as she opened it. Nestled in a bed of soft cotton was a tiny, delicate Crucifix on an equally delicate chain of gold.

Lifting it from the box, Scott put it around her neck. "Wear it in good health," he said softly. "And think of me when you do," he added, brushing his fingers across her cheek in a tender caress.

"It's beautiful," she gasped, swallowing the lump of tears lodged in her throat. "I'll treasure it always," she insisted, reaching up to press her lips against his cheek. Sliding her arms around his neck, she accepted his embrace when he picked her up and hugged her against him.

Joy bubbled up and escaped in irrepressible laughter when he swung her around once before setting her back on her feet. "I'm starving," she announced, slipping her hand in his as they continued walking toward the hotel.

"Me, too," Ace remarked.

Craig laughed. "You're always hungry," he teased his son. "We'll check out of the hotel and eat lunch before heading back," he promised, his words bringing a murmur of agreement from everyone.

"Can we stop at Nottoway Plantation on the way back?" Amber asked, once they were on their way out of the city.

"I don't know, Amber," Craig hesitated, eying Scott for his reaction.

Scott shrugged. "I'm in no hurry." He turned to Trina. "You don't have to go to work until tomorrow, right?"

She nodded. "At three."

"Please," Amber pleaded. "There's no telling how long it'll be before we get to go again."

Seeking his wife's gaze in the mirror, Craig saw the small nod of acquiescence and agreed.

The second tour of the plantation home and grounds was every bit as exciting as the first. They arrived at Scott's house that evening, tired but happy.

Katrina reached for her suitcase, as it was unloaded from the Suburban.

"You're not leaving?" Scott asked.

"Yeah, I'm ready for my bed."

"Stay," he pleaded. "There's plenty of room here."

She hushed his protests with a finger on his lips. "Visit with your friends, although, I feel truly blessed to call them my own." Her smile encompassed the entire family.

"Count on it, Sweetheart," Craig hugged her. "Even if you dump this lug, you're welcome to visit us anytime."

She laughed. "I'll remember that." Turning to Tamera, she hugged her.

"Thank you for everything," she whispered. Slipping one arm around Amber and the other around Ace, she hugged them to her. "I feel like I've gained a sister," she told Amber.

Amber smiled. "Does that mean I can call you if I ever need any sisterly advice?"

She hugged her again. "Any time. Scott will give you my number and address before you leave."

Scott walked Trina to her car while the rest of the family went inside. "I want you to stay, but I can see you want some time alone so I won't press. Call me as soon as you get home, okay?"

Smiling, she raised up on her toes, her arms sliding around his neck, her lips reaching for his. "Thank you," she whispered against his mouth, then savored the tenderness of his kiss.

"Keep this up, and I'll never let you go," he teased.

Laughing, she promised to call him as soon as she got home, and then left.

It's good to go, but it's good to be home, she thought with a sigh when she entered her apartment. After calling Scott as promised, she put away her things, took a long, hot bath and snuggled down in her bed to pray and read before drifting off to dream heavenly dreams; dreams of Scott and their future. A future blessed with love and laughter, one filled with joy and happiness and hopefully her one desire, children.

Chapter Eleven

Craig and his family had been gone for a little over a week. Scott and Katrina had barely seen each other since the trip to New Orleans. Both returned to their respective jobs on different shifts. Today was the first day in nearly two weeks they would actually be able to see each other. With a great deal of reluctance at having to cancel their plans, Scott dialed her number.

Katrina fumbled for the telephone whose insistent ringing yanked her out of a sound sleep. "Hello," she mumbled. It was Scott.

"Trina? Aw, Kitten, did I wake you?"

"It's okay." She yawned, stretched, and plumped her pillows into a firm pile behind her. "What time is it?" she asked, tucking the phone between her shoulder and ear while pulling herself into a sitting position.

"Nine o'clock," Scott answered. "I just wanted to let you know I got called in to work a double. I'm sorry I woke you, though. Are you okay? It's not like you to sleep so late."

"I'm fine. I stayed up late last night praying and reading, and writing in my prayer journal."

Scott smiled, loving the sound of her voice, husky from sleep. "Maybe I should have stopped by instead of calling. Then I could have awakened you with a kiss."

His low, deep voice sent shivers of delight through her sleep-drugged senses. Trina snuggled deeper into her mattress and hummed her agreement.

"Maybe next time," he offered.

She smiled to herself. "Be kind of hard without a key," she reminded a hint of teasing in her voice.

"Minor technicality," he remarked with a chuckle when she laughed. "We'll just have to remedy that little situation."

"Maybe."

"Did you dream of me?"

Again, Trina smiled to herself. "Maybe."

"I dreamed of you," he admitted, groaning when someone knocked on the door of the doctor's lounge and informed him an ambulance had arrived. "Gotta go, Sweetheart, call you later. Okay?"

"Okay. I want to go see my Mama today, and I have to register for school, but I've got to be to work at three. Call me when you get a chance."

"Okay. I love you, Kitten."

"I love you, too," she remarked, her voice soft and tender. Hanging up the phone, she pushed back the covers, slid into her slippers and padded into the kitchen to fix a cup of coffee.

Finishing her morning routine of prayer, Bible reading and breakfast before showering, Trina decided to get registration over with before visiting her mother. While waiting in line, she couldn't shake the feeling that her mother needed her. Slipping away, she used the pay phone and dialed the familiar number. No answer. Shrugging, she went back in line.

Checking her watch for the tenth time in just as many minutes, Trina felt her nerves grow taut. Something was wrong. Bowing her head, she prayed, silently...Lord, I've got this feeling that something is terribly wrong. Please, God, whatever it is, show me. Her mother's face rose foremost in her mind. Turning, she left her place in line and drove to her mother's house, praying all the way.

Elizabeth Fontenot dragged herself from the bed and to the door at the sound of her daughter's insistent banging and calling. "Mom! Open the door, Mom!"

Trina sighed with relief when she heard the doorknob rattling. The safety chain stopped her mother from opening the door all of the way. "Mom, is everything all right?"

Elizabeth sighed, hiding behind the door, shielding herself from her daughters view. "Yes, Katrina. How are you?"

"I'm fine. Can I come in?" she asked, frowning when her mother hesitated.

Rubbing her throbbing temples with trembling fingers, Elizabeth searched through the fog of pain in her head for a reason to turn her daughter away. "I'm not feeling very well today, Trina. Maybe you can come back later."

Katrina stuck her foot in the door to stop her mother from closing it in her face. "Open the door, Mama," she insisted. "I know something's wrong, so you might as well let me in."

Too weary to argue further, Elizabeth opened the door.

Pale, listless eyes gazed at Trina from sunken sockets surrounded by black, blue and purplish skin. Shock followed by rage coursed through her at the sight of Elizabeth clad only in a nightgown so thin it didn't begin to hide the bruises on her neck and torso, much less other signs of the trauma she had suffered. "Mama, what happened?" she asked, although she knew. There was only one way her mother would look so bad: her stepfather.

Her lip, swollen and busted, trembled slightly, but Elizabeth refused to answer her daughter.

"Tom did this to you? Why?" Trina rasped when her mother nodded. "Where is he?"

"He's gone, Trina. He's been gone a couple of days."

"This happened a couple of days ago?" she cried incredulously. "Mama, look at yourself! Have you seen a doctor?"

Elizabeth shrugged, she was so tired. "What would I tell them?"

"The truth!"

"I can't, Katrina. I love him."

Katrina fought the urge to shake her mother. "Oh, please! How can you say that after he's abused you all this time?"

"Please, Trina, don't start," her mother pleaded, looking far older than her forty-five years of age. "We've been through all of this before. He lost control. It won't happen again."

"Yeah," Trina snorted. "Till the next time. Mama, you've got to get out of here. You've got to get help. Please," she pleaded. "Let me help you. We'll go to my house. You'll be safe there."

"What makes you think that?"

Katrina sighed heavily. "Why do you think I've always come here instead of having y'all visit? No one knows where I live, Mama. Not even Jack knows where I live, and I can promise you, Tom doesn't either. You'll be safe there. And if you're not, I'll get you into the women's shelter where I stayed."

"And then what, Trina? I'm forty-five years old. I have very little education and no skills. What would I do?"

"You would live!" Katrina insisted, again fighting the urge to shake her.

"Mama," she broke off her tirade as her mother swooned.

Trina caught her as she slumped toward the floor. Though she weighed no more than ninety-eight pounds, Elizabeth was a heavy load to carry when she passed out in her daughter's arms. Somehow, Trina managed to get her to the couch. Picking up the phone, she called Scott.

"Can you leave?" she asked before he could greet her. "Scott, please, can you leave?"

"Whoa, hang on there. Where are you? What's the matter?" His blood ran cold at what she told him.

"I'm at my mother's house. He's beaten her again Scott. It's really bad. She fainted, and I can't wake her up." She began to cry.

"Call an ambulance, Trina," he insisted. "Have them bring her here. We'll be waiting." He promised. "Trina, do you hear me?"

She nodded then spoke. "Okay. Pray, will you? Pray she'll be all right." Hanging up the phone, she dialed 911. Kneeling by her mother's side, she prayed they would hurry, and that they would get her mother out of here before her stepfather decided to come back.

Thomas Fontenot cursed when he found his driveway blocked by his stepdaughter's car and an ambulance. Slamming out of the car, he swore violently. "What's going on here?" he demanded as a stretcher was wheeled out of the house carrying his wife. "Leave her alone! You can't take her without my permission!"

Katrina stopped packing a few of her mother's things when she heard the commotion outside. Banging the suitcase shut, she slammed the latches into place, grabbed it and flew out of the house. "Get away from her!" she screamed at her stepfather, shoving him away from her mother. "If you try and stop them, I'll call the police!" she insisted, stepping between him and the stretcher.

"If you even come near her, or the hospital, I'll report you," she assured him, climbing into the ambulance behind the stretcher.

Frustrated and angry that he had been bested by the child he'd raised from the time she was ten years old, he vented his fury on her car, ramming his into it several times. Entering the house where he had reigned as boss for twenty years, he continued his tirade, destroying nearly everything within its walls.

Between cases, Scott paced in the ER doorway, worried and concerned until the ambulance arrived. Talking with the paramedics, he barked out orders for x-rays and cat scans, blood work and IV's.

Katrina roamed the waiting room, her head bowed in prayer, anxious for some word on her mother's condition. She glanced up when Scott stopped by the admitting desk and handed the clerk some paperwork. The look on his face told her more than words ever could. Foreboding crept into her heart. Things did not look good at all.

Scott hesitated beside the admitting desk, preparing to speak the hardest words he had ever spoken to the woman he loved. His silent plea for Divine help and guidance didn't seem to rise past the ceiling as he watched her stop pacing and look at him with an expression of intense pain and unspeakable horror. The knowledge she had experienced similar treatment at the hands of the man she once loved filled him with a renewed fury at that man and the man who was her stepfather. God only knew how many generations of abuse had been handed down through the family. Taking a deep breath, he walked toward her, his heart continuing to plead with God for his words to be gentle.

Taking her by the arm, he led Katrina over to a seat. He cleared his throat, hoping to dislodge the lump of nerves clogging it. "Trina," he hesitated.

"Sweetheart, I don't know how to tell you this." He closed his eyes and prayed for strength. "It doesn't look good at all, Trina," he admitted softly.

"She's got multiple rib fractures and a punctured lung. She's malnourished and very weak. There's an infection somewhere and..." he pulled her close as she began to sob.

"She's in a coma. Honestly, Trina, I don't know how she survived this long. In my opinion, the only thing that helped her hang on was that she probably didn't get out of bed until you knocked on her door."

"Then it's all my fault!" she cried. "I should have prayed harder! I shouldn't have gone over there, I should have just prayed."

"No, Trina," Scott insisted. "It's not your fault. You getting her here is for the best. At least she's getting medical attention. If you hadn't gone over there, she may have died all alone."

"But, she's going to die anyway."

"I don't know that for sure Trina. She's in really bad shape. But we are doing everything humanly possible to treat her considering the extent of her injuries." He held her, rocking her gently while she sobbed into his chest.

"I've got to call Mac," she mumbled.

"It's done," he assured her. "I've called him and the police. They're on their way to your mother's house right now."

"Good," she muttered. "I hope they put him away for life."

"We'll see," Scott whispered, knowing that was probably not going to happen unless there was some proof her stepfather actually did the beating.

"Can I see her?" Trina asked.

"As soon as we get her admitted. Have you eaten?"

She shook her head. "I'm not hungry."

"Me, neither. But someone has to eat the food I had delivered for the staff. Maybe, between us, we can force down a few bites. You've got to, Sweetheart. You've got to take care of yourself so you can take care of your mother if she pulls through this," he insisted.

Pulling her up out of her chair, he led her into the doctor's lounge. Leaving her so she could wash her face, he went into the tiny break room where a smorgasbord of chicken, salads, pasta dishes and deserts graced the small table. Preparing a plate for each of them, he asked to be informed when Elizabeth was transferred to CCU and rejoined Katrina in the lounge. Urging, pleading and downright threatening, he managed to get her to eat some of everything on her plate.

The hours dragged, one into another. Elizabeth was moved from the emergency room into an isolation room in the Critical Care Unit. Katrina remained in the waiting area, praying away the hours between visits. Scott would come up every so often to check on them and keep her informed as to Elizabeth's condition.

The day wore into evening and evening into night but there was no change in Elizabeth's state. Thankfully, the emergency room wasn't overly busy and Scott was able to check on her and Katrina regularly. When the last patient in the E. R. had been seen and released, he joined Katrina in the waiting area, knowing he would not be able to rest as long as she was up there. Around four the next morning, he received a call to return to the E.R. When he was relieved at seven, there was still no change in Elizabeth's health.

He found Katrina curled up, sleeping, in the same chair she had occupied all night. Sitting next to her, Scott gently shook her awake. "C'mon, Sweetheart, let's get you home."

She shook her head. "I'm not leaving her."

"Trina, visiting hours are not until nine o'clock. I promise I'll leave my number with the nurses, and I'll contact you the minute someone calls to tell me there's a change in her condition. You have to get some rest," he commanded, when she shook her head no.

Trina remained adamant. "I don't want to leave."

His eyebrow arched in annoyance brought on by worry and lack of sleep. "I don't recall asking whether or not you wanted to leave."

Temper flared in her eyes. Katrina's chin snapped up in defiance. A tiny smile tugged at the corners of Scott's mouth in the face of her anger. He nodded slightly.

"Fight me all you want, little one," he urged, his voice deceptively soft. "I swore I'd never hurt you, or manhandle you, and I won't. But know this, I will do whatever is necessary to see to it you take care of yourself and right now that means getting some rest."

Katrina glared at him. "I can rest here."

Scott ground his teeth in frustration. "The atmosphere in this waiting room is not conducive for proper rest," he argued, then tried a gentler approach, placing his hand over hers.

"Look, I know you're worried and upset, but there's nothing you can do now but pray. You need to go home for a while and try to get some sleep."

Katrina jerked away from his touch. "You know?" she asked, her tone mocking. "You know what? Have you ever been held down against your will and beaten into a bloody pulp? Or forced to submit to some kind of vile punishment for an insignificant or imagined slight?" She snorted, nearly stomping her foot in agitation.

"You know nothing, Scott. You may have seen it, but you've never lived it. You have no idea what she's been through, how I feel or what I need, so don't bother telling me you know!"

Scott saw past the anger to the fear and it cut him like a knife. "You're right, Trina. I've never experienced it for myself and I probably don't know how you feel. But I do know this much, pushing yourself into a nervous breakdown is not going to help the situation at all. You need to take care of yourself. And if you can't, I'll do it for you. Remember, I'm the doctor here, and I say you need to get home and get some rest.

Katrina stormed to her feet. "Oh, right, the doctor, and let's not forget the big man," she sneered, her fists clenched at her sides, trembling with the intensity of emotions raging in her soul: anger, pain, helplessness.

"What are you going to do, Doctor?" she demanded, working herself into a fine fury. "Throw me over your shoulder and carry me, or drag me out by my hair?"

"Watch it, Trina," Scott warned softly, not willing to become a target for her anger against men in general and one man in particular. Forcing himself to remember how to effectively deal with the shock family members felt brought on by an unexpected illness or accident involving a loved one, he remained seated in order not to frighten or intimidate her further.

His calm demeanor broke through the turmoil of emotions. Trina flushed heatedly, ashamed at her outburst, and at the same time angry that she felt intimidated even though he never raised his voice. She turned on her heel, unwilling for him to see the tears in her eyes. "I want to see her."

"Visitation isn't until nine," he reminded in a quiet tone.

"I don't care," she bit out through clenched teeth. "You're the doctor. You're forcing me to leave. I want to see my mother, or I refuse to walk out that door with you."

Scott bit back on his own anger and frustration. Standing, he walked around to face her and gently lifted her chin with his finger. When she realized he waited for her to look at him, Trina warily raised her eyes to his.

The pain in those beautiful dark eyes neutralized Scott's anger and frustration. Stepping back from her, he held out a beseeching hand toward her. Her breath hitched on a sob and her hand trembled when she placed it in his. Pulling her into his arms, he stroked her hair in a gentle caress of comfort, whispering soft, sweet words of hope. He led her toward the closed doors of the CCU.

Stopping for a moment at the nurses' station, he spoke quietly to the head nurse then led Katrina in to see her mother.

Taking one of her mother's hands in both of hers, Katrina brought it to her cheek. "Mama," she whispered. "Scott's making me leave for a while. I'll be back later. I promise. Hang on, Mama," she pleaded, praying Elizabeth could hear. "I love you, and I'm so sorry I didn't go see you sooner."

Scott pulled her away when she started to weep, mumbling words of sorrow, anguish, and blame.

"Where are we going?" Katrina asked, when Scott turned in the opposite direction of her apartment.

"I'm taking you home."

"I live on West Jefferson, remember. You're going the wrong way."

He chuckled at her tone of voice. "I'm taking you to my house. I need some sleep too, and I refuse to try and sleep on that tiny couch of yours."

"I need a shower and clean clothes. I can't get those at your house."

"I'm sure we can find something for you to sleep in. I'll put your clothes on to wash then dry. We'll go by your house this afternoon."

"Huh," she snorted. "I'd like to know who you think you are, treating me this way." His soft laugh grated on her already raw nerves.

"I'm the guy who loves you. The one who's vowed to take care of you."

"Well," she snarled, "barging in and taking over my life is not what I consider taking care of me. I need to get my car," she huffed.

Scott shook his head and grinned. "Sorry, Sweetheart. Snack, shower and sleep are the only options on the agenda at this time. We'll get your car this afternoon, too. Are you hungry?"

"No, I'm not hungry. Not that it matters. You'll probably shove it down my throat if you think I need to eat."

Scott sighed. He had sparred with her as long as he cared to. "Your being upset is justified, Katrina, this childish petulance is not," he chided in a pained, gentle tone.

Katrina rolled her eyes, crossed her arms over her chest, and remained silent the rest of the way to his house.

Chapter Twelve

Scott pulled into his driveway with a weary sigh. One glance out of the corner of his eye confirmed Katrina was still furious. Her arms stayed crossed tightly across her chest, her chin was tilted in a defiant angle and her steadfast gaze remained locked on the window of the passenger door. Suppressing a growl, he leaned across and caressed her cheek with his hand, urging her face toward him.

"Kitten," he breathed, brushing a tender kiss across her forehead.

Her arms fell limply to her lap, but her fists remained clenched. Her breath hitched in a Herculean effort not to cry.

Scott ran his hand gently down her arm to grasp one of her clenched fists. Lifting it, he pried the fingers open, kissing them one at a time.

As usual, his tenderness was her undoing. She trembled violently in a last-ditch effort to suppress a sob, and failed.

With a muffled groan, Scott pulled her in his arms, soothing her ragged sobs with tender words and gentle caresses. When her sobs deteriorated into soft, hiccupping sounds, he released her. Climbing out of the car, he walked around to her side, opened the door for her and helped her out. Holding her firmly by the waist, he led her into the house, up the stairs and into his bedroom. Sitting her gently on the bed, he retrieved a large, dark T-shirt from the dresser.

"This should well cover you," he remarked, holding it up against her tiny frame. "And, if you're not comfortable sleeping in only this, I'll get you a pair of shorts."

Returning to his dresser, he withdrew a pair of jogging shorts. Holding them up, he eyed them, shaking his head with a weary chuckle. "Not a chance, they'll ever stay up. Wait, there's got to be something in here that'll work." He continued digging around in the drawer until he found a pair that had a drawstring in the waist.

"There! Now, you can take a bath or shower in here, or in the guest bath down the hall. Just throw your clothes out the door and I'll toss them into the washer."

Katrina stood, holding the clothes like a shield, firmly against her. "I guess I'll use the guest room down the hall."

Her voice was hesitant, meek. Scott nodded. "Okay. I'll pass by in a minute and pick up your clothes. Just leave them by the door."

She nodded and turned to leave. His soft voice, stating her name in a questioning tone, halted her exit. Without turning around, she waited for him to say whatever it was he wanted to say.

The chill in her stance struck him like a knife in the heart. Running a hand down her hair, he whispered, "I love you, Kitten."

"I know," she muttered, for some reason feeling unable to return the endearment.

Scott bit back his words and forced himself not to reach for her. Instinctively he knew she needed time and space to deal with her mother's situation and the emotions it evoked.

When he didn't touch her, or restrain her further, Katrina walked slowly out of his room and into the one down the hall. Stepping through the doorway she hesitated a moment, awed at the beauty of the décor and the serenity that reached out to envelop her.

It was large bedroom, light and breezy and undeniably feminine. Tiny rosebuds climbed the white wood paneling. Decorative molding trimmed the room in soft, pastel pink. Frilly curtains billowed in the breeze which flowed through the huge, airy windows. The bed, a four-poster antique, invited a body to curl up under the patchwork quilt and rest amongst the enormous, fluffy pillows.

Continuing on to the bathroom, which too, was a mixture of antique and modern, she was once again astounded at the peacefulness of her surroundings. A huge claw-footed tub was complimented by a double-sink vanity, modern shower stall, and a commode set in its own tiny cubicle. Furnished much like a fancy hotel room, the huge, fluffy bath towels were large enough to wrap around her small frame at least twice. There was shampoo, bubble bath, conditioner, a brush and comb set, mouthwash, toothpaste and an unopened toothbrush. The toiletries lay neatly on the counter top, ready for a guest who may have forgotten to pack something, or an unexpected guest who hadn't packed a thing.

Trina touched the items, surprised at how something so simple, so thoughtful could bring a measure of solace to a wounded soul. Running a tub full of water, she removed her clothes and left them by the door as Scott had requested. A sigh escaped when she sank into the welcoming warmth of the thick, frothy liquid. Allowing herself to relax, she soaked a few minutes, scrubbed up and emerged feeling somewhat better. Drying off, she donned the clothes he'd given her. Picking up the brush, she walked into the bedroom and got a glimpse of her reflection.

Color from the warm water infused her too pale cheeks like dark spots of rouge on a porcelain doll. Fear lurked in the depths of her eyes accentuated by the bright light of panic. Lines of worry and grief marred her complexion and she wondered if they'd be permanently etched there. The T-shirt fell in soft folds well below her knees. Had they not ballooned out around her hips due to the string drawn as tight as it possibly could around her tiny waist, no one would guess she had shorts on underneath it. A hysterical little giggle escaped, then another, followed by a sob as she desperately clung to her rapidly crumbling emotions.

Scott sat on his bed for long minutes absorbing the pain her cold acceptance of his comfort had wrought. After the sound of running water ceased, he took a shower. Going downstairs, he put a load of clothes, including Katrina's, on to wash. Numb from exhaustion, he started back up the stairs but paused at the sound of her weeping.

Without hesitation, he entered the guest room. He found her in a crumpled heap on the floor. Wretched sobs shook her slender frame.

"Trina," he groaned. "Trina, Love." Picking her up, he carried her to the bed, desperately searching for words to ease her grief and pain.

"I'm sorry, Scott," she mumbled between sobs. "My misery is no excuse to be rude. Not to you. Especially not to you. I'm just so angry! And so afraid," she wailed.

"I know, Kitten. It's okay. I understand and I forgive you."

"What am I going to do if she dies? What?"

"I don't know, Love. But, don't give up yet. All you can do at this point is pray. And, remember, I'm here for you, Kitten. Through thick and thin, I'll always be here."

"I don't even know how to pray right now, or what to pray for," she sobbed. "God seems so far away, so silent, so unconcerned."

"You know that's not true," Scott chided. "He's carrying you now. Believe in that. Trust in that. You've just got to let go of the anger enough to feel him. Please, Kitten, don't let what's happened harden your heart against God."

"I'm trying not to."

Wrapping his arms around her, Scott held her until she drifted into an exhausted slumber. Only then, did he allow himself to rest. He awoke five hours later to the sound of her whimpering. He watched, concerned, when she mumbled and turned away from him, curling up into a fetal position. A lone tear left a moist trail down her silky cheek. Even in sleep she couldn't find peace, he thought with a frown.

Careful not to disturb her, he rolled from the bed and covered her with the quilt. Making his way quietly down the stairs, he put the clothes on to dry, found his tennis shoes, slipped them on and took a run. Dark clouds floated in the overcast sky, thunder rolled in the distance. A sense of fear and foreboding filled his heart. He shook it off, praying for God's wisdom, guidance and direction, but mostly, that His will be done; whatever that might be. Despite his petition, instinct combined with experience warned him that no matter how the situation turned out, Katrina and her mother had a long, rough road ahead of them. Returning to the house, he took another shower, dressed and was making coffee and omelets when she came down the stairs.

"Hi," she greeted.

Scott smiled. "Hi."

She looked like a waif, lost, alone, afraid. Dark circles marred the delicate skin beneath her eyes; her hair tumbled in wild disarray across her shoulders and down her back. Dressed in his clothes, clothes which swallowed her small frame, her fragile beauty struck him anew.

When he continued to look at her, his dark eyes dancing with amusement, Trina cocked her head, a curious lift to her brow. "What?"

Scott chortled. "Do you know how adorable you look?"

She frowned. "Yeah, right. I probably look like a bum."

"That's gratitude," he remarked. "I loan you my best old clothes while yours are being washed and dried, and you call yourself a bum."

Trina couldn't help but smile at the pained expression on his face. His eyebrow arched, a grin played along his sensuous mouth, a chuckle sounded low in his throat.

"Was that a smile? I'm not sure. Can I have another one please? Just to be sure."

Unable to stop the smile tugging at her lips in response to his teasing, she slipped her arms around his waist. "Yeah, but don't tell anyone."

He laughed and swept her up in his arms, kissing her thoroughly. "Deal. If you promise to eat one of my famous omelets." He laughed when her stomach growled. "I heard that, so don't even try and tell me you're not hungry."

She wrinkled her nose at him. "Jerk."

Placing her in a chair, he served her before fixing himself a plate. They ate in silence for a few minutes.

"What now?" she asked in a scared, little-girl voice.

"I called the hospital, there's still no change. I thought we'd go get your car, then pass by your place and pick up a few things. I'm off until tomorrow morning. I was supposed to work evenings, but I called Mike to switch with me. That way, I can check on you often during the day, and bring you here or to your apartment at night. Oh, and, I called Mac and told him you probably wouldn't be in for a couple of days. He said to keep him posted."

She nodded. "Thanks. I can't believe you're being so nice to me after the way I've behaved." His smile remained tender, as was the light in his eyes.

"Love does not take offense, it is never resentful. It is always ready to excuse, to trust, to hope, and to endure whatever comes," he reminded gently, tracing her trembling lip with his thumb. "I love you, Kitten."

"I love you, too. And I am sorry."

"Shh, say no more. It's forgotten," he whispered, before replacing his thumb with his lips.

The buzzer on the dryer announced her clothes were dry. Insisting he stay seated, Trina rinsed the dishes and stacked them in the dishwasher. Slipping into the utility room, she changed. Within minutes she stood by his chair. "Will you hold me?" she queried, her voice soft, meek.

Scott's chair nearly toppled in his rush to make room for her on his lap.

"Any time," he assured, pulling her firmly in his arms.

"I'm so scared. It's like I know she's not going to make it. She's been hurt so many times..." she shrugged, not knowing how to express the anguish in her heart. "I'm so afraid," she repeated.

Resting his forehead against hers, he whispered a soft prayer. "Father, in the name of Jesus, we pray for Elizabeth. We trust in You, Lord, and we know Your will is perfect. Help us to accept Your will, whatever it may be, and heal her Lord. If not her body, then give her soul rest."

"Amen," Katrina chorused, her voice hitching on a sob. "It's strange how I feel God the most when I'm with you."

"Really?"

"Not always. There are times when I'm really aware of His presence, especially lately. Like in New Orleans. But, today, it's as if I can only feel Him while I'm in your arms."

Scott's smile was tender. "That's because you've let your guard down, Kitten. You've let Him in. Try and remain vulnerable and open, that's when you'll feel Him the most. And even if you don't feel like He's there, know He is. And know He's holding you when I can't."

"I'll try," she promised, reluctant to get up and get on with what she knew had to be done.

Scott held her, determined not to rush. Not that he would anyway. He'd hold her forever if she let him.

"Guess I'd better finish getting ready to leave," she mumbled, without moving a muscle.

"Whatever, Sweetheart." He cuddled her tenderly.

Taking a deep breath, she stood up. Before he could stand, Katrina placed her palm against his cheek and kissed him.

Scott's breath stuck in his throat at the wealth of emotions in that one kiss and forced himself not to pull her back in his arms.

Brushing her fingers through his hair, she smiled then turned to go upstairs to brush her hair and teeth and straighten up the bed. Squaring her shoulders, she tried to pray, sending up a silent plea for strength. Bible scriptures floated through her mind, giving a measure of comfort.

Come to me all you who are weary and heavy burdened and I will give you rest.

In my weakness, He is made strong.

Blessed are those who mourn, they shall be comforted.

"Thank you, Lord," she whispered, feeling a little more prepared to face another night. Until she got to her mother's house. The sight of her car, demolished by an angry man's rage, filled her with a fury unlike any she had known.

"My car! He's ruined my car!" she cried, bolting from Scott's vehicle before he could come to a complete stop.

"Trina, wait!" Throwing the car in park, Scott followed, worried her stepfather would seek retribution on her for taking his wife away from the house. He reached her as she banged on the front door.

"Tom! Open this door, you jerk!"

"Trina," Scott put a hand on her shoulder and tried to calm her.

She jerked away, banging on the door again. When no one answered, she turned away. "I want to press charges."

Scott nodded with a weary sigh. When, how would it end? "Okay. We'll go to the police station before we go to the hospital."

Before they could turn around, Tom drove up. One could tell by the dents in his car that he'd used it to destroy hers. Before Scott could stop her, Katrina flew off the porch and met her stepfather as he disembarked from his vehicle.

Only blind fury could prevent Trina from noticing Tom was crazy drunk, and give her the courage to confront him. "You!" she squealed, pushing at him.

He staggered and fell back against the car but came up on the defense. Grabbing her by the arms, he shook her. "Who do you think you are, Missy? You come to my house, and take my wife!"

Trina nearly vomited from the smell of sour whiskey on his breath and the scent of filth emanating from his clothing. She pounded her fists on his chest. "She's my mother, you jerk! You've practically killed my mother, and you've ruined my car!"

His hands were like steel manacles on her arms when he shook her again. On a surge of fear she pulled free from his grasp and retreated a couple of steps. Her chin jerked up in defiance. "You'll pay for this, Tom. I swear. If it's the last thing I do, I'll get you."

"Don't threaten me," he warned, taking an ominous step toward her, his hands clenched into tight fists by his side.

Scott stepped between them, shoving Trina behind him and placing a restraining hand on Tom's chest. "That's enough. If you put a hand on her, you'll answer to me."

At five-foot, ten-inches, Tom had to look up into Scott's furious gaze. It was a very intimidating feeling having to look up into such dark, dangerous eyes. So intimidating in fact that the old adage, ten foot tall and bullet proof didn't apply despite the whiskey he had drunk. He stepped back.

Katrina faced Tom once more, impaling him with an angry glare. "Stay away from my mother," she insisted in a low, fierce voice.

"Enough, Katrina. Let's go." Taking her gently but firmly by the arm, Scott urged her into his car. After they arrived at her apartment, Scott called the hospital to check on Elizabeth once more before taking Katrina to the police station where she attempted to press charges against Tom for the destruction of her car.

The officer took her statement and made out a report, but informed her there wasn't much they could do. Her car was parked on his property. They could charge him with destruction of private property, but chances are he wouldn't go to jail or stay there very long if he did.

"What about beating my mother? She's in a coma right now because of him."

"I'm sorry, ma'am. There are no witnesses to the beating. Until and unless she confirms he was the one who did it, we can't detain him."

"Confirm it? I can promise you he's the one who did it. He's beaten her for years! What more confirmation do you want?"

The young officer just shook his head. He had responded to the call the night before and had seen the damage done by Tom's uncontrolled rage. Gut instinct told him she was telling the truth. The problem was, they had no proof. "I'm sorry, ma'am."

"Well," she huffed. "Sorry doesn't get it. What's going to happen if she dies?"

Again he shook his head. "I don't know, ma'am. Unless you can get us some proof or a witness..." he trailed off at the look of horror dawning on her face.

"You mean if she dies, nothing's going to happen to him?"

"Not without proof, ma'am. There's no prior record of abuse so it's hard to say." He sighed wearily. "I'm really sorry."

Katrina turned away in an angry whirl. Scott put his arm around her and led her from the police station. Arriving at the hospital, he called a wrecker service and had her car towed to a body shop, while Katrina sat in a numb trance waiting for a chance to see her mother.

Day two slid by with agonizing slowness, melding into day three without the slightest change in Elizabeth's condition. By day four, her health began to decline, but she hung on.

Nine days after she was admitted into the hospital, Elizabeth Fontenot died.

Chapter Thirteen

Once Elizabeth's death was reported, Tom was arrested. The District Attorney did his best to have him charged and tried for murder, but his most vehement arguments were met with opposition from the courts. Even with the autopsy confirming she died as a result of the injuries sustained from a beating, there was no proof Tom had been the perpetrator. On top of that, there were no witness and no prior record of abuse. Other than a judgment against him for the damages to Katrina's car, Tom walked away a free man, all within forty-eight hours of his arrest.

But her mother was dead. Katrina couldn't begin to fathom the reality, the harshness, and futility of the justice system. In the funeral director's office, Scott held her as she absorbed the latest blow from the impact of her mother's beating. There was no burial insurance, no savings, nothing. Even with her meager savings and income, Katrina would likely pay on funeral expenses for a long time.

"No dignity," she sobbed into Scott's chest. "She had no dignity in life, and now there'll be no dignity in death. I can't even give her a proper funeral," she wailed. "There's no money, no plot, nothing! What am I going to do?"

Scott was at his wits end. He'd fought with Katrina, using every means available outside of sheer force, to get her to rest and take care of herself. Her constant emotional highs and lows bordered on depression to the extent he'd only witnessed, not dealt with on a personal level. His own emotional involvement rendered him less than objective. Tired, angry, and frustrated, he gave his best shot at comforting her. "C'mon, Kitten, let's go home. You don't have to make these decisions today. Give yourself a break," he urged.

"I can't."

"Let me help you."

She knew his offer meant more than emotional help. Mistaking compassion for pity, the thought infuriated her.

"Help? How? You couldn't help her; what makes you think you can help me?"

"That's not fair."

"You're right, it's not fair. Nothing is fair! It's not fair that I lost my mother. It's not fair the jerk who killed her, my stepfather mind you, is walking the streets. It's not fair that I was married to an equally hateful jerk for ten years of my life. It's not fair that it took the death of my child to make me see the light. And it's certainly not fair she died before I could help her see the light!"

Scott stood, fists clenched in a determined effort not to jerk her up out of the chair and shake some sense into her. Taking a deep, calming breath, he tried to talk reasonably to her. "I know this is hard on you, Katrina, but you've got to get some rest. You're not eating, nor sleeping, and you're certainly not thinking straight. Why don't you let me take you home, give you something to help you get a good night's sleep, and we'll sort this out in the morning."

"You go if you want to. I don't care anymore."

"Oh, you don't, do you?" Scott demanded, his control slipping dangerously. "Well, let me tell you something, Miss," he continued, pulling her up to where her face was mere inches from his. "I care. Whether you like it or not, I do care. And I'm tired of seeing you like this. If you don't get ahold of yourself, I'm going to have you admitted."

His arrogance grated on her already raw nerves. It was the final straw. Clenching her fists, she pushed herself out of his grasp. "Put me down, you jerk. I'm sick to death of your superior attitude. You have no control over my life. You can't tell me what to do, and I wish to God you'd stop trying to run my life!"

She couldn't have hurt him more had she stuck a knife in his heart. They glared at each other for long, tense, moments. Hanging on to his temper by a fragile thread, Scott walked away. The door slammed in his wake. Meeting with the funeral director, he handed him a hundred dollar bill. "When she's ready to leave, call a cab. Have him take her wherever she wants to go."

Having overheard their encounter, the funeral director nodded with a sad smile. "Grief is a terrible thing," he said softly.

Scott nodded, unable to speak, not knowing what to say if he could, and afraid of what he might say if he opened his mouth. At this point, he couldn't put two compassionate thoughts together. All he could think of was getting out of the building in one piece. Once seated in his car, he fell apart. He'd been the pillar of strength, now the pillar crumbled. Reaching for his car phone, he called the one person in the world who would understand.

Seeing Scott's number on the caller I.D., Craig answered with a smile.

"Hey, Buddy. How's it going?"

"If it gets any better, I don't think I can stand it," Scott answered, his tone reflecting all the misery in his soul.

The utter defeat in his friend's voice had Craig grabbing a chair. "What's going on, Scott?" he queried.

Scott unloaded, telling him of every single incident since Katrina called him from her mother's house two weeks ago.

Craig remained silent until Scott finished with what had just occurred in the funeral home. "You left her there?" he asked incredulously.

"I've had all I can take, Craig. I swear. Half the time I just want to hold her and take away every ounce of pain she's ever felt, and half the time I'd like to strangle her!" He sighed. "She's blaming me."

"What? She doesn't mean it, Scott. She can't mean that."

"I know." Scott swallowed convulsively trying to dislodge the lump in his throat. "I keep telling myself that. She's gone through the list, blaming herself, her stepfather, the law. Now, it's my turn. I was the attending physician. She called me from her house. She trusted me. Now she blames me. I couldn't help her mother. I couldn't save her." His voice broke. "I tried, Craig. I did everything humanly possible. I swear I did."

"I know you did, Buddy. She knows it, too. She's just going through some tough emotions right now. You've been a doctor too many years to let someone who's grieving like that make you second-guess yourself. Sounds like you could use some company."

"Oh, man, could you? I know y'all just got back from vacation and I know you have got a lot going on...."

"We'll leave within the hour," Craig interrupted.

"Thank you," Scott muttered. "Thank God."

"One thing though, Buddy," Craig interjected. "Don't leave her there alone. Go back."

Scott smiled ruefully to himself. "I'm in the parking lot on my mobile phone."

Craig chuckled. "Well, go back into the building," he insisted. They talked a few minutes longer then hung up. Leaning his head against the back of his seat, Scott closed his eyes and prayed, pleading with God for guidance and wisdom.

"Love and forgiveness, patience, gentleness, meekness, kindness, and self-control." The words were loud and clear, as though the Holy Spirit were seated next to him.

"I'm trying, Lord," he whispered.

"But the Spirit worketh in you, bearing fruit," the Voice reminded gently.

In that moment Scott knew when it all went wrong: When he started taking over, when he took it upon himself to be everything to Katrina—counselor, friend, rock, and comforter. He had been relying on his own strength, instead of cooperating with God and allowing the Holy Spirit to work through him to touch her heart and mind. He'd inadvertently set himself up to be God in her life.

The tears came, remorse overwhelmed, and with it, forgiveness. Cleansing. Renewing. Healing. Direction followed. Scott knew what he had to do. Climbing out of the car, he walked back into the funeral home. The director met him at the door, holding the money for him to take back.

Scott shook his head. "Keep it. Put it toward whatever arrangements she makes."

"You'll want a receipt, then."

"No. I trust you. And I trust you to keep this between us."

The man nodded.

"Where is she?"

"Where you left her."

Scott went back into the room and found Katrina sitting exactly as he left her. Kneeling in front of her, he took her hands in his, bringing them to his lips.

"I'm sorry," she mumbled. "I know you're not like other men."

"Are you sure about that?" he queried.

His voice was raw, his eyes fierce. Trina's eyes widened in surprised shock.

Scott smiled, self-mocking, though tender. "That's where you're wrong Katrina, assuming I'm so different than other men, so much better. Underneath, we're all alike. There's a very thin line between civilized and uncivilized, between man and beast. What makes us better than the beast is free will. We have a choice on how to behave. Just because I don't believe in violence doesn't mean I'm not capable of it. Only by God's grace am I different from the next guy. Not better, only different."

She began to cry softly. "I don't know what to do."

"You don't have to make these decisions today."

She shook her head. "I know, but I'd just as soon get it over with."

He nodded. "Okay, let's go. Whatever you choose, I'll stand behind you. Whatever financial arrangements he'll make with you are fine with me. But, Trina, at least let me guarantee them. If, for some reason you can't pay, please let me help. Everything I have is a gift from God, anyway, a gift I'm commanded to share. I choose to share it with you. I love you, Trina. Don't deny me the privilege of doing something for you."

Unable to resist without throwing his declaration of love back in his face and hurting his feelings again, she nodded.

Taking her by the hand, Scott gently pulled her to her feet. Placing an arm around her waist, they sought the funeral director. Arrangements were made for a simple but elegant funeral.

With the assurance her mother's body would be ready the next afternoon, Katrina let Scott lead her out and help her into the car. Once on their way, he informed her Craig and Tamera would be there sometime during the evening.

"That's nice," she mumbled, too numb to know whether she should be grateful or not.

"Your place or mine?" Scott asked.

"I don't care."

He frowned. "I hate that answer," he remarked, regretting it immediately when her eyes filled with tears.

"It doesn't matter. Really."

He reached over and caressed her cheek. "My place, then." Once there, he pulled her overnight bag out of the back seat of his car, helped her out and into the house. "First, a hot bath. You have clean clothes in here. If there's nothing comfortable enough to sleep in, let me know and I'll get you a T-shirt."

"There's not."

He nodded. "Okay, then, a T-shirt it is." So saying, he retrieved one for her. Leaving her to her preference of a bath or shower, he pulled back the covers on the bed then went downstairs and heated up a can of soup. Placing the soup, crackers and a glass of sports drink on the tray, he carried it up to her.

Katrina's stomach did a sick flip-flop at the sight and smell of the food. She shook her head. "I'm not hungry." She sat on the bed and began unbraiding her hair.

Scott placed the tray over her lap. "It's plain soup, Trina, mostly broth. Please try and eat just a bite or two. At least drink something."

Swallowing the nausea that was thick in her throat, she sipped on the drink until her stomach settled somewhat then contemplated the soup. After only a couple of spoonsful, her stomach revolted. Putting the spoon down, she pushed the bowl away. "No more. Please," she pleaded with Scott.

He nodded. "Okay." Removing the tray, he placed it on the floor by the dresser, but took the drink and put in on the table by the bed. "If you wake up, please try and drink. I'm worried Kitten. I don't want you to get dehydrated."

She nodded.

Taking the brush from her trembling hand, he turned her around and brushed her hair in long, soothing, strokes.

When it cascaded down her back in a silken mass of waves, he put the brush down. Encouraging her to lay down, he rolled her over onto her stomach. Pushing her hair out of his way, he brushed his lips across the nape of her neck and began massaging her shoulders. His hands roamed over her back and shoulders; his fingers kneaded the knotted muscles at the base of her neck. He continued, easing the tension from her muscles until he felt her body begin to relax beneath his hands.

Rolling her onto her back, he continued, kneading the muscles in her arms, thighs, calves and feet. The feel of her melting, soft and pliable beneath his hands, was sheer erotic torture, but Scott was determined she not mistake compassion for passion. He kept his hands light, his voice soft, urging, coaxing her into a deeper state of relaxation.

Katrina let go, and allowed him to pamper her. She felt herself unwind, as though she were floating on a soft cloud. The thought crossed her mind that he was trying to seduce her. She squashed it. He wouldn't stoop so low as to take advantage of her emotional state in that manner. A moan of pure appreciation escaped as she realized that. She closed her eyes, savoring the sensations. Her mother's face, bruised, battered and deathly pale, loomed in her mind. Her eyes jerked open.

As though reading her thoughts, Scott moved, cupping her face in his hands. He brushed his lips across her forehead, nose and eyelids as his fingers massaged her temples, down to her ears, along her jawbone, and back up to feather across her forehead. "I'm sorry," he whispered thickly. "I'm sorry I couldn't do more for her. I'm sorry I couldn't save her for you," he mumbled, as tears dripped down her pale cheeks.

"Thank you," she whispered, unable to open her eyes and face the pain she knew shone in his; pain she put there with careless, thoughtless, angry words. "I know you did everything possible, and I'm sorry I said otherwise."

He brushed his lips across hers, hushing further apology. "Shh. Say no more. Think no more. Just rest, little one."

Unable to soothe the emotions roiling within her, demanding release, he pulled her in his arms, cuddled her against his chest and prayed silently, letting her cry until she slipped into an exhausted slumber. Knowing he should, but not willing to leave her alone, he pulled the covers over them and slept with her wrapped securely in his arms.

* * * * *

Although Amber and Ace stayed home under the careful eye of the ranch foreman, it had taken no persuasion and very little time for Craig and Tamera to get things together and get on the road. They arrived at Scott's house around midnight. Though long, the trip was pleasant; a time of quiet interspersed with snatches of conversation as they prayed for their friends. Using the key Craig had been given years ago, they let themselves in the house.

Careful not to disturb anyone, Tamera went into the kitchen and fixed sandwiches and soup to suppress the gnawing in their bellies. With worry and concern for their friends urging them on, they hadn't taken the time to stop and eat along the way. Afterward, Craig went upstairs to check on Scott while Tamera cleaned the kitchen.

Finding him and Katrina asleep, he quietly removed the tray from the room and closed the door. Going back downstairs, he informed Tamera they were sleeping. Taking her by the hand, he led his wife into another of Scott's spare bedrooms and urged her beneath the covers with him.

Taking her in his arms, he thanked God for the blessings in his life, and prayed they would be a comfort and strength for their friends in the days to come.

Chapter Fourteen

Despite the late night, Craig was up at dawn. Careful not to disturb Tamera, he rolled out of bed and took a shower. After dressing, he went down to the kitchen and fixed a pot of coffee.

Scott awoke, surprised to find Katrina still sound asleep. The smell of fresh coffee permeated the air, luring him from beneath the covers. Careful not to disturb Trina, he slid from the bed and went into his bedroom to take a shower. Putting on fresh clothes, he went in search of a cup of the hot, enticing brew.

Craig turned at the sound of footsteps and greeted Scott with a smile. "Morning."

Scott felt as though a ton of bricks were being lifted from his shoulders. "Thank you for coming," he remarked, embracing his friend.

"Coffee?" Craig offered.

"Please." Scott sat as Craig poured him a cup. "When did y'all get in?"

"Around midnight."

"Why didn't you wake me?"

"You were sleeping so well and, from what you told me, I figured you needed it. Didn't want to disturb Trina either. How is she?"

"She's still sleeping. Thank God. Are the kids here?"

Craig shook his head. "No. The only way I'd have gotten Amber to leave Texas was to physically drag her."

Scott grinned. "What about Ace?"

"He's in the very capable care of his sister."

"Whose very capable care is she in?"

Craig's eyes narrowed. "Sam's."

Scott chuckled. "I'm sure Stanley will make sure everything's okay."

Craig glared at him. Hearing him laugh, even that strained little chuckle, was worth the effort it took not to explode at the mere mention of the new man in his daughter's life. "I'm sure he'll be sniffing around," he growled.

"Sam has strict instructions to watch that boy, and Amber has promised he won't stay past Ace's bedtime. It was the only way I'd agree he could visit at all while we're away."

Scott knew him well enough to know when to quit teasing. Now was that time. "And how's Tamera?"

"Tamera's fine," the woman in question answered, bending and slipping her arms around Scott's neck. She hugged him before greeting her husband. Placing her hand in Craig's she kissed him, refreshed their cups of coffee, and then poured herself a cup.

"How are you?" she asked Scott.

Scott knew she would see through anything but the truth. They both would. Tears pricked his eyes, and he shook his head. "To be honest, I'm not doing too well. It's been a hellacious couple of days, hellacious couple of weeks."

"What happened?"

Scott told them how Katrina had gone to visit her mother and found her beaten nearly to death. And how, after nine agonizing days in Intensive Care, Elizabeth had died. He told of Trina's stepfather banging up her car and not being charged with the death of his wife because there was no proof and no witnesses.

"Trina is taking it badly. Very badly. It brings back too many memories of her childhood and a marriage filled with the same kind of treatment. Makes me want to kill someone," he growled.

"And what would that solve?" Tamera asked a gentle rebuke in her tone.

"Nothing," Craig interjected. "But it would probably give him a sense of justification. I know exactly how you feel, Buddy," he assured Scott, remembering how he had felt when he found out Tamera had been engaged and abused before they met.

Tamera rolled her eyes. "Let's not go there," she insisted, remembering the same incident as though it happened yesterday.

Scott reached for her hand. "Thank you for coming, Tamera. I'm hoping you can help her. God knows I've tried. But," he hesitated, thinking. "I can't seem to reach through her grief and pain. It goes so deep. Maybe since you experienced something similar you can help her."

"I'll be here for her, Scott. That's all any of us can do. She'll have to deal with this in her own way and in her own time. But I'll be here if she needs me."

"What's on the agenda for today?" Craig asked.

"Elizabeth's body will be ready at one o'clock. The funeral is at two."

"So soon?" Tamera queried.

Scott shrugged. "It's what Trina wanted. She's so torn up, I'm not sure she realizes she may need more time to say goodbye. Then, again, she's been grieving since the day she found Elizabeth like that. She said more than once that she knew her mother wouldn't make it."

Tamera's eyes filled with tears. "Poor baby. How long do you think she'll sleep?"

"I hope she sleeps until noon." All three looked up when they heard the water begin running in an upstairs bathroom. "So much for hope," Scott murmured. "Guess I should be grateful she's rested this long."

Tamera got up from the table and began preparing breakfast.

* * * * *

Katrina stood a long time in the shower, letting the hot water soothe her troubled mind and wash the remaining lethargy from her body. Shutting her mind to the pain in her heart, she fought back tears, determined not to start crying. If she started crying now, she wouldn't stop, and she craved at least a few moments of peace from the emotional turmoil. Her heart pleaded with God for those few moments. She emerged from the shower feeling refreshed and somewhat calm. Pulling clean clothes out of her overnight bag, she dressed and went downstairs. Her heart lifted at the sight of Craig and Tamera.

"Morning, Sweetheart," Scott greeted, kissing her on the cheek.

"Hi," she answered, accepting hugs and greetings from Tamera and Craig. "Thank you for coming."

"We wouldn't dream of staying away right now. That's what friends are for," Tamera assured her.

Trina smiled gratefully and accepted a cup of coffee. Forcing the warm liquid past the lump in her throat, she put the cup down with a trembling hand. "I need to go to my apartment and get something to wear this afternoon."

Scott nodded. "We can do that."

Her voice trembled. "And, I guess I need to call Tom and see if he'll let me get a dress for Mama."

"Either that, or we can buy one," Scott offered.

Katrina's smile was wistful. "I imagine it's been a long time since Mama's had a new dress."

"Well, she'll get one today," Scott promised.

Trina shook her head. "Please don't be too sympathetic this morning. I don't think I can handle it," she pleaded in a tremulous voice.

"Feel free to cry all you want, Sweetheart," Craig insisted, giving her a hug. "We know exactly how you feel. We've all lost someone we love."

She sighed heavily. "I'm tired of feeling angry and depressed, and so very tired of crying."

"Well, don't then," Tamera urged. "For a little while this morning we'll forget. We'll find a salon that will pamper us for a change, and we'll both get new dresses, also."

Craig chuckled, winking at his wife. "Might as well hand over your wallet, Buddy," he told Scott, pretending to reach for his. "I know that look."

"Gladly," Scott insisted, getting up to put his dishes in the sink. "I'd gladly give her the wallet, everything in it, and anything else she wants." He slipped his arms around Trina's waist and pulled her trembling frame against his chest. "I'd give everything I own just to see her smile."

Trina's lips trembled into a tiny smile, but her eyes filled with tears. She blinked them back and forced down the lump in her throat. Urging his arms tighter around her waist, she leaned against Scott, gaining comfort from his strong embrace as he whispered his love.

After breakfast, Tamera took charge. They arrived at a salon where the stylists took pains to trim, wash and style their hair, then treated them to manicures and pedicures as well as complete facials. Grateful for the reprieve from the emotional roller coaster she'd been on, Trina allowed Tamera to lavish her with tenderness and affection. The hours seemed to fly by and before they knew it, it was time to bring Elizabeth's dress to the funeral home. By the time they returned to Scott's house, it was time to get ready for the ordeal ahead.

* * * * *

Trina stood a long time staring at her reflection. Rich velvet material graced the yoke of the deep mocha dress she wore, which was as close to black she could don without looking like death herself. Wrapped up into a French twist with wisps of curls framing her face, the hairstyle lent a soft radiance to her countenance. The facial she'd been treated to did wonders to erase the lines of stress from days of worry and grief, from her skin, but nothing could erase the depth of pain from her eyes. Blinking them, she fought down a wave of grief. Taking a deep breath, she squared her shoulders in an effort to maintain control. It didn't work. Sinking to her knees she cried out to God.

"Oh, Father, help me make it through this day," she pleaded, clasping the cross dangling from the gold chain around her neck. A sense of strength flowed through her, and she knew God had heard her prayer. He was near. He was listening. Reminded of the poem, Footprints, she knew He would carry her if necessary.

"Thank You," she whispered, clinging to those thoughts. "And thank You for the friends You have so graciously put in my life to support me through this ordeal."

Rising, she slipped her shoes on. At a knock on the door, she answered, "Come in."

Tamera walked in looking beautiful in the deep navy dress she had bought. "How are you doing?" she asked.

Trina smiled. "Okay, I guess. Thank you for taking me away this morning."

Tamera hugged her. "You're welcome, but I was just doing what the Lord asked of me. Please don't misunderstand. I love you, and I enjoyed our time this morning too. But we have to realize that sometimes it's God who provides a way to remind us of the beauty in our life, and the beauty all around us: good friends, nice people, pretty dresses, sunshine to warm away the darkness in our soul. Even if it's only for a little while."

"I never thought of it that way," Trina admitted. "I mean, I just finished thanking Him for your and Craig's friendship but... "She hesitated, unable to express all she felt.

Tamera smiled. "As Christians we are called to show God's love to a hurting world. I don't believe in coincidence as much as Divine Providence. Do you really think your relationship with Scott is just the result of an accidental meeting? Or that our ensuing friendship is a result of your knowing him?"

"I never really thought of it like that," Trina repeated. "Guess I have a lot to learn about the ways of God."

Tamera squeezed her hand, the gesture soothing and encouraging. "It'll come. Believe me; it takes a lot of time, a lot of prayer, many hardships and countless blessings to come into the full realization of God's grace and mercy. I don't think we ever really come into a full realization of it until we reach heaven.

"The Bible says we are changed from glory to glory and we suffer in order that we may grow in grace and in love. Jesus said the greatest commandment was to love God, and the second greatest was to love our neighbor. To get love you have to live love. I'm sure you've heard the old saying that love isn't love until you give it away."

She continued at Trina's nod. "Well, that holds true for a lot of things. Share love, you'll receive love. Share joy, you'll have joy. Share peace, and peace will abound in your life. But in order to do these things, you have to be rooted and grounded in Christ, and that takes time. When we are born again, it's the beginning of a whole new way of thinking and living. That's why we are challenged to renew our minds and be transformed. We are in this world but not of it.

"The Bible is full of nuggets of truth to guide our daily walk in this world—a world which has turned away from God and gone mad as a result, a world full of sin and violence and hatred. The only way we'll change the world as a whole, is to change the world we live in. The only way we'll do that is by being obedient to the commands of God, by loving our neighbors, by forgiving those who hurt us, and by accepting God's forgiveness for ourselves. Believe me, Trina; it's not as easy as it should be. We humans have made loving and forgiving one another a job instead of a joy."

A knock on the door interrupted their conversation. "It's twelve-fifteen, ladies," Scott informed them.

"We'll be out in a minute," Tamera called. Reaching for Katrina's hands, she took them in hers. "Promise me something," she continued. "You're going to be feeling a whole range of emotions today and in the days to follow: grief, pain, anger, bitterness, a whole lot of feelings that will eat you up if you let them. Promise you will hold on to Jesus. Promise you will let nothing hinder your relationship with Him."

"I promise I'll try," Katrina assured her in a soft, tremulous voice.

Tamera reached into the pocket of her dress and handed Trina an envelope. "It's a letter from Amber. She wanted you to know her thoughts and prayers are with you and how much she loves you. Read it tonight," she urged, knowing the words of comfort and hope her daughter had penned. "And read it often."

Trina fingered the pretty stationary, amazed that she could actually feel the love and friendship contained within the sealed envelope. Scripture came to mind, Acts 19: 11 & 12; of how people were healed simply by touching or being touched with handkerchiefs and aprons from the Apostle Paul. Her heart swelled with tenderness for the young woman who gave so much of herself to others. Though she had met her mere weeks ago, she knew deep down Amber Harris was a very special child with a tender heart, a heart for God.

Scott was halfway back up the stairs when the door opened to the bedroom where Tamera and Trina were talking. He stopped and stared for a full minute at the beauty of the women exiting the room. His heart skipped a beat when Katrina's gaze met his. He held a hand toward her, smiling when she placed hers in it.

"If there was ever any doubt in my mind that God is a god of beauty, you two gorgeous creatures just demolished it."

They heard Craig chuckle behind him.

"I second that," he remarked, reaching for Tamera's hand.

Tamera winked at Katrina. Taking his hand, she let her husband lead her downstairs, permitting Scott a few minutes alone with Trina. "How is she?" Craig asked, when they reached the foyer.

"I think she'll be fine. In time," she added, accepting her husband's embrace as he pulled her into his arms and lowered his lips to hers.

Scott took one more step, bringing him closer to the woman he loved. No words were necessary when he cupped her face in his hands and brushed his lips across her forehead before pulling her firmly in his arms.

Trina allowed his arms to enfold her and his love envelope her. She relished the feel of his strong arms around her, gaining comfort from the strength of his embrace and the warmth of his soothing voice as he whispered sweet words of love and tenderness.

Gazing up at him, she placed her palm gently against his cheek. "Thank you, for everything. I love you."

"I love you, too, Kitten."

"Guess its time," she whispered, reluctant to leave the comfort of his arms.

Scott glanced at his watch and nodded. "It's time," he agreed. "But know this; I'm beside you every step of the way. Through pain or sorrow, happiness or joy, I'll always be here for you."

"Thank you," she whispered, clinging to his hand all the way into town.

The funeral director met them at the door and led them down the hall. Scott hesitated in the doorway of the room where the director stopped. Bringing her hand to his lips, he gazed tenderly down at Katrina. "Do you want a few minutes alone?"

She shook her head. "Not yet. Maybe before we leave."

He nodded, put his arm around her, and led her through the door. Flowers of every kind and color filled the tiny stateroom. It didn't take a rocket scientist to figure out who had sent the dozens of yellow roses.

"Thank you," Trina whispered, her eyes filling with tears of gratitude at their thoughtfulness. Her eyes widened in surprise at the sight of her mother as they approached the open casket. "She's so beautiful," she gasped.

There was an angelic peace, an ethereal beauty to Elizabeth's countenance. The dress, a deep rose creation in the latest fashion, clung to her tiny frame. Her hair, which had been limp and dirty despite the daily brushing Katrina had provided, was clean and artfully arranged in a becoming style. Make-up had done wonders to remove the bruises which had marred her face and the pale discoloration of her complexion.

"Oh, Mama," Trina murmured. "I've never seen you look so beautiful." Tears slid unashamedly down her face as she touched her mother's hand, recoiling at the cold, stiffness of it. "I've never seen you look so peaceful," she whispered, stroking Elizabeth's arm. Forcing her fingers beneath Elizabeth's clasped hands; she clung to her mother, wishing she could lift that hand and press the palm to her cheek, wanting to feel her mother's touch, her caress, one more time.

One by one, Craig, Tamera, and then Scott moved away, giving Trina time with her mother. Bowing their heads, each said silent prayers for Elizabeth and her daughter. After a few minutes, Katrina released her mother's hand and knelt beside the coffin to pray.

The minutes dragged by with agonizing slowness. Trina rose from her knees to finger the spray of roses on the casket. Hearing her movements, Scott got up from his seat and walked to her. Sliding his arm around her waist, he held her firmly against his side before urging her to sit in the chair which had been placed beside the coffin. A movement at the door caught her eye, and Trina stiffened a cry of protest on her lips. Scott turned his attention to where she looked.

Tom stood in the doorway, pale and visibly shaken. Sensing the animosity radiating from Katrina, he hesitated.

"Trina," Scott's voice was soft. "Are you all right?"

"I don't want him here," she insisted.

Scott knelt before her, taking her hands in his. "Trina, look at me," he commanded. "She was his wife," he said gently.

"He killed her," she argued through clenched teeth.

"They were married for twenty years. There had to be some good to keep her there."

"She had no choice."

"Everyone has a choice."

"She didn't know that," Katrina insisted.

"Listen to me," Scott urged softly. "Let him come in, Trina. Let him pay his respects. Let him say good-bye. I promise, if he gets one step out of line, I'll personally escort him out. There has to be forgiveness," he insisted, when she shook her head.

"How can you say that? How am I supposed to forgive him?"

"I don't know, Kitten," he admitted with a ragged sigh. "It won't be an easy thing to do. All I know is that we're commanded to forgive, and until you can offer forgiveness, there's always compassion."

Biting back the many angry retorts which ran through her mind, Katrina jerked her hands from his, rose from the chair and walked stiffly to where Craig and Tamera sat. They made room between them, surrounding her with comfort and support.

Taking a deep breath, Scott got up off his knees and turned to face Tom.

He nodded in acquiescence, and watched as Tom made his way slowly up the aisle. Squeezing his shoulder in a tiny gesture of solace, he left Tom beside his wife and went to sit by Craig. Burying his face in his hands, he prayed God would intervene and that Katrina would forgive his interference.

Katrina sat stiffly between Craig and Tamera; her eyes shut tight, tears streaming down her cheeks. Clenching her fists, she fought the urge to lunge from her seat and attack her stepfather with all of the pent-up emotions in her soul. "There has to be forgiveness," Scott's words echoed in her ears.

"Forgive us as we forgive those..." words from the mouth of the Lord joined in convicting her heart while her mind cried out in angry denial.

She looked up when Tom slumped to his knees. Deep, heart-wrenching sobs shook his frame as he cried out in anguish. "I never meant to hurt her," he mumbled between sobs. He turned to face Katrina, his eyes begging for mercy and forgiveness. "I'd been sober for years. I don't know what happened. Honestly, Katrina, I don't. But I never meant to hurt her."

At that moment, Katrina's traitorous heart chose to remind her of a better day, a day when a little girl ran into the arms of a loving, gentle father. The man Tom once was. Twenty years of anger, fear and bitterness had made her forget the man he was when not drinking. In an instant she saw him for what he truly was: A man too weak and helpless to fight the demon of alcoholism. And alcoholism was what changed him from a gentle man into an angry beast. In that moment, it didn't matter alcoholism was idolatry and drunkenness a sin. Un-forgiveness was a sin too. Katrina didn't understand why God chose that particular moment to give her a revelation. All she understood was, the only father she had ever known, was hurting as badly as she.

"And on that day when you hear His voice, harden not your hearts," a Voice insisted gently.

Rising, she opened her arms, if not her heart, to her stepfather. Without a word of condolence, and with very little feeling of true mercy, she held him while he cried. Trina knew the day would come when she would have to choose forgiveness over compassion. But for now, compassion, if only a tiny spark, and obedience to the still, small Voice within, was all she could summon.

"I know you really don't want me here, so I'm not going to stay, Katrina," Tom said, stepping away from her. "Thank you for letting me come at all."

Trina kept her eyes lowered for fear he would see the anger and confusion in them and nodded. She sank weakly into the chair as he returned to Elizabeth's side for another brief moment. A collective sigh of relief could be felt when he left.

Craig put his arm around Scott when Tamera rose to comfort Katrina. A movement in the doorway caught his eye, and he tightened his grip on his friend's shoulder. "It's time to practice what you preach, Buddy," he told Scott softly, as Katrina's ex-husband walked into the room.

Scott's head jerked up, eyes narrowed and jaw hardened when Jack Simmons walked toward the casket where his former mother-in-law lay.

"Remember what you told Katrina," Craig warned. "If he gets one step out of line, I'll personally escort him out," he assured Scott, as they rose in unison while Tamera helped Trina to her feet.

Jack turned to face Katrina. For the first time in his life he realized what a life of over-indulgence could lead to. It could be her, the woman who was once his wife, in that coffin. It could have been him who put her there. His hand trembled as he reached for her; arm fell limply to his side when she took a step back from him, hugging herself in obvious fear.

"I'm sorry, Katrina," Jack mumbled, as Scott stepped up beside her and put a protective arm around her.

"Thank you," she whispered, grateful to feel Scott's strong frame beside her.

Scott glanced at his watch and then looked meaningfully at Craig.

Craig offered a hand to Jack and thanked him for coming, then escorted him out of the room.

Once again, Katrina sank weakly into the chair. Kneeling in front of her, Scott took her hands in his. "It's two o'clock, Sweetheart," he said gently. "Do you want to be alone a few minutes?"

"Please," she pleaded, unable to meet his gaze.

He hesitated a moment, but rose when Tamera placed her hand on his shoulder. Bending, he brushed his lips across Katrina's forehead. "We'll be right outside the door. Take as long as you need."

Katrina stood for long moments talking softly to her mother and weeping. Leaving the funeral home was the hardest part for her. Once they were at the cemetery and the simple gravesite service was over she felt more at peace.

Taking a single yellow rose from one of the many bouquets, Scott handed it to her and walked with her to Craig's truck.

"I need to go home," Katrina said, once they were on their way.

"I'd like for you to stay at the house with us tonight," Scott urged. "Please. I know you need time to yourself, but stay. Just for tonight."

"Okay," she relented with a sigh. "But I need to pick up some clothes and to check on things."

"We'll stop by," Craig offered, following Scott's directions to her apartment.

At her apartment, Trina gathered clean clothes and her un-opened mail then rejoined them for the drive to Scott's house.

Chapter Fifteen

Tense, emotionally charged silence filled the atmosphere in the air-conditioned Suburban. Everyone sat quietly, immersed in his or her own thoughts. Craig and Tamera contended with memories of their past losses mixed with concern for their friends as well as the children they left at home in Texas. Katrina's heart pounded in turmoil, her mind a jumbled mass of emotions.

Scott wasn't in much better shape. The doctor in him warred with the man. Torn between compassion, worry and relief that the worst was over, he watched in concern when Katrina massaged her temples with trembling fingers before wiping a tear off her cheek. Putting his arms around her, he cuddled her to him, whispering soft words of love and condolence.

Trina's hand trembled when he lifted it to his mouth, brushed his lips across it, then rubbed the silky skin against his cheek. Meant to soothe, his words only emphasized the pain and emptiness in her heart. Burying her face into his chest, she cried, grateful he didn't feel the necessity to shush her.

Once back at Scott's house and seated at the kitchen table waiting for a fresh pot of coffee to brew, she turned to him. "Would anyone be terribly offended if I excuse myself and go upstairs?"

"Not if you won't be terribly offended if one of us checks on you every two minutes," he teased gently, hoping to coax a smile from her.

His smile was tender as was the light in his eyes. Grateful for his efforts Trina smiled; a tiny, strained smile that didn't quite reach her eyes. "Make it twenty minutes, and you've got a deal."

Scott chuckled. "Five minutes."

She shook her head. "How do you expect to visit if one of you is running up the stairs every five minutes?"

Though reluctant to let her out of his sight, Scott understood she was asking for some time alone. He capitulated, reluctantly but graciously.

"Ten minutes, and that's my final offer."

Trina couldn't help but smile at his insistence. She rolled her eyes. "Whatever."

He chuckled. "Mind if I walk you up?"

"Do I really have a choice?" she asked, her voice laden with sweet sarcasm.

Scott laughed and shook his head no. They rose from the table together. Katrina turned and hugged Tamera then Craig. "Thank y'all for everything. Words can't describe how grateful I am for having friends like you."

"No words are necessary, Sweetheart," Craig assured her.

Tamera murmured her agreement, insisting Trina try and get some rest. Picking up the things she'd gotten from her apartment, Katrina took Scott's hand and let him lead her upstairs to the bedroom where she slept the night before.

Scott hesitated in the doorway, reluctant to leave her alone. He knew it was irrational, but its how he felt. Raising her hand to his lips, he kissed it. "Have I told you lately how beautiful you are, and how much I love you?"

"Many times and in many ways. I love you, too, Scott."

He smiled. "Is there any thing you need? Any thing I can do for you, or get for you? Something to eat or drink? A massage?"

Trina placed her hand against his cheek. "Only some time alone," she answered. "I know you're worried, but I'll be fine. I really just need to be alone right now."

He pulled her in his arms once more. "I hate the thought of leaving you alone, but I know it's what you need." He hugged her, kissed her tenderly, and then, with a great deal of reluctance, walked away.

Trina sighed with relief and shut the door. She kicked off her shoes, slipped out of the dress, slip and pantyhose, put on Scott's T-shirt, and then climbed up on the bed.

Thirty minutes later Scott went up to check on her. She slept, one hand clasping the cross around her neck, the other holding onto Amber's letter. She murmured, shifted and dropped the letter. He picked it up and read.

Trina, sometimes God sends special people to enhance your life. I've felt that way about you since the day we met. I know you're going through a really tough situation right now, one that has to have many horrible memories attached to it. I want you to know my thoughts and prayers are with you always. Love, Amber.

She followed that up with a page full of Scriptures beginning with: *Blessed are they that mourn, they will be comforted.* There were Scriptures about sowing in tears and reaping in joy, and sorrow lasting for a night but joy being found in the morning, words of hope and faith and comfort. Each Scripture was accompanied by little prayers or Amber's special thoughts of encouragement.

Scott's heart overflowed with love and gratitude that such a wonderful young woman was a part of their life. Sitting gently on the bed he prayed for both Amber and Trina. Unwilling to disturb her rest, he resisted the urge to touch Trina or take her in his arms, though he did cover her with the quilt. As quietly as he had entered, he left the room and went back downstairs.

"She's sleeping," he informed Tamera and Craig.

"Good," they murmured in unison.

Scott stretched, rubbing the back of his neck. "I can't decide whether to take a run or a nap."

Craig laughed. "You call that a choice. I'd choose a nap over a run anytime."

Scott chuckled. "That's why you're getting soft in your old age."

"I can take you on anytime, Buddy," his friend assured him with a grin.

Scott smiled, not doubting for a moment he could. There was nothing soft about ranching. "If you'll excuse me, I think I'll go for the nap."

Craig rose from the table to slip his arm around his wife. "We'll not only excuse you, we'll do the same."

Scott went into his bedroom while Craig and Tamera went into the guest room they'd occupied the night before. Craig put his arms around his wife, pulling her close. "How are you holding up, Sweetheart?"

Tamera sighed, blinking back tears. "Okay, I guess. I'm ready to be home, though."

"Me, too," Craig admitted. "I want to hug my daughter and wrestle with my son, and I want to see you smile again."

Tamera's smile wobbled. "I love you so much, Craig." He pulled her closer, whispering his love, his lips covering hers in a tender caress. Soft whispers and kisses flowed between them as they changed clothes and climbed into bed to curl up in each other's arms.

Tamera awoke several hours later. Woman's intuition told her something was wrong. Her first instinct was to call home where Amber assured her everything was fine. Ace was sleeping and she had just gone to bed.

"How's Trina?" Amber asked.

"About as well as can be expected, I guess," Tamera assured her.

"I don't know, Mama, I've had a heavy burden on my heart all evening to pray for her. Are you sure she's okay? And what about Scott?"

"They were both sleeping earlier. Just keep praying, Sweetheart."

Promising she would, Amber rang off.

Craig stirred. "What is it?"

Still unable to shake the feeling, Tamera got up and put on her robe. "Something's wrong. I'm going to go check on Trina."

"I'll check on Scott," her husband assured her, rolling out of bed and slipping into a pair of jeans. Seeing a light on downstairs, he went to see who was up. He found Scott in the living room, a bottle of whiskey on the table, an unopened letter in his hand.

"What's going on, Buddy?" Craig asked gently.

Scott nodded toward the unopened bottle. "I was just contemplating a drink. Want one?"

Craig shrugged. "Sure. I'll pour," he offered, retrieving two glasses and some ice from the kitchen. Returning, he opened the bottle and poured a liberal amount in each glass. "What's this all about?" he asked, handing him the glass.

Scott sipped the whiskey, slapping the letter gently against his thigh and shrugged. "Elizabeth's death has brought back memories." He held the letter toward Craig.

Craig recognized Scott's mother's handwriting on the envelope. "You've never opened this?" he asked, surprise evident in his tone. The letter had been given to Scott at the reading of his father's will. "Why not? Better yet, why now?"

Scott shrugged again. "Guess I was afraid to find out what's in it. Why would my mother write me a personal letter and give it to an attorney to hold until her death unless it was bad news?"

"What could be so bad, Buddy?"

Scott eyed him for a moment. "I'm a doctor; I deal in medicine and biology. I see natural siblings who don't favor each other as much as we do. I lived through the gossip and speculation about us as well as you did. So, you tell me."

"You think that's what's in the letter? The truth?"

"What else could it be?" Scott asked.

"Would it really be so bad?"

Scott leaned toward him. "Nothing could ever change how I feel about you, Craig. You've been more than a friend to me all of my life."

"Then what are you afraid of?"

Scott sighed, rubbing his tired eyes. "Do you ever wonder? Really? Your grandfather never would give you a straight answer when asked about us. Do you ever wonder if we've lived our whole lives as a lie?"

Craig shook his head. "No. I'm who I am, and you're who you are. I'm Adam Craig Harris the Third, and you're Dr. Richard Scott Hensley, neighbor, friend and confidant. There's no lie in that. I love you like a brother, and nothing can ever change what we share. Unless we let it."

"Well, I guess there's no point in opening this now, is there?" Scott remarked.

"That's up to you, Buddy. It's your letter. Let me tell you something, though. I may not be but a few months older than you, but I know how much your parents loved you. The truth of it is, your mother doted on you, and your father couldn't have been more proud of any son than he was of you. If opening that letter will cause you to doubt that, then don't do it. If opening that letter will cause you to second guess who you are, how you were raised and what you're all about, then don't do it."

The moments passed by in a thick, tense, wary silence; the only sound penetrating it was Scott tapping the envelope against his thigh. Craig took it from him and tossed it onto the table between them.

"Frankly, my friend, it wouldn't surprise me in the least to find out we are flesh and blood brothers. You knew my father; you know how no good he was. How your parents got involved would be another story." He shrugged. "Maybe you were adopted. They never did have any other children. Regardless, if finding out we share the same father would blacken the memory of your mother, or father for that matter, don't even consider opening the thing."

Scott sighed. "You're right. They loved me and raised me to be the man that I am. To be honest, I don't care how it came about God chose them for my parents and you for my friend. I'm just grateful He did."

"So am I, Buddy. So am I," Craig assured him.

While Craig and Scott were talking and reminiscing, Tamera tried desperately to comfort Katrina. She had walked into the bedroom to find Katrina sitting up in the bed; her head buried in a pillow across her raised knees, wretched sobs shaking her slender frame.

Tamera wrapped her arms around Trina, rocking her as gently as though she were her own child. When the sobs subsided into soft, hiccupping sounds, Tamera turned Trina where she could look into her eyes. "Are you all right?" she asked. Tears rushed to Trina's eyes, emphasizing the pain shining in the dark depths.

"I don't know what I'm going to do," she wailed, handing Tamera an envelope containing a check, a note and a pink slip. Opening the note she read...

Katrina, I know the timing is lousy and I'm sorry. I've held your job open as long as possible, but I'm forced to fill the position. Please accept my deepest condolences. The gang has pulled together and taken up a collection of funds to help you out. Added to your final check are two weeks severance pay and the money collected. Again, I apologize for the timing and, please, as soon as you get on your feet, come by and see me. I'll do my best to rehire you or to help you find another position. Sincerely, Mac.

"I've lost my mother and now my job. I've missed registration, thereby forfeiting a whole semester of school. What am I going to do?" she cried, burying her face in the pillow again.

Tamera took her in her arms once more. "God will provide something. I know He will."

"Please, don't tell Scott anything just yet. He'll feel like he needs to be the one to provide, and I want to make it on my own. Jack always said I couldn't make it on my own," she sobbed. "I guess he was right."

"No," Tamera insisted. "He's not right. You've had a set back, that's all. Listen to me," she urged. "Don't think Scott wanting to help you is because he wants to dominate you like Jack did. Scott is motivated by love, not some sick sense of ownership."

"I wonder how long it'll last. I've lost everything else, why should I believe I won't lose him?"

Tamera held her close, praying for the right words to comfort and reassure her. "You've got to hang onto the fact that he loves you, Trina. That's all I can tell you. Hang on to his love and God's love, and I promise, you will pull through."

"If Scott knew half of what I've been through and what I've done, he would drop me like a hot potato," Katrina insisted.

"I don't believe that for a minute."

Trina glared at her, suddenly angry at the world, angry at God. "Oh really? What do you think he'd say if he knew I've slept with men other than my husband?"

Tamera's heart dropped to her stomach. She knew with every fiber of her being God was testing her. He was watching, waiting to see if she would offer the same unconditional love He offers and commands.

"Maybe he wouldn't find it difficult to understand at all. It's no secret what your husband put you through. Not many people would blame you for seeking love and comfort elsewhere. I would imagine he'd want to know if that were the reason."

"Do you want to know the reason? Will it really make a difference? No matter what the reason, it won't change the fact that I'm guilty of adultery."

Tamera brushed the hair off Trina's cheeks. "No, it won't change that fact, but forgiveness does change everything. The Bible says the blood of Jesus washes us as clean as snow, and that God removes our transgressions from us as far as the east is from the west, and He remembers them not.

"When the Lord commands us to forgive one another, he wants us to forgive in that same way and to remember not the sins of the past. He also wants us to forgive ourselves in that same way. No matter what you've done in the past, or why, Scott loves you now. I honestly don't believe anything could change that."

Trina looked away, ashamed she had thrown that little tidbit of news at Tamera in such a way. She wondered if explaining to her what it was really like would ensure the forgiveness she talked about.

"It was horrible, Tamera," she ventured softly. "I'd been abused all of my life: physically, mentally, emotionally, but not sexually. I was a virgin when I married Jack. We were married only a few years, and I could tell he was getting bored with me. When he first suggested that we experiment with other couples, I was horrified, hurt and angry. He knew I was inexperienced. I thought being a virgin was the ultimate gift to him, one that would be cherished forever." She snorted. "Boy, was I wrong.

"Anyway," she continued. "I refused. He continued to bring it up. Then he started cheating on me. If that wasn't bad enough, he would tell me about it, taunting me with how much better the other women were, and how much more of a woman they were. He convinced me it would be a great learning experience, and it would make things more exciting for us. I loved him, you see, so I finally agreed, but it was under the condition that nothing would change between us. It would only be once, and if I couldn't go through with it, everything would be okay." She looked at Tamera to see how she was digesting all of this information and whether or not she believed her.

Tamera remained silent, careful to keep her expression politely blank, her heart weeping for the lost innocence of this woman.

"So," Katrina continued. "I agreed to give it a try. The experience itself wasn't so bad. The guy was really gentle and sweet, something I hadn't experienced in a long time, if ever, but I couldn't live with myself afterward. Ashamed and guilty, I cried for days." She began to weep, brushing the tears away while she finished her story.

"I knew it was wrong. It was a sin, but I couldn't convince Jack. He thought, as many do, that what goes on between a husband and a wife is nobody's business but theirs. We weren't religious at all, so I had no one to turn to for support. When I showed him the Scriptures to back me up, he threw my Bible in the trash. I dug it out, cleaned it up, and put it away. But I refused to experiment any more. That's when the beatings started." Her voice broke, but she held on, determined to tell the whole truth.

"I vowed he could beat me all he wanted, but I would never do it again. Things got progressively worse. Sometimes

I thought he would kill me. Other times I wished he had. He wouldn't even wait until I'd healed from one beating before he'd start in on me about doing it again. I thought about killing myself, or him, many times, but I just couldn't go through with it."

"My God!" Tamera gasped, unable to remain silent any longer. She pulled Katrina in her arms. "You can't blame yourself. True, you initially made the decision to go along with it. That was a mistake, but you can't continue berating yourself for something you had little or no control over."

Trina clung to Tamera while the offer of compassion was strong, wondering how long it would be offered at all. "After a while, he stopped harassing me about being with other men, but he continued to see other women. He was convinced, even had me convinced, it was my fault I couldn't please him in bed. I refused to do what he wanted, so I shouldn't hold it against him if he sought his pleasure elsewhere."

"That's horse manure," Tamera insisted, fury evident in her tone. "And that is not love. Love is gentle and kind."

"Love is always ready to excuse, to trust, to hope and to endure. Love bears all things," Katrina interrupted.

"You can't really believe that Scripture is meant to excuse that kind of behavior," Tamera argued, a gentle rebuke in her tone.

Trina shrugged. "Once upon a time maybe, but not any more. But you see, everyone says they don't know how a woman can stay in an abusive relationship. Even deep down Scott believes we have a choice, but you don't have a choice, Tamera. You really don't. You're caught up in a vicious cycle, and there's no real way out. They've got you convinced you're the one who's wrong, that it's entirely your fault, and that you can't make it without them.

"You saw how Tom was today, so pitiful, so repentant, so sweet. That's always the way they are. Even Jack seemed remorseful. So you believe them when they say they're sorry, and it'll never happen again. You cling to their every word, hoping and praying things will really change. Just when you believe you've done the right thing by standing by them and supporting them, bam! It starts all over again. Hell, half the time you don't even know what sets them off. It can be as simple as not getting their slippers fast enough or as ridiculous as their glass of milk not being as cold as they like it. But, no matter what, the harder you try, the less you're able to please them. And, when you've been around it your whole life, you don't know anything different. I mean, deep down you think there's got to be something better, but you don't really know for sure.

"It took the loss of my child to convince me to get out. Now I may never have a baby! All I've ever really wanted out of life was a good marriage and a family. I wanted someone to love me with the kind of love a child has for their mother. I wanted someone to need me and to depend on me. Now that may never happen," she wailed.

Tamera held her not knowing what to say. What words could erase the horror or ease the pain and the guilt? None that she could think of. So she prayed, pleading with God to give this woman, His child, the ability to accept the unconditional love He offers through Christ and through true Christian friendship.

She prayed He would put many people in Trina's path who would speak words of life and hope to her. And she prayed that Katrina would open her heart and put away the guilt and shame long enough to listen to those people, and to believe in God's word.

Tamera hugged her close. "Remember the woman caught in adultery who was brought to Jesus?" she asked softly.

Katrina nodded.

"Remember what the Lord said? He told her that he didn't condemn her. Then He told her to go, and sin no more. God knows the whole truth of what you went through and why." She looked into Trina's eyes and brushed the hair off of her face. "He doesn't condemn you, and neither do I," she assured her.

"Thank you," Trina whispered, accepting Tamera's embrace once more. She heard a whisper, deep in the dark...

"You are forgiven."

The voice was gentle and distinctly male.

Katrina glanced toward the door to see if Scott or Craig had overheard her confession. No one was there. Goosebumps rose on her flesh as she realized she had heard the audible voice of God. And He had forgiven her! She began to weep again, only this time they were tears of joy.

"Do you think I should tell Scott?" she asked Tamera, when she could speak clearly.

Tamera shrugged. "That's a decision you'll have to make on your own. I know Scott well enough to believe he would not condemn you either. However, it may be difficult to keep him from going for the kill where Jack is concerned," she warned. "All I can tell you is to pray about it. If you feel it's something God wants you to do, then trust God to get you through it. Just remember, Trina, the devil roams about like a lion, seeking to steal, kill and destroy. Be sure you're obeying God and not being deceived if you choose to tell anyone else. Be careful.

"There are many out there who would never understand. Many, who even claim to be Christians, would judge and condemn you. You've confessed your sins before God, and you've been forgiven. There are no other requirements you have to meet except to accept that forgiveness and to stand on it. Stand firm when the devil comes against you with feelings of shame and guilt for past sins. Rest assured that God remembers them not, so you shouldn't either."

"Do you think I should go to confession at church?"

"That's something else you're going to have to pray about. Personally, I believe it's between you and God and He already knows. I wasn't raised in your religion, though, so I can't really advise you on that issue. Listen to your heart. Let God lead you."

"Thank you," Trina whispered. "I really do feel like I've been forgiven. I mean, I've prayed and tried to believe I was forgiven, but I guess it took talking to someone who really walks a Christian walk to help me see the truth."

Tamera hugged her. "You're welcome. I'll admit I was shocked. But Trina, I've felt strongly for you since the day we met. As I said before, it's not by accident God put us together. I'm just grateful He found me a worthy vessel to extend His love and guidance to you."

"I pray He'll use me someday, too," Trina whispered, not daring to even hope God would ever find her worthy to use, although she honestly believed she was finally and truly forgiven.

"He will," Tamera assured her. "One day you'll be strong enough in your faith to be used by God. Just keep believing, keep trusting, keep growing and you'll see."

They turned in unison when someone knocked softly on the door.

"Hey," Scott greeted. "I was hoping you were awake."

"Why?" Trina asked.

"So I could kiss you goodnight," he admitted with a chuckle.

Katrina smiled. "You were hoping I was awake so you could kiss me goodnight?" She shook her head. "That's as bad as waking up a patient to give them a sleeping pill."

He laughed, reaching out to stroke her cheek. "Are you all right?"

Tamera squeezed her hand gently as Trina nodded, then slipped from the bed and left them alone.

"Better than I've been in a while," Trina admitted.

"You've been crying." And it tore his heart out.

She nodded, smiled. "But Tamera is wonderful. These are some really special friends you have here, Dr. Hensley. I'm truly blessed to call them my friends, now."

He sat beside her, his smile tender. "I know tears are to the soul what rain is to the soil: cleansing, healing, renewing. It's just that," he took her in his arms. "I want to be the one to hold you when you cry."

His voice was soft, husky, and filled her heart to overflowing. "I'm sure you'll get the opportunity many times in the future."

"Not if I have my way," Scott argued. "If I have my way, you'll never have a reason to cry, except maybe tears of joy."

For a moment, held in his strong embrace, Trina indulged herself in believing life could really be that way for her, and that she deserved it.

Chapter Sixteen

Katrina awoke to sunlight streaming through the windows. Turning toward them she listened as a bird sang joyously. Others joined in his melody, filling her heart with their happiness. Slipping from the bed she went downstairs, surprised to find that no one else seemed to be stirring. Careful not to disturb the tranquil atmosphere in the peaceful old house, she put a pot of coffee on to brew, poured herself a glass of milk and grabbed a honey bun. Taking the snacks with her, she returned to her room and settled in the chair by the window. Her heart overflowed as she remembered the events of the night before. She held the memory of God's voice close to her heart, letting it fill her with praise and thanksgiving.

"I wonder if Tamera will be as gracious this morning?" A voice taunted. "It's easy to offer God's mercy in the dark but things always look different in the light of day."

Trina shook her head. "I don't believe that for a minute," she whispered, knowing instinctively the voice taunting her mind was not the same voice she had heard in her heart the night before.

Instantly she understood what Tamera meant when quoting the Scripture that the devil roams about like a lion seeking to steal, kill and destroy. He was now trying to destroy her peace of mind and her sense of wholeness. "I will not let you steal the blessings and truths God gifted me with last night. The Bible says we are given the choice between life and death. You are trying to kill my faith in God and in Tamera. I won't let you," she determined.

She closed her eyes and heard God's voice again, urging her to believe and to trust. "Father, I believe. I believe You really spoke to me last night, and I believe Tamera will be the same today as she was last night. Your word says Jesus is the same today and tomorrow as yesterday. He lives in us. He lives in Tamera. Therefore, I know she will be as gracious and loving today as she was last night."

Immediately the voices were silenced. Joy rose up within her. Trina laughed softly to herself, praising God in her heart and mind. Glancing out the window, she thanked Him for the blessings in her life. A movement below caught her attention. She watched as Scott stretched, reaching heavenward then touching his toes. He stretched his calf and thigh muscles, preparing for his morning run.

Her heart leapt with joy, her senses hummed with excitement. He was a beautiful sight, the perfect specimen of man; tall, well proportioned and muscular with wide shoulders, narrow waist and long, muscular legs that would make any woman's mouth water and cause her to appreciate the opposite sex with greater clarity. He possessed good looks and a good heart, loving and pure. A heart after God's heart, and he loved her!

At the soft knock on her door, she turned to see Tamera peek around the frame before entering the room.

"Good morning," she greeted.

Trina smiled and returned the greeting.

"You look refreshed this morning," Tamera observed.

Trina laughed. "Refreshed? It's okay, Tamera, I'm not ashamed to admit I look happy, because I feel happy. This is a beautiful day the Lord has made. I will rejoice and be glad. Even if it's only for today," she insisted. "I feel like a whole new person. I've been cleansed by the blood of Jesus and made whole. I've been forgiven and made new. And the man I love is down there," she pointed with her thumb, "working up a sweat and oozing sensuality." Heat rushed to her cheeks. "You probably think I'm a slut for saying something like that, especially after last night."

Tamera noticed the quiver in Trina's voice, the flush on her cheeks and how her eyes sparkled with emotion. The epitome of a woman in love, she thought, reaching out to hug her. "Not at all, since I agree," she assured, with a chuckle. They glanced out the window as Craig joined Scott. "Quite an impressive sight, aren't they?" she asked, when the men took off at a slow jog.

Katrina hummed her agreement. "I didn't know Craig was a runner."

Tamera grinned. "He's not. Craig is into wrangling, roping and branding. I've always worked out in addition to riding. He teased me from time to time until I challenged him to run with me one day. I came back hot and sweaty. He came back winded." She laughed. "Since then, he runs a couple of days a week. Ranching keeps his muscles strong, but running keeps his heart and lungs strong."

"I love to run," Trina admitted. "I'm not real disciplined, and I haven't done it much lately, but I love it. One day I'll get a treadmill so I can run anytime I want, regardless of what's going on around me."

"Want to join them?"

Trina sighed. "I'd love to, but I don't have anything to wear. Except these," she picked up Scott's shorts which she had borrowed again a couple of days ago and giggled. "Even with the drawstring they swallow me."

Tamera laughed. "I always pack extra running shorts even if I only plan on being gone a day or two. Mostly out of habit and mainly because Amber usually forgets to pack hers," she admitted with a smile. "C'mon, let's get changed."

So saying, they changed and stretched. Taking off together at a jog, they gradually increased their pace until Craig and Scott came into sight. They could hear the men talking while they continued jogging. As if by silent consent, Trina and Tamera picked up their pace, eating up the distance between them and the men. With a nod of mutual agreement, they separated and ran up along side of them.

"Want to race, Cowboy?" Tamera challenged, picking up her pace.

"Hey!" Craig grinned at Scott as Trina issued her dare and joined Tamera ahead of them. Within moments they were running abreast of each other.

Scott had no intention of spending this morning racing against Katrina. His arm snaked around her waist and he pulled her to a sliding halt next to him. "Let's walk," he insisted, taking her hand in his.

"Walk? I was just getting warmed up," she protested. "What's the matter, Doc, getting too old to keep up?"

He tossed his head with a laugh, thrilled to have his Trina back. "Better watch it, Kitten, or I might be tempted to show you just how well I can keep up. And I don't mean running, either," he insinuated, his voice husky. Picking her up, he twirled her around in his arms laughing at the blush which stained her cheeks. "I love you," he whispered. "And I love having you here."

Trina kissed him. "I love you too, Doc. And I appreciate your generosity more than words can express."

Scott's smile was self-mocking. "Generosity? Call it pure selfishness, Honey. There's a certain agonizing comfort in knowing you're under the same roof as me."

She frowned. "Agonizing comfort? That's an odd choice of words."

He chuckled. "Let me clarify it for you, My Love. It's agonizing because I'd rather have you in my bed. Let me rephrase that," he insisted, when she blushed. "I'd rather have you in my bed as my wife. However, there is a certain comfort in knowing you're just down the hall instead of across town, alone."

Trina thought about the letter she had received from Mac, and wondered how long she'd actually be able to keep her apartment across town. She shrugged it off, determined to think only happy, positive thoughts today. She smiled up at Scott. "Well, Doctor, put ever so sweetly, I think I understand your reasoning."

"You think? What exactly, My Dear, did I not make clear enough for you? The fact that I want you here, or the fact that I want you as my wife?"

Her heart did a somersault. "I believe you've made yourself perfectly clear on both counts," she answered. "And I'm sure we'll discuss them at length sometime in the not too distant future."

Scott raised her hand to his mouth brushing his lips over her knuckles. "Just say yes, Sweetheart, and your wish is my command."

Trina laughed, her heart doing a slow swirl into her stomach. A sweet lethargy infused her limbs, her knees weakened. "I thought my wish was already your command," she teased breathlessly, surprised at the surge of desire assaulting her system.

He chuckled, forcing back his response to the heat in her gaze, positive she was unaware of the need glowing in her eyes. "Got me figured out," he admitted. "Let's go start breakfast. I'm sure Craig and Tamera will want to get on the road as soon as possible this morning."

"I don't blame them, though I wish they could stay longer." She sighed. "Life goes on, I guess."

"And a good thing for us it does," Scott insisted. "I wish they could stay longer too," he admitted. "I've got to go to work this evening, Kitten. I know you've got a lot of loose ends you want to tie up, but promise me something." He pulled her close, tilted her chin up with his finger and kissed her tenderly. "Promise me you'll take it easy and get some rest today," he pleaded.

"I promise," she replied.

"Don't think you have to do it all in one day. It takes time for things to get back to normal," he cautioned. "Grieving is a process, don't rush yourself through it."

"I won't."

"Promise me something else."

She waited expectantly.

"Promise you'll call me anytime you need or want to, and promise you'll let me hold you when you feel like crying."

"If you promise me the same," she insisted.

He chuckled. "You've got it, Sweetheart."

They went into the kitchen. Trina poured him a cup of coffee, insisting he sit while she cooked breakfast. "You've been taking care of me, now it's my turn."

Scott didn't argue. He just sat back and enjoyed the sight of her puttering around in his kitchen. He'd meant what he said about having her in his house, and he'd meant what he said about having her as his wife. When the time was right, he would propose properly. Until then, he was satisfied knowing she understood what his intentions were.

Craig and Tamera walked in, hand-in-hand. They went upstairs to take a shower and gather their belongings so they could get on the road as soon as breakfast was over.

After breakfast Trina ran upstairs to change out of Tamera's shorts and into a pair of jeans. Tamera tossed them into the bag containing her and Craig's dirty clothes before enfolding Katrina in her embrace. "Take care of yourself," she urged, every ounce of tenderness she felt evident in her voice.

"I will," Trina promised. "If Scott will let me," she added with a grin.

Tamera laughed. "That man's got it bad, Honey," she admitted. "Don't be surprised if he gets all bossy and arrogant if he thinks you're doing too much too soon," she warned, remembering all to well how over protective both men were when someone they loved was hurting.

Having experienced it first hand herself, Trina giggled. "Thank you, so much, for all you've done. You've been more than a friend these last days. I don't know how I'll ever thank you enough, or repay you for your kindness."

Tamera brushed the hair off her face with a gentle caress, the touch of a mother, a sister, a friend. "You're welcome. You'll repay me by being kind to someone else in the future, and by being kind to yourself. Just hang in there, Trina. Keep trusting, keep believing and keep growing. Grieving is a process; don't rush yourself through it."

Katrina smiled. "Scott told me that earlier, in those exact words."

"Heed them," Tamera insisted. "Remember, joy in the Lord is your strength. He'll help you through your grief; if you let Him."

"I will," she promised. They walked outside, arm-in-arm where the men were standing by the truck, talking.

Trina accepted Craig's hug, thanking him while Scott hugged and kissed Tamera, urging them to be careful on the road. Turning to Craig, Scott offered his hand to his friend, thanking him for all he had done. Their eyes met and held. A lifetime of friendship passed in a split-second look that said it all. Handshakes turned to hugs, and then they were off.

Three days later Trina received a book of prayer and meditation from Amber, and a Scripture-based book on emotional healing from Tamera. In a note, Tamera acknowledged that, though what she had experienced in her life was not as devastating as what Trina had been through, the book had helped her. The Scriptures had aided her in developing a deeper relationship with God, and had helped her to understand and to believe He alone could create beauty from the ashes in any life.

If only we believe. If only we trust.

* * * * *

Trina brushed and braided her hair and dabbed a bit of makeup under her eyes to hide the black circles from lack of sleep, and the puffiness from crying. She was meeting Scott for breakfast when he finished his graveyard shift at the hospital. Nearly two weeks had passed since she'd buried her mother. She hadn't found another job, and she had yet to tell Scott of her note from Mac. He just assumed she was taking some extra time off. Which, in his mind, was good. Trina hated deceiving him in any way, but she had hoped to find another job before confiding in him the fact that she'd lost the last one. She took a deep breath and blinked back the tears that rushed to her eyes. Things weren't going too well today, and it was barely six o'clock in the morning.

In the days since she had returned to her apartment, Trina clung tenuously to her faith, finding comfort in the memory of that last night at Scott's house, and the morning after. The book on emotional healing Tamera sent had been a great help. She'd held it to her heart more than once, finding comfort in the fact that her friend had done the same. Pages containing ink splotches from Tamera's tears, or notes she'd written in the margins, had been more of a comfort to her than anything else could have been, except the Bible.

Today, though, Trina had no idea what God wanted her to do or what He intended for her life. She had no job, and her savings were dwindling quickly; she'd missed registration, thereby missing a whole semester of school. If things didn't change in a hurry, she might not be able to go next semester, either.

Taking a deep breath, she prayed. "Lord, I know You're there, and I know Your will is perfect. Your Word says that You have a great plan for my life, a plan for my good and not my destruction. I need You to show me the way."

"Go to the cemetery." The words were plain and very audible.

I'm planning on going after breakfast, Trina thought.

"Go now."

Trina knew it was best to obey the voice of God, whether He spoke in a still, small voice or in a very audible one. Glancing at her watch, she figured she had enough time before she met Scott. She only hoped he wouldn't call her apartment and then worry when she didn't answer the phone. Oh, well, she thought, I'm counting on You, Lord, to keep him from worrying.

The overcast sky was a perfect reflection of the turmoil in her soul. Only the bravest rays of sun could penetrate the dark clouds hanging ominously above. The scent of rain hung heavily in the air. Trina prayed she wouldn't get soaked while on this mission, whatever it may be. Turning into the tiny cemetery, she took the small, winding road to the solitary gravesite on the last row. The lone, gaunt figure kneeling beside her mother's grave seemed familiar. Just great, she thought, recognizing Tom and cringing at the sight of him. A strange little pain pierced her heart, and she immediately regretted the angry notion. God had brought her here for a reason. The least she could do was open her heart and mind to find out what it was.

Deep down she knew Tom was part of the reason. She had experienced so many emotions over the last few days, one of which was a deep-seated anger at him and Trina knew the time was drawing near when she would have to reach out to Tom with the same forgiveness God had extended to her.

"Please, Lord," she prayed softly. "Help me. I can't do it without Your grace."

Climbing out of her car, she walked toward her mother's gravesite. As she drew nearer she could tell Tom was crying; deep, heart wrenching sobs which shook his frame. Her heart clenched, not in pity or compassion but anger, and Trina understood God was testing her. She was determined to pass the test. Closing her eyes, she stood still and waited for His leading. Tom's continued sobbing began to drown the seeds of anger and bitterness that had taken root in her heart, despite her efforts to stop them.

Only a few steps separated her from reaching his side. Taking a deep breath, she closed the distance between them and, reaching down, put a hand on his shoulder. "Tom?"

He turned and stood, wiping his face with a handkerchief. "Trina, I was just leaving."

"It's okay; you don't have to leave on my account."

"I know you're still angry with me. I'm angry with myself. I still can't believe this has happened."

Wrapping her arms around her middle, Trina hugged herself. The stench of alcohol and filth emanating from him didn't frighten her as usual, but filled her with an overwhelming sadness. "I am angry, Tom. I can't believe it either. I can't believe the injustice of it all. I'm trying to forgive you, but I'm not sure how to do it."

Tom hung his head. His chest tightened, stomach roiled with unease. He'd been drunk for a week but even that hadn't been able to stop the guilt and condemnation from eating him alive. He wanted to walk away but felt immobilized. It would certainly be better for her if he did. The least he could do was disappear from her life forever. "I can't forgive myself, and I certainly don't expect you to forgive me."

Trina heard the bitterness in his voice and cringed inwardly. "It's not what we expect from each other that counts, but what God expects of us," she said softly. She knew what He expected of her, but couldn't bring herself to say the words. Her heart cried out for mercy. *God, please, help me!*

"Forgive as I have forgiven you."

How?

"Just say the words, and trust Me to bring the fulfillment of them."

Doubt and uncertainty mixed with bitterness and fear lodged the words in her throat. Trina swallowed hard. *I don't know if I can! I want to. I know I have to. Show me how*, her heart pleaded.

Death and life are in the power of the tongue and they who indulge it shall eat the fruit thereof.

Trina didn't know where those words came from, she assumed she'd read them somewhere in the Bible. She only knew there had to be truth in them, for this was a moment of truth. Could she refuse to offer Tom the same mercy God had offered her? Would she? *No*, she determined silently.

Reaching out she touched Tom's arm. "I forgive you, Tom."

The words were soft, barely audible, and Trina wondered if she had actually spoken them aloud.

Tom's head jerked up in surprise. Hope was evident in every plane of his face, and Trina knew he had heard. In that instant she understood the power of words. She knew those words had the ability to offer life to Tom, a new life in Christ. It was not her place to judge or condemn or to seek justice, it was God's.

"God will forgive you, too."

"How, when I can't forgive myself?"

"Because He is merciful and kind and slow to anger. God is love, Tom, and He loves you."

Hope and disbelief collided in his heart. Tom began to cry again. "I am so sorry," he sobbed. "Truly. If I could take it back or trade places with her, I would. If I could only turn back time, I would change everything."

Oh, how she wished she knew what to say to him!

Tamera's words echoed in Trina's heart. They had changed her life, so she used them, hoping they would change his also. "We can't change the past, but forgiveness changes everything. The Bible says God forgives our sins and remembers them not. He expects us to forgive each other and ourselves in that same way."

Tom shook his head. "Maybe so, Trina. And maybe someday I'll be able to believe that. Thank you for sharing that with me, and thank you for saying that you forgive me. I hope, someday, I'll be able to forgive myself." He took a deep breath and handed her an envelope. "I wasn't sure how to get this to you. I guess it's a good thing you came here today."

Trina's hands shook as she opened it. There was three thousand dollars in the envelope. She looked at Tom, waiting for an explanation.

"I sold the house. It's not much, I know, but you can't get much for an old, run-down house in a not-so-great neighborhood. Anyway, after I filed succession, paid off all of our debts, the expenses to fix your car, court costs, lawyer fees and your mother's funeral bill, there wasn't much left. I split it between the two of us. I hope you don't mind."

Trina shook her head trying to comprehend everything he'd said. "But where will you live?"

He shrugged. "I don't rightly know, yet. I'm leaving. I just want to start over somewhere. I'll write if you want me to. If not, I understand."

Shocked, all she could do was nod.

"Well," he hesitated, wanting to reach out to her, not knowing how. "Goodbye, Trina. I'll go to my grave wishing I'd been a better husband and a better father."

Trina stood in shocked silence as he turned and walked away. He was over halfway to his car before it dawned on her that he didn't have her address. The only father she had ever known was leaving town, and he didn't even know how to reach her! Running toward him, she called his name. "Tom!" He stopped, turned, and waited for her to reach him.

Trina stopped just short of flinging herself at him. He had shunned any expression of affection from her so many times, she was afraid to show any now. "You don't have my address."

Tearing the flap off the envelope, she reached for the ink pen that he always carried in his pocket. Writing quickly, she handed both to him. "Please, do write."

A ghost of a smile tugged at his lips. "Thank you."

"Take care of yourself."

"I'll try."

Acting on impulse, Trina kissed his cheek. "I'll be praying for you," she promised.

He touched his cheek reverently. "Thank you," he repeated, not knowing what else to say.

Trina watched as he drove away, wondering if she would ever see or hear from him again.

Chapter Seventeen

Trembling set in the minute Trina climbed into her car and sat behind the steering wheel. Her mind replayed the incident and she knew she had done the right thing. Her heart whirled with excitement and hand shook when she put the envelope Tom gave her into the glove compartment. God had provided for her. He had used her!

Taking a moment to compose herself, she started the car and drove—praying and praising all the way—to the restaurant where she was supposed to meet Scott. Her heartbeat accelerated the minute she saw him, so handsome in his scrubs, his hair tousled from the rain-laden breeze. Though nary a drop had fallen, the sky still threatened to open up at any minute and douse every living thing with much needed moisture.

Scott halted his pacing when Trina pulled into the restaurant parking lot and smiled when she approached him. "Hey, I was getting worried."

"I went by the cemetery."

Putting his arm around her waist, he led her inside. Once seated in the nearest booth, he took her hand in his. "Are you okay?"

She smiled, shook her head. "Yeah. I am. Don't I look okay?"

There was something different about her. A glow. A peace. An excitement. Scott nodded. "You look like you're in love."

Trina grinned. "That about sums it up. I'm in love. With two very special men."

He arched a dark brow at her, trying to ignore the quick stab of fear and jealousy. "Oh, really?"

Laughing softly, Trina nodded. "Yes, really. One is a very special man who lived a long time ago, and who died that I might have life today."

She squeezed his hand. "And one is a very special man today. Someone with a generous heart and a loving spirit."

He raised her hand to his lips. "I love you, too, Kitten."

She giggled. "Did I say it was you?"

Scott chuckled. "Better be me. I'd hate to have to chain you to my side." He thought a moment. "Then again, maybe not."

Trina giggled. "You're not going to believe what happened today."

"So tell me."

She thought a moment. "I don't know where to start."

"How about at the beginning."

She grinned. "I'm not sure where the beginning is."

Charmed by her playful mood, Scott shook his head and laughingly reached over and brushed the back of his hand across her forehead then cheeks as though checking her for fever. "Are you sure you're feeling okay? You're making absolutely no sense."

She laughed. "I'm feeling wonderful. I guess the beginning would be the night we buried Mama." She told him about her talk with Tamera, omitting only the darkest details of their conversation. She also told him about the note she got from Mac. She saw the anger flare in his eyes, followed by pain and held up a hand to ward off his rebuke. "Please, Scott, hear me out before you get upset."

"You should have told me. You know I would have helped you."

"I know," she said softly. "And maybe I should have. Maybe I was too proud or too ashamed or too scared. But, Scott, let me finish telling you what happened."

He nodded.

She told him about the struggles she'd had over the past two weeks, the answers she had gotten that morning at the cemetery, and the money Tom had given her. "So you see, I had to learn to trust that God will provide. Now I know He may use you to provide for me, but I had to learn to trust Him first. Does that make any sense?"

Scott hesitated a moment before answering. "Yes, Kitten, it makes sense, so long as you understand that God uses people in many ways. The Bible says He will pour you out a blessing that there is not room to receive, and that He will cause men to give unto you. There is no shame in asking for help, and even less in asking me for help. I love you, I want to provide for you, to take care of you. I want to marry you. All you have to do is say the word."

Her smile was tender as was the light in her eyes. "I know, Scott. I love you, too. There are just so many things about my future I'm unsure about."

"Like what?"

"School, us, or more precisely, me. I do love you, but I'm still afraid of making a mistake. I made a mistake the first time and paid dearly for it. Now I know you are nothing like Jack, but I just need more time to find out who I am before I become Mrs. Scott Hensley."

"What's school got to do with it?"

She shrugged. "I started with every intention of finishing. Now that I've missed a semester I'm not sure I want to go back. It was never my dream to be a bookkeeper or anything else for that matter. My only dream was to be a wife and mother. I've been forced to look out for myself and I know I need some kind of formal training to do so. I'm just not sure what I want to do, yet."

"Why don't you let me see if I can help you get on at the hospital," he offered. "They're always hiring."

Trina smiled. "Thank you, but no. This is something I need to do for myself." She sighed wondering how she could make him understand her feelings when she was so unsure of herself. Their meal arrived, giving her a few minutes to pull her thoughts together. "I really appreciate all you've done, and all you want to do for me, but please try to understand. All of my life, I've been dependent on someone other than God and myself. I need to be able to trust, not only in Him, but in myself."

Scott nodded. "I do understand, Trina, but I want you to know something. Financially you'll never have to worry about taking care of yourself once you become my wife."

"It's not just financially." She blew out a frustrated breath, hoping to explain only to have her words cut off by his finger on her lips.

"I know that. You didn't let me finish saying what I wanted to say," he chided.

She apologized.

He continued. "I understand you have a lot to sort out. You've been hurt in ways I may never understand, but I want you to know I will never hurt you. I'm sure we'll have our differences, but I will never intentionally hurt you. I will never put a hand on you in anger, I will never cheat on you and I will never desert or abandon you in any way.

"And," his voice softened. "I will never think less of you for your dreams or ideas. I'll be here to guide you and support you in all that you desire. Your every wish is my command."

"I believe you, Scott. I truly do. And I believe you will never intentionally hurt me in any way. It's not you. It's me. I'm just scared and unsure and..."she trailed off. "I don't know why, but I'm just not ready to make that commitment again."

Scott nodded. "Just so you know I'm not going any where. I'll be around when you are ready. I love you, Katrina, more than I ever thought I'd love anyone."

Trina felt a moment of fear that she would never measure up to that kind of love, and that she didn't deserve it.

Scott saw the flash of fear and insecurity in her eyes and felt a wave of irritation followed by disappointment. He wished silently that they were someplace private, someplace where he could take her in his arms and kiss away the fear and doubt lurking in the dark depths of her eyes. Forcing himself to speak past the lump in his throat, he asked what her plans were for the rest of the day.

Trina smiled and shrugged. "I have no idea."

"Spend the day with me," he urged. "We'll go to my place. I'll take a short nap after which we'll do whatever your little heart desires."

"Anything?" she teased.

Her voice was as enticing as silk and just as alluring. Her excitement set fire to his blood. "Anything." he assured in a thick voice.

His smoldering gaze, as tender as a caress and just as potent, lowered to her lips, lingered, then raked over her in a hungry gesture before returning to capture hers in a heated embrace. Trina felt as though he was touching her in the most intimate of ways. Her cheeks grew hot, her breath lodged in her throat. Desire washed over her in angry waves. She swallowed hard and tucked trembling hands in her lap, desperately trying to form a coherent sentence. "Please, Scott, don't look at me like that."

Scott could actually feel her trembling response across the table. His voice lowered another notch. "Like what?"

Trina shook her head. "Like you're starving to death and could eat me up. Didn't you have enough food?"

Pushing his plate away, Scott stood and held his hand out to her. Trina placed a trembling one in his firm grip. Pulling her gently to her feet, Scott raised it to his mouth, brushing his lips across her knuckles. "Food is not what I'm hungry for," he informed her in a husky whisper.

Trina waited as he paid for their meal then followed him to the parking lot as gracefully as possible on legs that wobbled. He paused and in a silent gesture, signaled for her to give him her car keys. His fingers brushed sensuously over her wrist and palm, grasping hers gently when she placed them in his hand.

Locking his heated gaze with hers, Scott raised their clasped hands to his lips, this time lingering over the kiss. He nibbled on her knuckles, teasing the back of her hand with his mouth, then, in one swift movement, turned his attention to the sensitive flesh of her palm and wrist, relieving her of her keys and her senses.

Trina felt the caress to the very core of her being. She moaned, leaning against his hard frame when he pulled her closer. His heat enveloped her until she burned with him, for him. And his lips had never even touched hers.

Need battled with control. Scott held her firm against him while he maneuvered them around so that he could unlock and open her car door. Guiding her onto the seat, he buckled her in, allowing his hands to linger where they touched. He fought to control his raging senses when she slumped against the seat, pleading with him to stop while her trembling body screamed the exact opposite of her words. His lips brushed across her cheek in a rapturous journey to her ear.

"I'll follow you," he whispered, the husky words punctuated by an intimate caress of mouth against flesh.

If I'm strong enough to drive, Trina thought and heard him chuckle as though he'd read her mind.

Scott hesitated, reluctant to squelch the desire running rampant between them. In a quick, decisive move, he unbuckled her seat belt. "Better yet, we'll leave your car here and pick it up later."

Trina shook her head. "If you touch me again, you're going to have to carry me to your car."

He chuckled. "It would certainly be my pleasure."

She glared at him. "We can't just leave it here. What if something happens to it? What if you get called out in an emergency or something?"

He frowned. "You're right. I'll follow you."

She stopped him from buckling her seat belt again. "I'll do it."

He chuckled again, gave her another intimate caress, whispered his love then stood up, nodding in approval when she buckled the seat belt before closing the car door.

Trina's hands trembled when she picked the keys up off her lap and slid them into the ignition. She rested her head against the steering wheel for a full minute, willing calm to her raging senses before leaving the restaurant parking lot.

"Quite the bitch, aren't you?" Jack's voice rose from somewhere deep inside her mind to taunt her.

"I am not." Trina spoke aloud, hoping to silence the hated words.

"Look at you, all hot and bothered over him. You're nothing but a harlot."

"That's not true. I love him. He loves me."

By the time Katrina pulled into Scott's drive, the dark emotions battering away at her mind had reduced her to a trembling mass. Tears streamed down her cheeks. She slumped against the steering wheel unable to think or move because of the confusion, pain, and anger screaming through her, warring with the passion aroused by Scott's kisses and the desire to believe in his love and in her worthiness to accept it.

Scott pulled into the driveway along side of Katrina. All the way home he had ignored the voices in his head telling him to slow down and take it easy, warning that he may scare her off or push her too soon into a more intimate relationship. He loved her and was determined to show her how desperately true his feelings were. He wanted to replace her past pain with pleasure and make her feel totally cherished. When she didn't disembark from her car, he expected she was thinking of all sorts of ways to postpone the inevitable.

What he didn't expect was to find her slumped against the steering wheel, sobbing. He opened the door. "Trina?" He reached for her. She jerked away from his grasp.

"Don't touch me. I'm not fit for you to touch me."

"What?" She looked at him, and the devastation in her eyes tore his heart out.

"I feel so defiled. So dirty. So unworthy."

Scott pulled her out of the car and into his arms despite her protests. "Let me love you, Trina. Let me show you how beautiful you are, how beautiful love can be. I love you, Kitten." His lips covered hers in a desperate plea.

She shook her head, pulling away from his searching lips. "You wouldn't if you really knew what I've been through and what I've tolerated in the name of love."

"I don't care," Scott insisted. "That was then. I love you now! Haven't I shown you how much I care? How very desirable I find you?" He pulled her closer. "Feel what you do to me," he urged. "Feel how much I love you and how much I want you."

What she felt frightened Trina as much as it excited her. Images of violence and abuse filled her mind. Jack's voice returned to haunt her. Her heart raced with panic. She pushed herself out of his arms with an angry snort. "That's what it always boils down to, isn't it? Lust and the overwhelming need to dominate and prove your manhood!"

Scott felt the blow as though it were physical. He stepped back, restraining himself from shaking—or kissing—some sense into her. "Is that what you really believe?" he asked, his voice deceptively soft. The pain turned to anger he couldn't stop or suppress. His eyes narrowed into dangerous slits, teeth ground in frustration, fists clenched as he fought not to touch her. A low growl sounded in his throat.

"For months I've been patient and loving, showing you in numerous ways how much I love you and you think it's all some kind of ploy to get you in my bed? Well, let me tell you something, Ms. Simmons, had I *only* wanted you in my bed you'd have been there long before now!"

Trina stared at him, her eyes wide with shock at his declaration and the sting of truth in it. "Oh, really?" she asked, barely able to articulate that simple question for the emotions rioting within her soul. "Mighty sure of yourself aren't you? Or is it just me you're so damn sure of?"

Scott nodded, took a step closer, and reached for her. "Both."

Her reaction was instinctive, fueled by fear and fury and a multitude of other conflicting feelings. Her hand connected with his cheek in a resounding slap. "How dare you? You think you can just will it, and I'll crawl into your bed like some kind of bitch in heat?" She whirled away, flung herself into the car and jerked the door shut. "Never!"

The ignition roared to life, spurring Scott into action. "Trina, wait!" he called, as she backed out of the drive. She pulled away, her tires spinning on the pavement with an angry squeal. He stood there, stunned to realize how deep and raw her pain and insecurity still was.

And he had thrown it in her face that he could have her anytime he wanted, as though she didn't have a choice.

Scott barely made it into the house before he collapsed into a crumbling heap on the floor. Oh, God, he thought, what now? What more can I do? How can I convince her what I feel for her is deep and pure and true? His heart breaking, Scott wept for the lost innocence of the woman he loved.

Chapter Eighteen

The miles streaked by in a blur of tears and anger. When she stopped in her driveway, Trina glanced around and wondered how she'd made it home in one piece then thanked God that she had. Fumbling with her keys she managed to unlock the door to her apartment before collapsing under the weight of guilt and condemnation. Only by the grace of God had she not blurted out the sins of her past, throwing them in Scott's face like so much dirty laundry. Oh, why couldn't she get over this? Why couldn't she just accept his love and revel in the pleasure his arms offered? Why couldn't she trust him? He had done nothing but love and support her since the first day they met!

Trina wondered if he would ever do so again.

Making her way blindly into the bathroom, she threw up the breakfast she had so thoroughly enjoyed, then washed her face. Carrying the wet washcloth with her, she crawled into bed praying for deliverance from the demons which haunted her mind, praying for deliverance from herself.

She awoke later to the sound of someone knocking on her door. Please, God, she prayed, if it's Scott, show me how to apologize to him. He doesn't deserve for me to treat him so badly, and I don't deserve his love, nor Yours. Please forgive me. Please help me.

She opened the door to find, not Scott, but a police officer standing there. Something about him seemed familiar. A memory fleeted then gelled. Unease settled in her gut. "Can I help you?"

Officer Robert Johnson recognized the young woman immediately. He'd thought her name was familiar. The moment she opened the door, his worst fears were confirmed. Less than a month ago he'd responded to a domestic violence call. Her stepfather had been the perpetrator; her mother had been the victim. He remembered the horror and the helplessness of that day; and the next as though it were yesterday. He cleared his throat nervously.

"Ms. Simmons?"

She nodded.

"Ms. Katrina Simmons?"

Katrina nodded again. "Yes."

"I'm sorry, ma'am, but I need you to come with me."

Fear sharpened her gaze. "Where? What for?"

Robert shook his head. There was no easy way to tell her his reasons for being here. "I'm sorry, ma'am, but I need you to come with me to the morgue."

She blanched. "What? Why?"

He grimaced. "Thomas Fontenot's body was pulled from the Mississippi river about an hour ago. His car was parked on top of the bridge. Eyewitnesses saw him jump. We found your address and his wallet on the front seat of the vehicle." He handed her the wallet. "I need you to identify and claim the body and the vehicle. That is, if you want to."

Trina nodded then said she'd be back in a moment. When she returned she had shoes on her feet, her blouse had been changed and her hair swept up into a ponytail.

Robert helped Katrina into his patrol car and assisted her in strapping on the seatbelt. Once seated and buckled in himself, he backed out of the drive and headed toward the Police Department. In all of his training, one of the most important things he'd learned was to read people; expressions, body language, nuances, and it hadn't taken more than a single glance to note she was miserably unhappy. Sadness lurked in the dark depths of her swollen, red-rimmed eyes. Paleness replaced the healthy glow of her peaches and cream complexion. Despite this, the woman was breathtaking. He couldn't help but remember the fiery passion she'd exhibited that day not so long ago when she'd attempted to press charges on Thomas Fontenot for the destruction of her car and for beating her mother.

He stole another glance. The air of desolation surrounding her was a tangible thing, tugging at his heart. "Is there someone I can call for you?"

Trina shook her head. "No. Thank you."

The thought of her completely alone in the world filled him with an inexpressible sadness. "What about that doctor friend of yours?"

Tears filled her eyes, her lip trembled. "He'll probably never speak to me again."

Though Robert doubted there was even an ounce of truth to the declaration, the words, spoken barely above a whisper, seemed to echo within the confines of the car. Reaching up, he retrieved an envelope off the sun visor and handed it to her. "It's customary for us to search the vehicle when something like this happens. I found this in the glove compartment. There's an awful lot of money in there, and a note I found on the floorboard."

Trina knew without looking in the envelope it contained Tom's half of the money left over from the sale of her mother's house. "Thank you," she whispered, and slid it into her purse.

The whole ordeal took less than an hour. She drove Tom's car back to her apartment in a numb state of shock, and walked around, wondering what to do next. Her mind replayed the conversation with him that morning at the cemetery. Picking up the phone, she called the funeral home where her mother had been, and made arrangements for his body to be picked up and prepared for burial.

* * * * *

Scott fumbled around, searching groggily for the phone whose insistent ringing jerked him out of a restless, troubled sleep. "Hello?"

"Dr. Hensley?"

"Yes."

"This is Officer Robert Johnson, Lafayette P. D." He cleared his throat. "I remembered you from a few weeks ago, and, I may be way out of line here, Dr. Hensley, but I'm calling out of concern for Ms. Katrina Simmons."

Scott came instantly awake. "What about her?" What the officer told him had Scott up, dressed and out of the house quicker than an emergency call from the hospital.

Breaking every speed limit between his place and hers, he arrived at her apartment in record time. In a single fluid motion, he parked and disembarked from his car then practically flew to her door, banging on it and calling her name. "Katrina!"

He rattled the knob, counted to ten and forcefully refrained from putting his foot through the thin wood. "Katrina, open the door!" When she did, her eyes were wide, haunted, devastated.

"He never even made it across the bridge." Her lips trembled, her voice broke, tears streamed down her cheeks and her shoulders began to shake with sobs. "He never even made it across the bridge."

Scott picked her up, held her close and stroked her hair in a soothing gesture. "I'm sorry, Kitten. I'm so sorry."

"You don't know how many times I've thanked God that He gave me the grace to forgive Tom this morning," she cried. "And how many times I've prayed He would allow me the opportunity to apologize to you, and to beg your forgiveness for what happened between us."

Scott carried her to the couch, cuddling her against his chest. "Shh. It's okay. There's nothing to forgive," he soothed, which only made her cry harder.

"Yes, there is. I have no right to treat you that way!"

"Nor I, you. I'm sorry, too. Let's forget it," he whispered, stroking her back and shoulders in a soothing caress.

"I wish I could," she mumbled in a heartbreaking whisper. "You just don't know how much Jack's voice haunts me; telling me how no good I am. How worthless and trashy."

Scott's hand halted in mid-stroke. He clenched his fist, silently wishing he'd done away with Jack Simmons when he'd had the chance, then immediately repented of the thought. It wasn't his place to seek vengeance or justice, it was God's. Shifting Katrina slightly in his embrace, he cupped her face in his hands and gazed into her tear-drenched eyes. His heart clenched at the pain and fear he saw there.

"Ignore his voice, and listen to mine. None of us are worthy of love and forgiveness. God blesses us with it anyway, and gives us the ability to offer it to one another. I love you, Katrina. I think you are very beautiful, very desirable and very precious. I love you. I want to make you my wife, to take away the pain and tears of your past and replace them with joy. I want to restore your shattered dreams, give you new ones, and make them all come true."

He shifted again, pulling her more firmly against him. His body tightened with need. Running his hands down her back, he cupped her tiny waist in his big hands and locked his gaze with hers. "I want to revel in your arms and wallow in the taste of your lips and skin. I want to feel your body against mine, and your hair on my flesh.

"Lovemaking is a very precious gift from God, Trina. I want to show you how beautiful it can be. I want to plant my seed within you, and watch you grow lovely and round with my child, our child. Don't listen to his lies anymore, Kitten. Let me show you the love you so richly deserve, and I so desperately feel."

Katrina buried her head in his shoulder. "I wish it were that easy," she whispered.

"It can be, Trina. To quote Scripture: I've put before you life and death...choose life. Choose to believe my words of life, and not his words of death."

"Jack was never satisfied with me. Not as a wife, nor as a woman."

Scott snorted. "Jack was-correction-Jack is an idiot. You are a beautiful, passionate woman. He wasn't man enough to appreciate what he had. I'll never be so stupid," he vowed.

"I'm so afraid," she whispered.

Scott cuddled her once more. "I know you are, Kitten. And the only way I can think to help you conquer that fear is to show you my love." He chuckled softly and quoted Elizabeth Barrett Browning.

"And how do I love thee? Let me count the ways—physically, mentally, emotionally. My love for you is all those things, Kitten, and more."

His lips covered hers in a tender caress. "I feel like you're part of me. You're the woman of my dreams, and I'm only half a man when I'm not with you."

He hesitated a moment, praying silently for the words to reach past her mind, deep into her heart and release her from the bondages of fear and guilt she carried so heavily. God answered, and Scott knew what to say. "Every time you go to church, Trina, you say a little prayer right before Communion. Do you know the one I'm talking about?"

She nodded.

He joined in when she repeated the words: "Lord, I am not worthy to receive You but only say the word and I shall be healed."

"He's saying the word, Trina. He's speaking to your heart right now. Will you listen? Will you believe Him? Will you believe me? What other words do you need? What more can I say?" He hesitated a moment, praying again. Once again, God answered, and he knew what to say.

"I often wondered why you all say that prayer every week. I think God has just given me a revelation. It's not a prayer to remind us of our unworthiness, but to remind us of the healing power of His grace, mercy and forgiveness.

"God has forgiven you for whatever it is you're so desperately afraid you did wrong, Trina and, regardless of what it was, I forgive you. You don't even have to confess anything to me. I can only imagine how horrible life with Jack was for you. So whatever it is, give it to God right now, Trina. Let Him take it away. Let Him heal you."

Katrina buried her face in his shoulder and succumbed once more to the hot tears pouring from her soul. Scott's words echoed in her mind, cleansing, healing, and filling her heart with renewed hope.

Scott held her and continued to stroke her body in a soothing caress. Each ragged cry tore at his heart, but he didn't shush her. When her sobs subsided into soft, hiccupping sounds he rose with her cradled in his arms and carried her into the bedroom.

Katrina stiffened in his grasp. "What...?"

"Shh," he whispered, brushing his lips over her forehead. "I just want to hold you. Trust me, Kitten," he urged and felt her relax in his arms.

Laying her gently on the bed, he crawled in beside her and pulled her close. His mouth covered hers in a tender caress—searching, tasting, teasing, urging a deeper response until he heard her soft, sweet moan of surrender, and she wrapped her arms around his neck. The sound and the feel of her yielding, soft and pliant against him, sent a sweet ache through his entire being. Scott reveled in the feeling.

Trina closed her eyes and gave herself up to the tenderness of his touch. When Jack's voice rose in her mind, she shook her head. "Talk to me, Scott," she pleaded. "I don't want to listen to him any more. I only want to hear your voice."

"You are so beautiful," he whispered. "So precious and sweet. The Bible says you are a new creature in Christ and that the old things have passed away. Believe in His word Trina. You are cleansed and made whole by the blood of Jesus. A new creature. A new woman. I love you."

He continued to stroke her body, speaking softly; sweet words of faith and hope, of love and desire, determined when he left, she would be assured of the depth of his feelings. When he moved to unbutton her blouse, she stopped him with a firm hand.

"Will you marry me in the church?" she asked, her eyes wide and pleading.

Trina saw the hope and joy flare in his eyes and her heart skipped a beat.

Scott smiled and brushed his lips over hers. "Honey, I'll marry you barefoot on the bayou if that's what you want. Just name the date and time."

"Can we wait until our wedding night to make love?"

He gently removed his hand from her grip and tugged the buttons of her blouse open. "No," his voice was soft. "I intend to make love to you every chance I get."

At her look of wide-eyed surprise, he chuckled, nuzzling her cheek and teasing her ear with his mouth.

"Lovemaking is more than sex, Kitten, so much more than the joining of bodies. Lovemaking is a connecting of hearts." He traced hers with his finger and felt her tremble beneath his touch. He caressed the silky flesh of her slim throat. His fingers moved over the smooth skin of her cheek to tuck her hair behind her ear.

"It's a meeting of minds and a touching of souls," he whispered, while pressing feathery kisses across her face. Once again he locked his gaze with hers.

"By the time our wedding night arrives and we complete the physical act of joining of our bodies, you will know you are truly and deeply loved," he vowed. "Completely and unconditionally."

Trina heard his sharp intake of breath when his gaze left hers to travel the length of her.

Scott's breath backed up in his lungs. She lay before him like a feast. He could feel her need; see it in the dark depths of her eyes and in the faint flush just beneath her skin, turning her complexion a rosy pink. His mouth watered for the taste of her silky flesh. His senses leapt in response to the depth of her desire, desire evident in the throbbing pulse at her throat and the slight trembling of her body. His control slipped dangerously.

"You are so beautiful," he whispered, his voice so thick he could barely get the words past his raw throat. "I love you so much." He caressed the length of her with a shaking hand, down her throat, over her chest, across the taut muscles of her abdomen. Her soft moan of pleasure nearly broke the tenuous hold he had on his control. Scott buried his face in her hair with a groan, and prayed to God for the strength to stop now, determined to do as she asked and wait until after the wedding to consummate their love.

The fire in his eyes and the heat of his touch seared the remaining shreds of doubt and fear in Katrina's heart. Her hands trembled when she ran them up his strong arms, across his broad shoulders and buried them in the silky thickness of his black hair. "I love you," she whispered, a heartbeat before her lips covered his in a tender caress.

Scott knew he'd finally won. The relief was so overwhelming he could have wept. Holding her tight against his chest, he rolled over, pulling her atop his long frame. Sinking his fingers in her hair, he buried his lips on hers for a long, sensuous taste of her sweetness.

Drawing on the last shred of self-control he possessed, Scott ended the kiss and buried her face in his chest. "We have to stop this, Katrina. Now. Before there's no stopping."

The agony in his voice made her giggle. Never had she been wanted with such sweet desperation. The thought filled her with joy. She sat up and ran her hands over the taut muscles of his firm chest. "What if I don't want to stop?"

Scott ground his teeth in frustration. "Jesus Christ, don't say that." She looked like a little girl who had just discovered a hidden cache of sweets; innocence combined with pure, sensual pleasure. His hands fisted in the folds of her blouse. "Lord, help me," he groaned.

Trina laughed, raising her arms overhead. She closed her eyes with a deep sigh. "I feel brand new," she said in a soft, tremulous voice.

In one swift movement Scott rolled her over, pinning her beneath him. "You are brand new, Kitten." He chuckled and tugged her blouse closed, concealing that luscious body from his view.

"And you're all mine," he assured in a husky whisper.

Chapter Nineteen

The next morning, Trina awoke with a smile on her lips and a song in her heart. She turned on the radio to the local Christian music station and rolled the volume to high. Her prayer time was spent in thankful praise and worship.

Scott had stayed with her all afternoon and late into the evening, leaving sometime after midnight. They'd talked and laughed and cuddled until Trina understood to a deeper degree what true love was all about. She'd heard his voice in her dreams, felt his touch as though he lay beside her, and awakened to the joy of love reborn. He was due to pick her up later this morning and accompany her to the funeral home.

There would be only a short graveside service for Tom, but Katrina was determined he be laid to rest with as much dignity as possible. She had requested a cemetery plot beside her mother for him. Picking up his car keys, she felt an overwhelming sense of grief. He had been so lost! She prayed for him.

Walking out to his car, she opened the trunk and searched for a suitable outfit to bury him in. Pressing the clothes to her face, she inhaled the scent of his cologne and felt a crushing regret that life hadn't been different for him, for them.

I press forward, not looking back but looking ahead to the high prize of Jesus Christ. The words of the Apostle Paul echoed in her soul, convincing Trina there was no point in looking back. The best thing she could do was look forward to the future God had planned for her, and pray Tom had found forgiveness and peace before his death.

Gathering the things she would need, Trina closed the trunk of the car and walked back into her apartment. Remembering the envelope Office Johnson had given her the day before; she retrieved it from her purse and counted the money. Just as she suspected, there was three thousand dollars. She would use it to pay for Tom's burial expenses.

Pulling out the note which appeared to have been crumpled then smoothed, she read...

Trina, you don't know how much I regret all that has happened. Thank you once again for talking with me this morning. Thank you for your vow to pray for me. I can't go on living with myself. If there really is a God, I only hope that He and you will forgive me one last time.

It was signed in a weak scrawl.

Trina collapsed into a chair. Holding the note to her breast she let the tears come, cleansing her of the remaining shreds of bitterness and anger she had harbored toward Tom. She prayed hard he'd found peace, and that he'd found Jesus, in those last few moments of life. When Scott arrived a few minutes later she showed him the note.

"I wonder," she whispered, "when he faced God, whether he found judgment and wrath, or forgiveness, love and peace?"

Scott took her in his arms. "What do you think?" he queried. "Before you answer, consider the thief on the cross."

Trina thought about all she had learned of God's grace and all she'd experienced of His mercy and forgiveness. She nodded at Scott. "This note is proof of his sorrow and repentance. I believe he found a loving, forgiving Father. I believe he found peace in the end. I only regret it came at such a cost."

"So do I," Scott whispered, his lips covering hers in a tender caress.

The next few weeks passed with explicit swiftness. Scott was always there when Trina needed him the most. He helped her through the emotional as well as legal process of disposing of Tom's belongings. She gave his clothes to the Salvation Army and his car to the women's shelter where she'd stayed while awaiting her divorce from Jack.

With the passing of time Trina grew stronger in her faith, faith in God, in herself and in Scott's love. She learned the true meaning of putting on the armor of God and faced each day with a new resolve to rise above her past. Whenever Jack's voice returned to haunt her, she squashed it with a healthy dose of determination to rid herself of it forever. She combated the death in his words with words of truth by turning the radio up loud with songs of life, and by turning on the memory of Scott's declarations of love. When that wasn't quite enough, she telephoned Scott, seeking verbal and physical confirmation of his love and her worthiness.

Less than a month after Tom's death, she went on a church retreat to spend three days alone with God. There, in the atmosphere of reverential quiet, she discovered God's purpose for her life: to minister to those like herself. She wanted to reach out to battered women with God's love and mercy, and to offer them hope in a deeper way than any had ever heard of, much less experienced. She shared her dream with Scott, and he vowed to support her in every way possible. He even went so far as to volunteer to be on call for the shelters whenever medical attention was needed.

To better prepare herself, Trina took a job as a receptionist at the shelter. This enabled her to be closer to the women and to get to know their individual situations as well as share her own story. She then embarked on a serious study of the Bible, taking advantage of others' experiences by purchasing learning materials, concordances and different translations of God's Word. She counseled with local ministers, absorbing information like a sponge. More than anything else, she relied on prayer and guidance from God, submitting herself to the instruction and wisdom of the Holy Spirit.

As usual, just when Trina thought she had a handle on things, her faith was tested again. She and Scott were having dinner one evening when Jack approached their table. Scott stood, halting Jack in his tracks.

Jack held up a hand in a gesture of peace. "I don't want any trouble." He turned to Trina. "I just wanted to talk to you a minute." He looked back at Scott. "I won't touch her, man, I swear. I just want to talk."

Trina could tell he'd been drinking, but there was something different about Jack this time. He seemed quieter, less violent, sad. She looked up at Scott, as Jack said he would wait by the door for five minutes. If she didn't meet him, he would leave.

She took Scott's hand. "I feel like I need to hear what he has to say."

Scott shook his head. "I don't want you near him, Katrina."

She hesitated, praying silently for guidance. There was no denying the sense of urgency that she should talk with Jack. "I have to, Scott." She rose from her seat and touched his cheek. "Aren't you the one who said there had to be forgiveness when my stepfather killed my mother? There has to be forgiveness now," she said when he nodded. "How can I teach other battered women about the value of forgiveness if I don't forgive him?"

Scott fought a surge of jealousy and fear. She was right. He knew this, but damn it, he didn't have to like it. He kissed her hand. "Stay within my sight, Trina. Don't let him talk you into walking out with him."

"I won't," she promised.

Trina prayed the entire two minutes it took to reach Jack's side, hoping to quell the fear coiling into a tense knot in her stomach. "What is it, Jack?"

He reached for her. She took a step back.

Jack's hand fell in limp defeat by his side when she recoiled from his touch. "I just wanted to say how sorry I am, Trina, for everything. I heard about Tom. It's made me think. A lot. I know there is no hope for us. I killed that a long time ago. Now, you've found someone else. It's obvious you love him, and that he loves you. He's very protective of you. That's good."

He hesitated. Tears rushed to his eyes; he blinked them back.

"I'm trying, Trina. I only hope you can forgive me. I wish you all the happiness you deserve and I'm sorry I wasted so many years of your life."

Trina knew in her heart what an effort it took for Jack to say those words. She swallowed past the lump in her throat and fought the urge to hug him. She was still afraid to trust him, even a little. Afraid if she offered that hug in a spirit of forgiveness, he would take it to mean something else and he would snap, and force her outside with him. God only knew what might happen before Scott could rescue her. Wrapping her arms around her waist, she took another step back from him.

Jack noticed the fear in her eyes, felt the tension emanating from her, and experienced a terrible sense of loss. He turned away, hesitated. "That's all I wanted to say."

Trina's voice stopped his retreat. "Thank you, Jack. I'll be praying for you. I do forgive you, and I hope you'll be happy someday, too."

Trina knew she would have to continually depend on God to make those words true in her heart. There would still be times when she resented the years of abuse and loss, but she was determined to overcome and be victorious through Christ.

Returning to the table where he waited, Trina shared with Scott all that was said between she and Jack. She was glad she'd talked with him, and vowed to continue praying; for as long as he lived, hope remained that God would reach him.

* * * * *

Time marched on to the steady beat of life. The holidays came and went. Though Scott had to work on Thanksgiving, he was off for Christmas. He and Trina spent the holiday in Texas with the Harrises. It was a lovely, exciting experience, especially when Amber received an engagement ring from her young beau. Exciting and lovely for everyone, that is, but Craig, who still resented the fact that his little girl was growing up.

Scott was on call New Year's Eve, but luckily he didn't get called out. He and Trina shared a quiet candle-lit dinner at his house. When Trina went into the kitchen to retrieve dessert and coffee, he placed a tiny gift-wrapped package beside her plate.

Trina's hand trembled when she put down the serving tray and picked up the box. Knowing in her heart what it contained didn't stop the quick surge of butterflies in her stomach. She sat down and opened it with trembling fingers. Her eyes filled with tears at the engagement ring sparkling vividly against a backdrop of black velvet. Scott reached over and gently took the box from her shaking hands.

"I love you, Kitten," he said. "Tomorrow's a new year, a new beginning. Let's start it out together." So saying, he took the ring from its nest of velvet and placed it on her finger before raising her hand to his lips.

"You want to get married tomorrow?"

He grinned. "Why not? Can't let Amber beat me down the aisle."

"I can't plan a wedding in less than twenty-four hours," she protested. "Besides, I thought we were getting married in the church."

"Okay, let's set a date then. And make it soon," he insisted.

Trina smiled. "I'll talk to the Priest tomorrow morning after Mass, and we'll set it as soon as possible."

They spent the remainder of the night laughing and talking, planning the rest of their lives. Early New Year's morning they called Craig and Tamera, who agreed to be the best man and matron of honor at the ceremony. After Mass, Scott and Trina spoke with the priest. They organized a shortened version of the marriage counseling required by the church.

When asked by the priest if he would allow Katrina to continue practicing her faith and raise their children in the church, Scott replied, "Under one condition." His gaze met and held the priest's for a full minute before searching Katrina's.

"That you promise to never put the church before God. Many people get so involved in the structure of their faith that they neglect a personal relationship with the Lord. It is for this reason I, personally, find more fulfillment in a one-on-one relationship with Christ instead of organized religion."

His gaze returned to Father Jacob's. "I have grown to appreciate the beauty and uniqueness of Catholicism, but I also understand why so many call it ritualistic. I don't want Trina to become so involved in the church's teaching that she forgets God's teaching. Now, I know the church's teachings are Scripturally based, but like all religions they are man enforced, and, too many times, enforced with judgment and criticism instead of the mercy commanded of us by Christ. I don't want that to happen to Katrina or my children."

Father Jacobs considered the doctor's words a full minute before replying. "You're correct. Many do substitute religion for God. And many cling to their religious beliefs to the extremes you've mentioned. All we can do for those folks is pray truth will illuminate their lives. I see it all the time, even in my own congregation. That's why we offer Bible study and prayer meetings, and why I encourage our parishioners to seek God on a personal level."

He addressed Katrina. "I, too, encourage you to continue doing the same. And I extend an invitation to both of you to take advantage of the many programs offered by the church."

Katrina listened to the conversation between Scott and Father Jacobs. Closing her eyes, she felt her love for God, so real, so deep, so alive in her heart. "I will never put anything or anyone before You," she vowed silently. "Never."

Chapter Twenty

Scott jogged along the bayou, his breath panting out as tiny wisps of fog in the cool, crisp air on the late January morning. The Harrises had arrived yesterday evening. He'd slipped off early for his morning run, wanting a few minutes of peace and quiet to contemplate the day ahead. His wedding day. His heart swelled thinking about the days, and nights, ahead when Trina would be his wife.

Desire, ever ready, sprang to life at the thought of his bride-to-be. His body tightened with need. Scott picked up his pace in a desperate attempt to ease the tension coiled like a tight fist in his gut. When his legs burned and lungs screamed for air, he slowed to a jog then a walk, watching the sun break over the horizon with the promise of warmth that was not unusual for Louisiana weather.

Filled with love and gratitude, he began to pray, thanking God for the blessings in his life and the blessings to come. Oh, how he hoped he and Trina would have a child soon. Nine months from today would be just about perfect.

* * * * *

Trina walked around her apartment, which was bare except for the things she would need today. Excitement shivered through her body when she thought about the day ahead. Soon she would be Mrs. Richard Scott Hensley.

The ceremony, set for eleven o'clock a.m., would be a small, intimate affair with only the Harrises, Amber's fiancé Stanley, and a couple of Scott's co-workers attending. Craig, Tamera and Mike Guidry would sign the marriage certificate as witnesses to the nuptials. The reception was lunch, after which the Harris family would head back to Texas, and then she and Scott would have the first of many afternoons and evenings alone, together.

In Scott's arms, Jack's voice had ceased to exist for Katrina. The voice she heard now belonged to Scott, and it was his touch she felt in her dreams.

In the weeks past, he'd kissed and caressed her until she thought she would faint with want; loving her to the point of being ready, even anxious for the physical joining of their bodies. When she cried out in frustration, tempted to ignore her desire to wait until their wedding night, he would hold her tenderly and gently coax her back to the edge of reason. Her heart swelled with hopeful anticipation that a child would be conceived this very day as she and Scott celebrated their love and consummated their wedding vows.

Tamera arrived at precisely nine-thirty to help Trina dress before accompanying her to the church where everyone else would be waiting. "Where did you get this dress? It's beautiful!" she exclaimed, while helping Trina slide into the slinky, velveteen material.

Trina smiled. "I had almost given up on finding the perfect dress. I shopped at all the big stores but couldn't find anything I liked. Then I went to a tiny boutique just a few miles out of town. The minute I laid eyes on it, I knew this was the dress for me."

Picking up her bouquet of yellow and white roses, Trina stared for long moments in the mirror, pleased at what she saw. The rich, cream material was floor-length but sleeveless. Though semi-formal, the dress could be worn again to a party or to church. The matching bolero was lined for warmth and had tiny yellow roses embroidered on it. A halo of baby's breath and more yellow roses encircled the crown of her head. Tamera gave her a necklace as something old. Amber provided a delicate gold bracelet as something borrowed. The dress was new and a lacy blue garter completed her ensemble.

Tamera smiled at Trina's reflection. "Scott will be beside himself." She glanced at her watch. "Especially if we're late."

Trina giggled, made one last search through the apartment to make sure nothing was left behind, then followed Tamera out to the car. Upon arriving at the church, she waited in the outer foyer while Tamera made a quick check to confirm everything and everyone was ready and waiting.

Candles lined the aisle filling the building with a soft, romantic glow. Muted sunlight filtered through the stained-glass windows, creating tiny rainbows in the air. Large arrangements of yellow and white roses graced the altar. Huge yellow and white bows hung on the end of each row of pews. Scott and Craig stood next to Father Jacobs. Amber, Ace, Stanley and the other guests sat at the very front of the church. Excitement and anticipation shimmered in the atmosphere. Tamera shook her head with a smile when everyone turned, hoping to get a glimpse of the bride.

Closing the doors behind her, she returned to Trina's side and took her hand, giving it a light squeeze. "Remember how we rehearsed last night," she whispered. "Stay back where no one, especially Scott, can see you until I get to where I need to be."

Trina nodded and whispered thank you.

Tamera opened the doors again and waited until Father Jacobs signaled for her to begin her walk up the aisle.

Standing in the shadows, Trina pressed a trembling hand to her stomach and said a short prayer to still her racing heart. As soon as Tamera reached her place beside the altar, the organist began the bridal march. Trina moved into the doorway and everyone stood in anticipation of the bride's entrance.

Scott's eyes widened when he saw her. She was a vision of loveliness, and he realized how lucky he was to have found her. The dress clung in all the right places, accentuating her tiny form. Candlelight reflected off her rich, red-gold hair, turning it into a fiery mass of silken waves that cascaded across her shoulders and down her back. Her eyes sparkled and a soft flush covered her cheeks. Luminous didn't come close to describing how beautiful she looked, and he was infinitely grateful for the flashbulbs going off all around him. He took a step toward her, only to be detained by Craig's hand on his arm. He glared at his friend.

Craig shook his head and grinned. "That's not how it's done, Buddy," he whispered, chuckling softly at the quick frown he received.

Scott's gaze returned to his bride and remained locked with Trina's while he waited for her to join him at the altar. She took slow, measured steps, each one bringing her closer to him and he had to restrain himself from urging her to hurry. He wanted the formalities over, lunch finished and he wanted her home, alone, in his arms. His whole body ached with the realization that his dream was coming true. Within moments she would be his wife. His smile was tender when she reached his side. He took her hand, raised it to his lips then slipped his arm around her waist, turning with her to face the Priest.

The vows were blessedly short. Scott cupped Trina's face in his hands, whispered his love and lowered his mouth to hers before Father Jacobs gave him permission.

The Priest chuckled and cleared his throat. "You may kiss the bride," he said, amidst the soft laughter surrounding them.

The groom grinned, said thank you, and kissed her again. Offering his arm to her, Scott led his bride back down the aisle as the Priest pronounced them 'husband and wife.'

Everyone gathered at the church's entrance to hug and kiss and offer best wishes to the bride and groom. A limousine awaited the newlyweds to carry them to the restaurant. The Harrises and Stanley followed in Scott's car and Craig's truck, while Mike and the other co-workers declined the invitation to dine with them. Lunch was a lively affair with champagne and little heart-shaped cakes for the bride and groom to share with their guests. After lunch they gathered outside.

Craig opened the door to the limousine for Trina. "We'll just see you two home, then head on out," he told Scott, as the groom climbed in beside his wife.

Scott sighed with relief while Craig gave directions to the driver. Making sure the tinted glass was raised between the driver and them Scott clicked the button and locked the doors then pulled Trina firmly in his arms. His lips covered hers in a tender caress. A soft, primitive grunt escaped him when he cupped her tiny waist in his hand and pulled her closer. "Trina," he breathed, his hand moving over her in a subtle caress, urging her closer still as his mouth captured hers in a hungry gesture.

Trina ended the kiss and buried her face in his chest. "I have no desire to consummate this marriage in the back seat of a car." She giggled. "Limousine or not."

Scott chuckled and released her from his heated embrace. "Neither do I. You know I love my friends, but I sure hope they don't hang around for long."

Trina laughed.

"Do you know how incredibly beautiful you look today?"

Trina smiled, running her fingers through his thick, black hair. "I only hope I look half as good as you do all dressed out in a tux."

He chuckled. "I think we look real good together." His voice lowered to a suggestive whisper, "We'll make pretty babies too."

Trina nearly whimpered with the onslaught of emotions his tender words wrought, love, desire, need. She could almost feel the gentle tug of her child nursing, and prayed once again that she would conceive on her wedding day.

The driver lowered the window a notch. "Excuse me, but we're here," he remarked, as he turned into the driveway at the address he'd been given. Within moments he had parked the car, climbed out and was holding the door open for the bride and groom to disembark.

Scott climbed out of the car and stopped, stunned to find his yard packed with vehicles. "What in the world?" he muttered.

"What is it?" Trina asked, climbing out of the limousine without her husband's assistance. "Oh, my goodness. What's going on?"

Mike Guidry came from around the house followed by what looked like the entire hospital staff. "Surprise!" They yelled in unison.

Craig laughed and slapped Scott on the back. "You didn't really think we'd let you off that easily, did you?" he asked, pleased at the surprise on their faces.

Offering an arm to his wife, Craig led the way around the house where a reception was in full swing. A white satin runner, flanked by rows of flower arrangements, led the way to a huge tent where a band was playing. Tables had been set up. One was laden with food as well as a three-tier wedding cake, the other overflowed with gifts.

People gathered, throwing rice and birdseed as the bride and groom made their way into the tent. The band immediately began playing the wedding march followed by Jole' Blanc, a French waltz better known as the Cajun National Anthem. With no choice but to participate, Scott took his bride in his arms and danced with her. Other couples joined in about halfway through the song.

The afternoon gave way to evening. A bonfire was lit and the party continued as workers from the hospital arrived and departed between shifts. Just before midnight Craig poured glasses of champagne and handed them out. Raising them in toast to the bride and groom, he repeated what Scott had said to him on his wedding day. "To you, my friend, and your bride. May the Lord bless you with a house full of children; boys just like you and girls as lovely as your beautiful wife."

Cheers went up, filling the night sky with sounds of joy and celebration. Scott hugged his friends then turned to his bride. Swinging her up in his arms he carried her out of the tent. Trina laughed and tossed her bouquet over her shoulder. It landed neatly in Amber's hands.

"Thanks a lot!" Craig called after them.

Scott turned, a quirky smile tugging at his mouth. "Serves you right."

"Hey, what about the garter?" Mike yelled.

Scott shook his head. "Ain't no one gettin' a look at these legs but me."

"Aw, c'mon man, that's just plain wrong." Mike argued, his statements confirmed by enthusiastic, light-hearted comments from the crowd.

"Besides, it's tradition."

"He's right," Craig interjected.

"Forget tradition," Scott insisted, watching his pretty wife blush from all the attention.

Craig winked at Tamera then turned back to his friend with grin and shook his head. "Oh, no, you can't ignore tradition."

Putting down his glass of champagne, he pulled up a chair and sat down. "Bring her here," he told Scott, patting his thighs, laughing at the glare he received.

With a reluctant sigh, Scott placed Trina on Craig's lap. "Keep your hands where I can see them," he warned, the words bringing another round of laughter and teasing from the crowd. Kneeling before them he cupped Trina's foot in his hand and took off her shoe.

"What'd you do that for?" she gasped, feeling the heat of his touch from the bottom of her feet to the roots of her hair.

"Didn't want to tear it on the heel," Scott replied, dropping the shoe in her lap before returning his attention to the task at hand. Locking his heated gaze with hers, he clasped her foot with one hand, and slid the other over her calf in a slow, torturous quest for the scrap of lacy blue elastic located about two inches above her knee. Slipping a finger beneath the material, he caressed the circumference and felt a quick rush of pleasure at her trembling response. Removing the garter with a flourish he twirled it around for all to see and then, in a quick, decisive move, tossed it over his shoulder and stood, sweeping Trina up into his arms as he rose.

Amidst the laughter, he turned around and carried his wife to the house, across the threshold, up the stairs and into their bedroom before putting her down. Waiting while she removed her other shoe, he took her by the hand then walked with her to the window and waved at the guests that had gathered below.

Scott stood behind her, slipped his arms around her waist and pulled Trina firmly against his chest. "It wasn't my plan to spend our wedding night with a house, or yard, full of guests," he whispered.

Trina smiled, hugging his arms tighter around her waist. "Mine either. It's been lovely, though. The whole day has been absolutely beautiful."

"Yeah, it has," Scott agreed. "But not near as beautiful as you," he whispered, brushing his lips across her ear. Reaching out, he pulled the shades, chuckling at the cheers and laughter coming from below. A simple tug on the cord closed the drapes. He turned Trina in his arms, his lips covering hers in a thorough caress. "I have something for you," he said, before leading her to the bed where a gaily-wrapped box, about the size that holds a large pizza, awaited.

Trina laughed and took a deep, inhaling breath. "It doesn't smell like pizza. Pepperoni or sausage?"

Scott chuckled. "Open it and find out."

Her hands trembled when she slipped off the bow and lifted the top of the box. A large wooden hoop encircling a web-like net, which was decorated with beads and feathers of various designs and colors, lay nestled in the soft tissue. "It's beautiful," she breathed. "Almost too pretty to touch."

"It's a dream catcher," Scott told her, as he gently lifted it out of the box. "The Native Americans put a great deal of value in them. The hoop represents strength and unity; the spider-like web represents the web of life. Depending which tribe you're talking to, the dream catcher either catches the good dreams and lets the bad ones escape, or just the opposite. Certain tribes believe the dream catcher holds the destiny of the future.

"If you think about it, the dream catcher could even symbolize God. The hoop could represent His unending, eternal love for us. The web of life would represent God himself, who is the Creator of life and the maker of our dreams."

He hung it on the wall behind their bed while continuing to speak. "The Bible talks a lot about God speaking to us in dreams and visions. I told you before that I want to take away your broken dreams, give you new ones, and make all of them come true. I believe the Indians have always been very spiritual people. Though they may not have known exactly who Jesus Christ and God were when it was invented, I think they were on the right track in believing the dream catcher holds the destiny to the future, because God—the dream maker—holds the destiny to ours."

He took her in his arms, kissed her tenderly then slipped the bolero off her shoulders. Picking her up, he laid her gently on the bed, climbed in beside her and took her in his arms once more. "When you lay in my arms at night and dream about our future, rest assured that, God willing, all of your dreams will come true," he vowed, tugging at her dress and leaving soft whispers of fire on her skin where his fingers or lips lingered.

Their vows were consummated in a tender celebration of love.

The dream catcher captured the newlywed's dreams and dedicated them to the web of life to be released in God's time, while the broken dreams of the past slipped away.

Dear Readers,

Abuse of any kind is a terrible thing, but to be abused and betrayed by one you've vowed to love 'till death do us part' is a difficult thing to live through much less emerge from unscathed. But there is always hope. Not the kind you find in drugs or alcohol or any other form of escapism but true hope. Hope and healing that can only be found in the shed blood of Jesus Christ.

It is my prayer that if you don't already know Him, you'll seek Jesus as your Lord and Savior and if you do, you'll pursue a closer walk with Him. And remember, delight yourself in the Lord and He will give you the desires of your heart.

Once again, until later, may God bless and keep you—and yours—in the palm of His loving hand!

Sincerely,
Pamela S Thibodeaux
"Inspirational with an Edge!"
http://pamelathibodeaux.com

Get a Sneak Peek at Book 3 in the
"Tempered" Series!

Tempered Fire

Amber Harris is a good girl on the brink of womanhood. Stanley Morrison is a young man at the start of his life. For each other, they have always felt the fireworks that two people in love should feel. However, the questions about his past, his pride, and Amber's father might be the end of what could be a strong relationship. As the two try to protect their budding romance, some unlikely but powerful forces conspire to keep them apart. Will they survive the wishes of everyone around them with their relationship intact?

Prologue

Since Stanley Morrison arrived in Bandera, Texas a few weeks ago, the Annual Charity Rodeo hosted by the Rockin' H Ranch had been the talk of the town. Anticipation floated in the air, excitement brightened every eye, and enthusiasm animated every conversation. Now that the day had finally arrived, Stanley understood why. He'd watched all day as riders with skill and style equaling professional rodeo cowboys, and girls, performed on animals of the highest quality to turn around and donate all of their winnings to charity. There had been generous donations, considering some of the top prizes ranged up to five hundred dollars, and he was proud to be a part of it, if only as a hired hand. Though he'd gained employment at the Bar S ranch for his ability in working with horses, today Stan filled the capacity of groom, tack-hand and babysitter.

He looked up from his chore of shortening stirrups as the roar of the crowd increased when the last contestant in women's barrel racing shot into the arena. As usual, the first thing he noticed was the magnificent specimen of horseflesh, but his eyes were invariably drawn to the rider. Despite the distance between himself and them, he saw beauty in the

i

young woman. Long legs encased in designer jeans rested comfortably in the saddle. Pulled into a French braid, dark hair hung like a thick rope down her back. Though her brow was tense with concentration, the fine, porcelain-like skin of her face appeared soft and lustrous despite the thin veil of dust hanging in the air. Style and grace lined every fluid movement of horse and rider as they rounded the barrels in the fastest and smoothest exhibition he'd seen in a long time, if ever. A nudge from the boot resting in the stirrup he was supposed to be shortening, reminded him of why he was here.

"A kiss for luck?" The young girl in the saddle leaned down to brush her lips across his cheek.

Surprised, Stanley stepped back and eyed his boss's daughter. She was a pretty young thing, blond-haired, dark-eyed and would turn fourteen just days before entering her freshman year of high school. "You're too young for anyone but your father to be kissing you, for any reason."

Lori Strickland's eyes narrowed into tiny slits of black fire. She grunted in a very unladylike manner. "You sound just like my father." With that, she whirled her horse around and headed for the paddock to take her place in line for the pole-racing event

Stanley shook his head with a sigh and rested his elbows on the fence to watch the winner of the barrel-racing contest return to the arena. His heart stopped then thundered in his chest when her name blared over the intercom. Her horse bowed and she blew a kiss to someone in the crowd before turning the big stallion around in a fancy whirl and exiting. Intrigued, Stanley found himself looking forward to his first and only, year at Bandera High School.

* * * * *

Craig Harris ambled up the stairs to his daughter's room. At sixteen, Amber Nichole, was usually busy helping her mother this time of day. Today she seemed oblivious of that fact. She'd been in her room for the last several hours.

"What!"

ii

A frown marred his forehead at the frustrated tone which bade his entrance. He opened the door, his eyes widening in shock and disbelief at the mess he encountered. Clothes covered every available inch of her bed. Shoes were strewn carelessly around the room.

Amber was having a problem.

"Is 'what' any way to welcome someone coming to your door?" Craig asked. "What in the world is going on?"

A sound of pure frustration escaped his daughter's lips when she drug her hands through the thick mass of black hair, shaking it off her shoulders so that it settled around her waist.

"I can't figure out what to wear tomorrow."

Craig grinned. "Ace doesn't seem to be having a problem. Since when did it matter so much?"

She snorted. "The only thing Ace is worried about is how he can get his new boots dirty before he gets downstairs," she growled, referring to her baby brother, Adam Craig Harris the Fourth, which was shortened to A. C., then evolved into Ace. "It's always mattered. I've just never worried about it before."

"And what good does worrying do? Does worrying add one more hour or day...? " He stopped quoting the scripture and laughed at the frown she bestowed on him.

"Don't come in here spouting Bible scriptures and don't laugh at me."

Craig's eyebrow quirked in concern. Despite the horror stories he'd heard about raising hormonal teenagers, he'd never had a problem gauging his daughter's moods and coaxing her out of them. Though passionate about many things, he'd never imagined that his mature, well-rounded, normally composed child would be in a tizzy over what to wear. Nor had he *ever* considered her taking that tone with him.

"The best book I know," he countered.

Amber heard the concern in her father's voice and rubbed her throbbing temples. Taking a deep breath she let the scripture flow through her, bits and pieces reaching through the turmoil in her mind and soothing her frazzled nerves...

Therefore do not worry saying "What shall we eat or what shall we drink or what shall we wear?" for your heavenly Father knows that you need these things... what good does worrying do, does it add one more hour or one more day... Therefore, do not worry about tomorrow; tomorrow will take care of itself...

Everything took on a new perspective. She sighed, smiled. "Okay, I'll just pray about it tonight and the first thing I grab in the morning will have to do."

"That's my girl," her father soothed, stroking her cheek. "Now, about this room...." She looked around. Surprise registered on her face when she realized the mess she'd made.

"Daddy," she purred slipping her arms around him and resting her head against his chest.

Craig tossed back his head with a laugh. "Oh, no you don't. You made the mess, you clean it," he teased, disengaging himself from the arms around his waist.

She pouted prettily but her eyes were sparkling. "Mean old Daddy."

"Dinner's almost ready," he informed her, making his escape, then paused in the doorway. "Amber?"

When she looked up from her chore, he continued. "No matter what you wear tomorrow, you'll be the most beautiful girl there," he assured, love and pride evident in his voice.

She grinned. "Thank you. And your opinion is in no way biased I'm sure," she teased. "I love you too, Daddy."

Nervous and excited about entering her junior year of high-school, hearing her father's wolf whistle pleased Amber when she came downstairs the next morning dressed in a royal blue denim skirt, western blouse, and boots.

"Go change. You look way too good to leave the house without me."

His eyes glistened with pride. Amber laughed and kissed his cheek. "It's the first thing I grabbed," she said, moving out of the way as, dressed in new jeans, cowboy shirt and boots, Ace barreled down the stairs on his way to the table. Nearly nine years younger than she, he was entering the second grade.

Though she had her driving license and the use of a car, Amber respected tradition. Her mother would drive them today and quite possibly the first week or so, however long it took for Ace to get comfortable with his new class and Tamera to get comfortable with letting him go. As her baby, long awaited and desperately wanted, she was protective of her son. Sometimes too protective, but, considering what she went through to have him, it was allowed. Amber harbored no jealousy, nor did she feel slighted in any way. She and her mother had a very special relationship. Her father, on the other hand, was her life. He was the one that she would miss the most today, she thought. Little did she know that very soon things would change drastically between them.

* * * * *

Craig lingered over a second cup of coffee on the clear October morning. The days were getting shorter already and cooler. Another year was nearly over. Amber had just rehearsed the evening's events with them for the hundredth time.

"Amber, we've been through this twice before already," he chided in a gentle, teasing tone. "Relax."

She fidgeted, unable to keep still for the excitement curling in her gut. Being Junior Maid on the Homecoming Court was not all that was causing her heart to flutter and her stomach to clench like a nervous fist. She was used to that, being both Freshman and Sophomore Maid before. But the boy she had noticed, really noticed, for the first time last night had her as nervous and excited as an untrained filly.

"I met the guy I'm going to marry last night," she remarked, raising sparkling eyes to her father's teasing gaze.

Her voice was soft, husky. Craig grinned. "Oh, yeah? Who's that?"

"Stanley Morrison."

v

She practically sighed over the name, Craig noted, his grin fading into a frown. "You can't date until your twenty-one or marry until you're thirty-five. What makes you think this boy will hang around that long?"

"By the time I'm thirty-five, you will be a grandfather," she assured, rising from her seat. "Several times over," she added her smile smug.

Craig's jaw dropped and eyes widened as much from her remark as the way she looked, all breasts and hips and curves, with incredibly long legs in an extremely short skirt. He couldn't have been more surprised had she sprouted wings or horns. "You can't wear that, it's indecent!"

She laughed, placing a kiss on his cheek. Short skirts and boots were all the rage. "It's the style," she said, wiping the pale mauve lip print off his freshly shaven skin before walking away.

"To hell with style, it's too short! Who determines style anyway?" Craig demanded, and heard her answering laughter.

"Nobody's father that's for sure! Don't have time to change. Come on brat," she called to her brother. "We're going to be late."

Placing a quick kiss on his mother's cheek and slapping his father's hand with a high-five, Ace ran to meet his sister. "I'm not a brat," he countered in the familiar morning banter.

"Yes you are," she argued, placing a kiss on his silky blond head. "You've been a brat since the day you were born," she concluded, her blue eyes dancing into his gray ones as she helped him into his jacket.

The door closed behind them before Craig found his voice. "Why didn't you tell me?" he demanded of his wife, who was nearly doubled over in a fit of giggles.

"Tell you what?" she asked, gasping for breath. "That she's growing up?"

"That she's built like a..." he stuttered, flushing at the description that came to mind, positive it *wasn't* appropriate for his daughter.

"And who in the hell is Stanley Morrison?"

Tamera's giggles turned into shouts of laughter. "Oh man, I wish I had a camera, the look on your face is priceless," she remarked, once she'd caught her breath. "Did you expect her to stay five forever?"

Craig didn't think that was funny one iota. His eyes narrowed, jaw muscle twitched. "No, but I didn't expect her to grow up overnight. Do you know anything about this boy?"

His wife's blonde hair bounced off her shoulders when she shook her head, her eyes laughed and mocked him.

"I'm glad you think this is funny," he growled, throwing her into another fit of giggles.

"Aren't you the least bit curious?"

Tamera wiped tears of hilarity off her cheeks before answering her husband. Like thunderclouds rolling in over an otherwise clear sky, his glittering gray gaze had darkened with emotion. The muscle in his jaw throbbed as it usually did when he was angry or upset. A shiver of pleasure shook her at the pure, male, animal magnetism he exuded.

"Not really. I'm sure he's just some new kid at school. We'll find out soon enough."

Craig watched the play of emotions on his wife's face and in her gaze. Sparkling like rare, precious gems those expressive blue eyes changed from shining sapphire to smoky, midnight blue. Shifting from laughter to soothing to something more basic, more primitive in the span of a heartbeat, she still had the power to capture him with a single look. Pushing back his chair, he walked to where she sat.

"Ride with me today," he urged, pulling her into his arms.

"It's too cold," she argued. "Stay home today," she countered, slipping her arms around his neck while pressing her body against his in blatant invitation.

His daughter's appearance was forgotten. So was the work he had planned for that day.

Book 4 in the 'Tempered' Series

Tempered Joy

All around rodeo cowboy and heir to the Rockin' H Ranch, Ace Harris is determined not to fall in love. He's only loved one woman in his life, his mother, and no one can even come close to filling her boots. Lexie Morgan thinks rodeo cowboys have rocks for brains and a death wish for a soul. A broken childhood and the death of her father and best friend leave her doubting and questioning God (despite her years of religious upbringing) and afraid of love. Can two young people who clash from the onset learn to trust in the healing power of God and find love and happiness amidst tragedy and grief?

And Don't Forget Book 1 ~ ***Tempered Hearts!***

Rancher Craig Harris and veterinarian Tamera Collins clash from the moment they meet. Innocence is pitted against arrogance as tempers rise and passions ignite to form a love as pure as the finest gold, fresh from the crucible and as strong as steel. Thrown together amid tragedy and unsated passion, Tamera and Craig share a strong attraction that neither accepts as the first stages of love. Torn between desire and dislike, they must make peace with their pasts and God in order to open up to the love blossoming between them. It is a love that nothing can destroy when they come to understand that ***only when hearts are tempered, minds are opened and wills are softened can man discern the will of God for his life.***

About the Author

Pamela S. Thibodeaux grew up in the town of Iowa, Louisiana and currently lives there with her husband, Terry. They have four children between them. A deeply committed Christian, Pamela firmly believes in God and His promises.

"God is very real to me and I feel that people today need and want to hear more of His truths wherever they can glean them. People are hungry for practical (and real) Christian values, not some 'holier-than-thou' beliefs that are impossible to believe and impossible to live up to," Pamela says.

"I do my best to encourage readers to develop a personal relationship with God. The deepest desire of my heart is to glorify God and to get His message of faith, trust and forgiveness to a hurting world."

Email Pamela at: pthibo7@gmail.com
Visit her website: http://www.pamelathibodeaux.com
Or blog: http://pamswildroseblog.blogspot.com

Other Titles by Pamela S Thibodeaux

Love is a Rose

Music is the magical entry into the spirit world; the golden gate into the Kingdom of God. But we mustn't be of the mindset that God only uses Christian music to reach out and touch our mind, heart and spirit. God uses any and every means available to speak to His children.

Our job is to be open and receptive.

In this devotional, Pamela S Thibodeaux shares how God opened her spirit to a deeper understanding of the abundance of His grace and mercy through the words of the song, The Rose sung by Country & Western artist Conway Twitty.

Pamela offers Seeds to Ponder and a prayer as she parallels the love of God and the Christian life to each verse of the song.

Lori Strickland (introduced in Tempered Fire) has always been known as her father's "wild child" with no desire to change until she meets ex-bull-rider-turned-preacher Rafe Judson. Her attempts to change her wanton ways come to naught until she realizes redemption only comes with true repentance. Can she find redemption and win the heart of the cowboy preacher? Find out in ***Lori's Redemption***

A visionary is someone who sees into the future Taylor Forrestier sees into the past but only as it pertains to her work. Hailed by her peers as "a visionary with an instinct for beauty and an eye for the unique" Taylor is undoubtedly a brilliant architect and gifted designer. But she and twin brother Trevor, share more than a successful business. The two share a childhood wrought with lies and deceit and the kind of abuse that's disgustingly prevalent in today's society. Can the love of God and the awesome healing power of His grace and mercy free the twins from their past and open their hearts to the good plan and the future He has for their lives? Find out in **The Visionary** ~ Where the awesome power of God's love heals the most wounded of souls.

The Inheritance is about the chance we all long for...the chance to start over. Widowed at age thirty-nine and suffering from empty nest syndrome, Rebecca Sinclair is overshadowed by grief and loneliness. Her husband has been deceased for a year, her oldest child has moved to New York in pursuit of an acting career and her youngest child is attending college in France. Having spent over half of her life as a wife and mother, she has no idea what God has in store for her now. Will an unexpected inheritance in the wine country of New York bring meaning and purpose to her life and give her the courage to love again?

US Postal worker Raymond Jacobey has been in love with the little widow since he first set eyes on her. A wanderer searching for the ever-illusive soul mate, Ray has never stayed in one place too long. Raised by self-centered, high-power executives, he's longed for the idyllic life of residing in a cozy house in a small town with the love of his life. Will he gain the heart of the lovely widow or will he lose her to the wine country of New York? Find out in **The Inheritance**

Single mom Cathy Johnson is tired of running her life alone...what she needs is a well-trained angel to help out. Jared Savoy gave up the dream of having a family when he discovered he is sterile. Can a confirmed bachelor and the mother of four find love amid normal daily chaos? Find out in **Cathy's Angel**

Best-selling novelist and songwriter, Camie Rogers has penned numerous accounts of the secret love she holds in her heart. Country-Music Superstar Kip Allen has changed from the shy, humble boy, to the epitome of "star." Can the two rediscover each other after one night of his Home is Where the Heart is Tour? Find out in **Choices**

Anthony Paul Seville is known as the 'most eligible bachelor' in New Orleans, possibly even the entire state of Louisiana, but finds himself alone—completely and explicitly alone. Jessica Aucoin is a writer on her way to fame and fortune, but is haunted by a man from her past. Will the "champion" lawyer and the author of romantic suspense find love written in their future? Find out in ***A Hero for Jessica***

Sienna has survived what most succumb to - the death of a spouse and child and has maintained her faith despite her troubles. William has never met anyone who actually lived out what they say they believe. Is it true love between the faithful optimist and broody pessimist or simply ***Winter Madness?***

Grade school teacher Carson Alexander has a gift—a gift that has driven a wedge between him and his family. Worse, it's put him at odds with God. Feeling alone and misunderstood, Carson views God's gift of prophecy as the worst kind of curse...that is until he meets Lorelei Conner, landscape artist extraordinaire, and perhaps the one person who may need Carson and his gift more than anyone ever has. Lorelei Connor is a mother on the run. Her abusive ex-husband has followed her all over the country trying to steal their daughter. Distrusting of men and needing to keep on the move, she's surprised by her desire to remain close to Carson Alexander. Through her fear and hesitation, she must learn to rely on God to guide her—not an easy task when He's prompting her to trust a man. Can their relationship withstand the tragedy lurking on the horizon? Find out in ***In His Sight***

Jason Stockwell has been commissioned to interview Kylie Erickson and to review her books. Only problem is, she won't give the time of day much less an interview to someone whose type of writing she deems not worthy of respect. Can they suspend their judgmental attitudes and find true love? Find out in ***Review of Love*** (A FREE read from White Rose Publishing!)

**Temperance
Publishing**

www.ingramcontent.com/pod-product-compliance
Lightning Source LLC
Chambersburg PA
CBHW070453120726
47910CB00003B/1035